In Sea

Terri Mackenzie

Contents

1.

2.

3.

4.

5.

6.

7.

8.

9.

10.

11.

12.

13.

14.

15.

16.

17.

18.

19.

20.

21.

22.

23.

24.

25.

26.

27.

28.

29.

30.

31.

32.

33.

34.

35.

36.

Chapter One

Nathanial Hardinge, The Duke of Norfolk, was not usually in the habit of receiving visitors before noon, a fact his butler knew well. Mornings were opportunities for him to rise, breakfast in comparative peace, and read his newspaper before the demands of the world took hold.

He was unprepared, therefore, to receive his mother, Her Grace, the Dowager Duchess of Norfolk at the tender time of half past ten. She, accompanied by his three older sisters, swept into the room like the proverbial ships, their sails fully extended.

The Duke laid down his newspaper. "Mama," he said, regarding that lady with a frown. "It is not yet eleven."

The Duchess, an imposing woman for whom age was an inconvenient and oft-disregarded truth, sat. His three sisters followed suit, and all four bosoms swelled in what he could only presume was indignation. "Well!" his mother said.

"Elinor," he said to his eldest sister, nodding at her. "Cassandra. Penelope. As you have all three stirred outdoors at such an early hour, I can only assume it must be a matter of great importance. Tell me, has someone died?"

"Don't be ridiculous, Nathanial!" Elinor said, plucking at her shawl. At thirty-seven, she had not fully lost her beauty, but five children and the iniquities of age had stolen much of her sweetness. "It is hardly early."

The Duke merely stared at her before turning to Cassandra, who at thirty-three, had all the roundness of an expecting woman. "*Has* someone died, Cass?"

"The mourning period for your father ended a month ago," his mother said.

"And as you can see." He gestured at himself. "I am not in mourning."

"Don't be so provoking," Cassandra snapped. "You know we're here to discuss your forthcoming marriage."

"How intriguing." The Duke rose and strode to the fireplace so he could better survey his family. All looked at him with ire in the same grey eyes he had inherited. "I was not aware I had committed to the act. With whom will this event take place?"

His mother didn't scowl—she never did anything so uncouth—but she allowed her dark brows to descend forbiddingly. "You know as well as I do that there are plenty of eligible young ladies available. Why, the Earl of Canterbury has a daughter out this Season."

"Lady Rosetta?" The flash of a smile lightened his face. "A pretty child, but I have no interest in schoolroom conversation."

"Perhaps, then, Lady Regina Bolton?" Penelope suggested. Closest in age to the Duke at thirty, she was—or had been—the sister he was most disposed to confide in. Until, of course, this rather distressing betrayal.

"Lady Regina is older, I grant you, but she has a hooked nose."

"Nathanial!" Elinor said, caught between amusement and irritation. "Don't be so crude."

"Let me understand you," Nathanial said, resting a hand against the mantlepiece. This was a meeting he had expected for quite some time, but he had not suspected all his sisters would take up arms against him. "You would have me marry any young lady, no matter her appearance, for what purpose?"

"As the Duke of Norfolk, it is *essential* you have an heir," his mother said irritably. "You have no brothers, and you know Montague is the next in line to inherit."

Nathanial's lips tightened. He had no particular desire to talk about his marriage prospects, but he had still less desire to discuss his cousin. "Montague is away on the Continent, Mama, and I think it unlikely he return for quite some time."

"So you say," his mother said, "but he has the unfortunate habit of arriving where he is least wanted."

"And he is *not* wanted here," Penelope added. Her hands fluttered anxiously in her lap. Before she married Lord Peterborough, she had fancied herself in love with Montague Radcliffe. And perhaps with an eye to inheriting, he had encouraged her affections.

To Nathanial, that was not the worst thing Montague had done, but for the rest of his family, it was perhaps his greatest transgression. He released a long breath. "Montague poses no threat to us. I will ensure it."

"And if," his mother enquired, "you should die without issue? You are the *only* male in the family, save for Montague, and I can guarantee he is eager to take the title and your father's wealth."

"It is my wealth now," Nathanial said irritably. "And my title. If you all recall, Montague killed a man in a duel and was forced to flee to France, where he has been these past seven years. I have not so much as received a line from him. Society has forgotten his existence, and my title is safe." He held their gazes, one at a time. "Your requirements I find a wife are somewhat precipitous. I am hardly on my deathbed."

Penelope swallowed. "Neither was Father."

"He suffered from apoplexy," Nathanial said, gentling his voice. Their father had been a kindly man, and his death had shook the family. Including, although he would never admit it, Nathanial. He had not thought he would inherit the title, and all the responsibilities it entailed, so *soon*. A wife would be yet another shackle.

In time, he would be prepared for that. But Montague, of all people, was not the man to force his hand.

"You are almost thirty and a duke to boot," Elinor said. "You have responsibilities."

"I am twenty-eight and have been Duke less than a year," Nathanial countered. "And, might I add, I have seen no sign of Montague."

His mother sniffed. "Nevertheless, a marriage is extremely important for a man in your position. It is expected."

Nathanial, by nature, did not consider himself overly irresponsible. He had, after all, done his duty by his title and his estate, and handled any number of business matters since he was abruptly made Duke. But this was too far.

Penelope held out a hand to him. "Marriage is the most felicitous of states. Mama wants to see you marry so you may have an heir, but I just want to see you happy."

"Then I shall be sure to marry for love," he said dryly, taking her hand and squeezing it. There was little to no chance he might do so, but if his family was convinced he was searching for the girl of his dreams, perhaps his mother may let up.

"Have you considered Lady Isabella?" she demanded, fixing him with a glare.

Or perhaps not.

Seeing it would be unprofitable to argue, Nathanial took a seat and listened to his mother list every eligible girl currently in London, noting their various accomplishments, beauty, and family name.

"For of course," his mother added, "her family is important. This is an alliance, Nathanial."

"I thought you wished me to marry for love?"

"You may do both."

Nathanial tapped his fingers against his thigh as he cast a glance at his clock. His policy when it came to his family was that visits could not last more than an hour. Five minutes before they were due to exceed this arbitrary time-limit, he rose. "Grateful as I am you have chosen to come all this way to lecture me," he said, "but I'm afraid this is all the time I have to spare you."

"I have invited all eligible young ladies to the Norfolk ball next week," his mother said. "I expect you to consider your position carefully."

"I presume I am not expected to make a choice by next week?"

His mother's sternness only deepened at his flippancy. "I would hope you at least make your preference plain."

Elinor also rose, smoothing down the rose-patterned muslin she wore. "You know it's the best thing for the family if you marry soon and well."

Penelope took his hand again. "You must overcome this flippancy, this passivity, if you are to find love," she urged, looking up into his face. "It does not come looking for you."

A relief, in Nathanial's opinion.

"And as the Duke," Cassandra said, "your obligation is first and foremost to the family."

"*Even* at eight-and-twenty." With that forbidding statement, his mother surged from the room. His sisters followed, Penelope throwing him a sympathetic glance as she did, and the door closed behind them. Nathanial stretched his long legs before the fire with a groan.

It was inevitable that he would eventually have to choose a wife. His mother was right about one thing: without children, Montague posed a threat. Marriage, perhaps, would be a revenge of kinds, but that could wait, at least until Montague had returned. Until then, he would continue as he had, enjoying the freedoms he was currently at liberty to enjoy.

8

As the eldest of two daughters, Lady Theodosia Beaumont was expected to marry well. As her father's estate was heavily encumbered, she was expected to marry *richly*. These were two unavoidable truths of her station, and if she secretly dreamt of a handsome gentleman to sweep her off her feet, she did not expect to marry for love. Such was the fate of a poorly dowered lady.

She did not consider it reasonable, however, for the rich and eligible gentleman in question to not possess teeth.

Lord Weston was, she estimated, in his fifties, and he had not aged gracefully; jowls wobbled as he talked and broken veins were scattered across his nose. He also appeared to be missing three teeth. Theodosia had counted them over the course of their conversation thus far. Two silver and one gold. The gold was placed so prominently in his mouth that she suspected it was supposed to attest to his wealth.

As far as she was concerned, it merely attested to his age. *Young* men did not suffer from golden teeth.

He leant forwards, shaking hands clinking the china cup he held. If he toppled over and died in her drawing room, would she be held responsible? And would it, more pertinently, affect her hopes of making a match?

"Do you like to ride?" he asked, and Theodosia was assailed both by the foulness of his breath and the unfortunate image of the Earl attempting to throw himself on a horse.

"No," she said, and thought she saw a flicker of relief in his eyes. "I mean—yes. I love to ride. Do I not, Annabelle?"

Her sister, sequestered by her mother at the other end of the room, looked alarmed to be addressed in such a way. Especially considering the question at hand was a direct falsehood.

"I, er—" Annabelle flushed. At eighteen, this was her first Season, and she still became tongue-tied before gentlemen, regardless of their physical prowess.

"So you see," Theodosia said, turning back to the Earl with as insipid a smile as she could muster, "I simply *love* to ride. Any form of exercise, in fact. Walking, riding, walking." She quickly realised she

had run out of exercises. What did gentlemen do?
"Hunting."

"You enjoy hunting?" He pulled out a large,
speckled handkerchief and mopped at his forehead.
She looked at the gathering beads of sweat with
horrified curiosity. "How very—well, I suppose it is
not so unusual for young ladies to enjoy hunting these
days."

"And shooting," she continued, ignoring the glare
her mother directed at her. "I do so wish my father
would let me shoot."

"Shooting? Young ladies ought not to shoot, Lady
Theodosia."

She beamed at him. "You sound just like my
father." *And you look like him, too.* When he
spluttered, she rose and tugged on the bell pull. "Are
you well? I shall have some more refreshments
brought in."

"No, there is no need—I do not—thank you, Lady
Theodosia, but I am quite well."

"Are you certain? My father finds he suffers from
gout on occasion, and I declare I could spot it from
anywhere."

"I do not suffer from gout," he said, a little sharply. "My health is perfectly satisfactory."

Theodosia let the silence drift uncomfortably before she smiled. "Of course, sir. How do you like to read?"

"Read?" He blinked as though the idea were entirely foreign. "Do you mean novels?"

"What else? I read as often as I can, although I am so busy of late I hardly have the time. Mrs Radcliffe's novels are my favourite. A female author? Can you imagine?" She did not give him the chance to reply, although he opened his mouth hopelessly in the attempt. "I find it positively charming that ladies can be authors, too."

"Sensationalist fiction," he said, mopping his brow once more.

"And yet so very compelling. I could read *The Mysteries of Udolfo* a thousand times over."

"Theodosia," her mother said, approaching them from the corner of the room. "Are you letting your tongue run away with you again?"

"How can I help myself when I feel so comfortable around Lord Weston?" Theodosia said. "He makes me feel quite as at ease as Papa."

"Enough." Lady Shrewsbury's tone was quiet, but the expression in her eyes promised trouble. "Thank you for calling, Lord Weston. I do hope we'll see you again."

I don't, Theodosia thought.

"Yes, well." He rose awkwardly to his feet, giving Theodosia a rather unfortunate view of the way his waistcoat strained at the waist. "I'm afraid I have some business. Urgent, you know. I'm sure I shall see you again."

"Will we see you at the Norfolk ball tomorrow?" Lady Shrewsbury pressed.

"Well, I." He mopped at his face once more. "I expect I shall attend, but I cannot be certain—I cannot make promises."

"Of course. I quite understand." Her mother gave him a tight-lipped smile that made no pretence at humour. "Goodbye, Lord Weston."

"Indeed. Lady Shrewsbury. Lady Theodosia Beaumont." He bowed. "Lady Annabelle."

All three ladies curtsied and he left the room. As soon as he did, Theodosia flopped back on the sofa. "Goodness," she said into the silence. "I thought he would never leave."

"Theodosia Charlotte Beaumont."

"Yes, Mama?"

"What were you doing?"

Theodosia blinked innocently. "Why, discussing the benefits of modern literature with Lord Weston."

Her mother's eyes narrowed. "You know *precisely* what you were doing, young lady, and I shall not have it."

"But he was so old, Mama," she said, casting her sister a pleading glance. "And did you see? He barely had any teeth."

"That is not the matter at hand."

"It should be," she muttered. "I understand my duty, Mama, but surely there is *one* gentleman in all of London prepared to marry me who is also in possession of his teeth."

"A gentleman who is prepared to overlook your lack of dowry?" Lady Shrewsbury's tone was sharp. "You cannot be squeamish, Theo."

Theo did not believe her requirements—a man younger than her father who retained his teeth, faculties, and all his limbs—were squeamish. But she ducked her head. "Yes, Mama," she said, staring at her fingers and the red prick where she had stabbed herself during the morning's sewing. "May I go for a walk with Annabelle?"

Her mother agreed, provided they were accompanied by a maid, and the two ladies set off, arm in arm.

"You shan't find your hero in Hyde Park, Theo," Annabelle teased as Theo watched every passing face. "Even if he *does* exist, he won't be lurking on the promenade."

"You don't know that."

Annabelle regarded her sister with laughing blue eyes. "Heroes don't do anything as unromantic as lurk."

"Much you would know on the subject," Theo returned. "Besides, as apparently the only gentlemen prepared to court a dowry-less lady are over the age of forty, I must try something."

"I hardly think this is how to find a husband. Try looking at the Norfolk ball. Your future husband is more likely to be in a ballroom than among the bushes."

Theo groaned. "But you know as soon as I enter the room, the Earl of Whitstable will pounce. I just know it."

"He's far too old to pounce," Annabelle said with a giggle.

"*You* may find my situation funny, but I do not."

"If it came to it, I'm certain you could outrun him."

She pinned her lips together, but the thought of her fleeing the ballroom with the elderly Earl lumbering after her was too much, and she burst into a peal of laughter. "If I know the Earl, it shall certainly come to it," she said. "But—oh, just imagine if there was a tall, dark, handsome stranger there, prepared to sweep me off my feet and carry me away."

"That sounds more like a kidnapping to me."

Theo pinched her sister's arm, but despite the chance she would see the Earl of Whitstable, she could not help hoping she might also get at least a *glimpse* of her hero.

Chapter Two

Norfolk House on Berkeley Square was a grand affair. Carriages lined the street, and in the second one along from the front door, Theo plucked at her gloves nervously.

"Stop fidgeting," her mother said. "We've known the Norfolks for years."

"Not in company," Theo muttered. Company was entirely different from running around their country estate as untamed children.

Her father, a slim man with a preoccupied air, frowned. "Out of mourning already?"

"It's been a month, dear," his wife reminded him.

What a way to celebrate returning to society, Theo thought as she peered at the house. Every window—and there were many—blazed with light, and young ladies like jewels mounted the steps to the door.

They alighted with the help of a footman and ascended into the house. Theo had only ever been inside their Havercroft residence in the country: an entirely more modest manor house, with a rambling old wing that had been there, or so she had been told, since the Civil War. Whenever she had visited, that had been her favourite place.

This house did not resemble that wing. The ballroom alone was far larger and grander than anything she could have conceived, and no expense had been spared. Chandeliers dripped from the ceiling, their crystals sending candlelight skittering across the walls, and ivy had been wound around the pillars. Fresh flowers interrupted the scent of hot bodies.

Almost immediately, Theo began her scan of the guests. In the crush, it was difficult to discern individual features, but this was her last chance, and she needed to find a partner before the insatiable and persistent Earl of Whitstable found her.

Any partner would do tonight as long as it was not him.

"Nathanial," her mother said as they approached their hosts. "Phillipa. How lovely to see you again."

Theo curtsied, meeting Nathanial's gaze. He sent her the shadow of a wink and she bit back a smile. "Lord Shrewsbury, Lady Shrewsbury," he said to her parents. "Lady Theo. Lady Annabelle. I hope you do not find the ball too crowded. My mother took a great deal of pleasure in organising this event, as you can see."

"It's lovely," Theo said, wondering if everyone else could hear the insincere note in her voice. From the twinkle in Nathanial's eye, he, at least, had. "And very . . . bright."

Very bright? That was the best you could do?

She had, apparently, grown so used to repelling her suitors that she had forgotten how to compliment with sincerity.

"Indeed, there are an unreasonable number of candles," Nathanial said. His lips twitched.

"Lady Isabella has just arrived," the Duchess said pointedly. "Pray excuse us, Mary."

"Not at all," Theo's mother said, and took hold of her arm. "Come, Theo."

"Mama—" With horror, Theo realised where they were going. "Please no. I beg you. I will dance with *any* other gentleman."

"The Earl of Whitstable is willing to reach an arrangement with your father. You know with your father's . . ." She stopped before she could say something like 'compulsion to game', although Theo knew it was true. Her father had gambled away his fortune and there was nothing left. Her family's survival relied on her marriage. "It won't be so bad, my love. You'll see."

"Not so bad? Mama, he is *bald*."

"There are worse things."

At that present moment, face to face with the Earl of Whitstable, she could think of *nothing* worse. He was older than she remembered, with a few straggling grey hairs across his shiny head, and a sweaty top lip. The large golden buttons on his waistcoat seemed in imminent danger of flying off any second.

"Lady Shrewsbury," the Earl said in a plummy voice as he bowed. "Lady Theodosia. What a pleasure to see you here tonight."

"We could not have missed such an event," her mother said.

For the first time, Theo wished they could. She fanned herself vigorously. "It is so crowded tonight. And warm!"

"The Norfolks are excellent hosts," he said as though he knew them intimately. Theo knew he did not. "May I ask for the first dance, Lady Theodosia?"

"She would be *delighted*," her mother said with an accompanying glare.

He is willing to reach an arrangement with your father.

Thankful she was wearing gloves, Theo allowed the Earl to lead her into the centre of the floor where a minuet was beginning. One dance. She could manage one dance.

"Now, my dear," the Earl huffed, tightening his grip on her hand. "You look charming this evening."

"You mean to say I do not look charming any other time?"

The Earl did not so much as blink; she may as well not have spoken at all. "I have spoken to your father, and he is amenable to the match. I understand your *lack of a dowry*"—this was delivered in a stage whisper that made her flinch—"may have been a deterrent for other suitors, but I assure you it is not a consideration for me."

Perhaps you should have invested in a golden tooth as proof of your wealth, she thought viciously. "Are you certain?" she asked. "I have nothing, you know."

"Quite certain."

Drat. "I—"

"Before I am carried away with my ardour," he continued, "I must also inform you I am more than

21

happy to render your father any financial assistance he feels is necessary."

This was going all wrong. Knowledge of her father's expectations was supposed to discourage potential suitors—especially the unappealing ones. "It is likely to be considerable," she said.

"That is of little matter. I will consider myself amply recompensed." His gaze flicked over her body. "Your beauty and accomplishments will decorate my drawing room most pleasingly."

If she'd had a little more breath, she might have educated him on what romance was supposed to look like. The great heroes of literature did not mention financial matters or a woman's accomplishments; they pledged themselves body and soul to their loves.

They did *not* refer to said loves as being mere *ornaments*.

"Your charms may tempt the most reticent of men," he said, his hand dropping dangerously far down her back. "I look forward to our wedding with the greatest anticipation."

"You are hasty, sir," Theo said, wiggling away from his wandering hand. "You may have spoken to my father on the matter, but you have not spoken to me."

He frowned, thick lips puckering. "What further is there to say?"

To her relief, the dance came to an end, and she slipped free of him under the pretence of curtsying. "I should speak to the Duke, my lord. Pray excuse me." Without waiting for his response, she turned and ploughed through the crush.

Her mother would rebuke her for this, but surely— surely—she would not be expected to marry the Earl of Whitstable.

She found Annabelle in a corner, her dance card all but empty, and with a glass of punch in her hand.

"There you are," Annabelle said with a wide smile. Blonde where Theo had dark hair, the sisters appeared as opposites except for their blue eyes. "Did you manage to run from him after all?"

"He has spoken to Papa," Theo wailed. "And it seems all but settled. Anna, what am I to *do?*"

"Can you not repulse him?"

"He is immune to any repulsion I can offer."

Annabelle twirled a curl around her finger as she thought. "If Henry were here, he might be able to intervene."

"What use is an older brother when he's abroad fighting for King and Country?" Theo gave a frustrated sigh. "Besides, if this *is* the only chance at saving the estate, he'd probably feel the same way, seeing as he'll inherit."

"You could always refuse to go through with the wedding."

"I *could*." And Theo had thought about it, dreamt about refusing to walk down the aisle to her doddery husband-to-be.

Then after, inevitably, came the daydream that followed. She failed to find a husband and her family lost everything—their house, their final remaining carriage, what little respect they still held in the *ton*. If she refused the only offer of marriage that she had, she was condemning her family to poverty.

Annabelle squeezed Theo's hand sympathetically. "In that case, the only thing for it is to find another gentleman prepared to propose. Someone younger—though just as rich."

"I'm looking for solutions, not miracles," Theo said dryly. If finding someone to marry her was as easy as that, she would have done it by now.

Annabelle glanced behind her and winced. "The Earl is headed this way."

"Make my excuses." Theo darted past a lady with an oversized fan, past a vase mounted on a pedestal, and out to the patio doors. She slipped between them, thankful for the brisk air. She leant against the wall and tilted her head to the sky.

Peace. Quiet. *Finally*.

"Theo?" Nathanial asked. "Are you all right?"

She jerked, knocking the back of her head against the stone, and rubbed it ruefully as she looked at her friend. The dark concealed the details of his face, but she knew them regardless: brown curls above grey eyes, a straight nose, thin lips. Handsome, in a careless way.

"You scared me," she said. "What are you doing creeping around like that?"

"What are you doing hiding on the patio?" he countered.

"If you must know, I'm hiding from the Earl of Whitstable. He's already forced me into one dance, and you may be certain he will force me into another." Theo looked into Nathanial's shadowed face. "And you?"

"My mother is determined to see me dance with as many eligible young ladies as possible," he said, mimicking her stance and leaning one shoulder against the wall. "I'm almost tempted to develop a limp."

"At least you do not *have* to marry them."

"My mother would disagree."

Theo laughed, then sighed, gazing across the garden. Flaming torches seemed to coax more shadows from the darkness than they revealed. "Mine, too. She is determined to marry me to the Earl."

Nathanial's gaze returned to her face, suddenly intense. "The Earl of Whitstable?"

"The very same."

"But he must be above fifty."

"Yes, but he's rich and prepared to marry me without a dowry," Theo said. "And you must know I need to marry well."

"I see."

"Do you? You are the Duke of Norfolk." She stiffened. "And I should have mentioned again how sorry I am about your father. I know you had not thought of being Duke quite so early."

"I had not, but one grows accustomed to things after a while. It's an incomparable honour—at least according to my mother."

"I suppose I should be a countess if I married the Earl," Theo said miserably. "And perhaps in time I would not mind *quite* so much that he is so . . . old." She brightened. "Although perhaps his age will mean he will die soon and leave me a rich widow."

Nathanial laughed. "I'm sure he would be flattered to hear it."

"I must find some solace where I can. After all, I cannot find it in his age. Or his hairline." As for his teeth—she hadn't even *seen* them. She supposed she would be lucky if he possessed any at all. "And he will not be deterred by my lack of dowry."

"He doesn't want you for your money," Nathanial said dryly. "He wants an heir. His estate is entailed away to his nephew, if I remember rightly, but with the help of his son, he could break the entail."

Well, that explained the way he had looked at her hips. She suppressed a shudder of disgust. "I don't *want* to bear his sons. If we even have sons at all. What happens if I don't? I become his third deceased wife?"

This was all starting to sound very Tudor.

Beside her, Nathanial's eyes were fixed on the distant trees. The quartet started up again in the ballroom, and the sound of mirth carried on the wind.

"We should return to the ball," he said suddenly, offering her his arm. "If my mother sees me with you, at least she will not accuse me of shirking my duties."

Theo snorted. "Only if you're on the cusp of proposing. Doesn't she want you to marry?"

He stiffened, and she looked up into his face, cursing her stupid, loose tongue. He guided her through the doors again, and she stumbled over her words.

"Did I offend you, Nate? I'm sorry."

"Not at all," he said with a wry smile that didn't reach his eyes. "Enjoy the remainder of the ball." He bowed over her hand, and Theo watched his tall figure as he strode away, exiting the ballroom despite the debutantes that trailed in his wake like abandoned

28

flowers. They sent her scornful, jealous glances as they dispersed in search of better prey, and she returned to avoiding the Earl of Whitstable.

Chapter Three

Nathanial entered his study with a thoughtful air and poured himself a glass of port from his crystal decanter. The ball was still in full swing, and no doubt his mother would notice his absence and scold him for it, but he needed space in which to think.

Only if you're on the cusp of proposing.

He had not been on the cusp of proposing. The idea of marrying Theo, a girl he'd known since she was in muddy petticoats, was a preposterous one, and he had no sooner dismissed it than it had taken hold.

Really, Beaumont shouldn't be forcing his daughter into marrying lecherous fossils. Then, there would be no need for Nathanial to even consider matrimony, and he could go back to his life as a carefree bachelor.

As carefree as anyone could be with a mother like his breathing down his neck and insisting he marry.

He tossed the drink back as he sank into his favourite armchair. Marriage was a serious business, and not one he contemplated lightly, but if he married Theo, it would free him from his mother's attentions. And Theo would no doubt suit him better than the insipid young ladies his mother had presented to him this evening.

Of course, this was assuming Theo would accept his suit. He would have to make his intentions plain; he was offering to save her from Whitstable on the understanding that this would not be a love match. Considering her choice was between him and Whitstable, however, he flattered himself that she would not reject him.

He poured himself another glass of port, decision made. Tomorrow, he would call on Theo.

In dedication to his newfound cause, Nathanial prevailed upon himself to call on Theo the next morning at around noon. To his relief, he found her alone in the drawing room, unaccompanied by either her younger sister or her mother.

She looked up as he entered, and her face creased in confusion. "Nate? What are you doing here so early?"

"I see my reputation precedes me." He noticed her eyes were a little red-rimmed, and he extended a hand, which she took at once. "Are you all right?"

"Yes, of course. That is—well." She smiled wanly at him. "Why don't you sit down and tell me why you're here. How did you contrive to avoid Nott?"

"I told him I would see myself in," Nathanial said, accepting the seat beside Theo and retaining his grip in her hand. "He and I are old friends. But tell me, Theo, what's the matter? Are things so terrible?"

"Oh, not *terrible*. Or," she added, "Mama would not say it is so bad. I'm to be a countess, you know, and that should make up for . . . Well, for everything else."

He watched her face, not missing the way she sniffed defiantly, as though daring him to comment on her unhappiness. "How would you prefer to be a duchess?"

"A duchess?" At this, she laughed. "If I thought the Duke of Wessex would dispose of his wife and ask me, I would be a deal sight more cheerful. He isn't above forty, you know, and he has his teeth."

"You have a preoccupation with teeth," he said, frowning. "I can't think what has brought this on."

For an instant, laughter brimmed in her blue eyes. "No, I daresay you can't. Why are you here, Nathanial? If Mama ever finds out you came to see me—alone, at that—and did not see her, too, she'll be quite put out."

If Nathanial had once had misgivings about his purpose, the sight of her woebegone face would have been enough to banish them entirely. "As it happens," he said, extending his legs in front of him, "I came with a solution to your problem."

Her mouth turned down at the corners. "You can't have done. I've thought it all through, and there's nothing for it. No one else has offered, and Papa is desperate, you know. Lord Whitstable is the *only* man to want to marry me enough to propose, if you can call it that, and if I don't accept, we shall have to return to the country."

Nathanial found himself conscious of both shock and anger. He waited until his voice was steady before saying, "Immediately?"

"Oh, we're quite undone," she said candidly. "If he did not gamble so much—but I shouldn't know about that."

Considering her father did so little to hide his vices from his family, it was hardly surprising Theo knew about them, but the thought still irritated Nathanial. He pushed it aside. "You shouldn't," he said, "but that's not the point. My solution is drastic, but I think you'll find it preferable. I, at least, am in possession of all my teeth, the last time I checked."

She looked up at him in blatant shock, and Nathanial encountered his second surprise of the day when he discovered that little Theo, whom he had seen more as a grubby child than a young lady, was remarkably pretty.

"Good God," she said. "You can't be suggesting what I think you're suggesting."

"This is extremely disheartening."

"Nate, you—" She swallowed. "You must be joking. Why would you want to marry me?"

"You must learn to accept your proposals with a little more grace, my dear."

She squinted suspiciously at him, and it was all he could do to keep a straight face. "Are you being serious?"

"I have never been more so."

"And you are not drunk?"

His control snapped, and he laughed. "Brat," he said, chucking her under the chin. "No, I am not drunk, and I'm not teasing you. I'm in want of a wife, or at least my mother believes me to be—which, I have on authority, is the same thing. And you are in search of a more eligible husband than a man easily old enough to be your father."

"Twice over," she muttered.

"So, will you accept?"

Her eyes were wide, the blue a crisp, wintry shade. "Do you think my father would accept?"

"I shall ensure he does."

"Only . . ." She hesitated, toying with the edge of her book. "I believe the Earl offered to pay some of my father's debts."

Of course he had, Nathanial thought grimly. And of course that was why Lord Shrewsbury had accepted the match. Still. "You need not fear," he said. "My fortune is large."

"We have been friends long enough for me to know *that*. But Papa is . . . And there is Oliver to consider. He is due to go to Oxford next summer, and—"

"I know where Oliver is in his education," Nathanial said wryly. "He will go to Oxford if he wishes. But there is one final thing we must discuss before I speak with your father, Theo."

"Oh?"

There were many ways he could have approached this subject, but Theo was his friend—of longstanding nature—and she deserved the truth. "This is not a love-match," he said. "Nor will I lie to you about the nature of my affections."

"I thought you were going to say something terrible!" she said, releasing the breath she'd been holding. "Are your affections engaged?"

"Not presently."

"I suppose it would have been unfortunate if they were."

"Yes," he agreed with a smile he could not help. "Are yours?"

"Not yet. Although I had . . ." She dropped her gaze, a becoming flush high on her cheeks. "I had hoped to find—someone."

Ah, so his little Theo was a romantic. "That brings me onto my next point, then." He waited until she looked up at him again before saying, "I intend to continue the lifestyle I enjoy now, largely." Alongside the obligations that a wife would necessitate. "And I have no objection if you find . . . distraction elsewhere, as long as you're discreet."

A second ticked by, then another, and for a moment, he didn't think she was going to understand his meaning. But then shock swamped her eyes. "Are you—*Nathanial*. Are you saying what I think you're saying?"

"That entirely depends, but I believe so. And you should know that while I will, of course, want children in time, I have no intention of expecting you to perform any wifely duties at present."

This time, his name was uttered in a voice of confusion. "Wifely duties?" she said. "What has that to do with anything?"

He sighed. This was not a conversation he had relished, and it was turning out to be just as bad as he had envisaged. "Usually, when a man and woman wed, he visits her bed. I shall make you no such visit."

Her brow creased. "I see."

"It is not perhaps a traditional situation, but I think we will get along well enough together."

"Unless," she said wickedly, "I hope for romance."

"I am afraid you will never find that with me."

"I see." She pursed her lips in an oddly charming gesture before relaxing into a smile. "Well, if you're certain you mean it, I shall be glad to accept."

"I mean it."

"I can't think what a sacrifice it must have been," she continued, her face remarkably straight, "offering for me over all the young ladies vying for your hand."

"Wretch."

Amusement danced in her eyes, dissolving the winter into summer warmth, and a lopsided dimple popped in her cheek. "Not a wretch. Your future wife."

If that wasn't the most terrifying thing he had heard all day. He ruffled her hair. "You may stop moping now," he said. "I'm about to visit your father, and all being well, I should have an announcement in the papers tomorrow or the day after."

"I wasn't *moping*," she said indignantly as he went to the door. "And Nate—do not be too angry with Papa."

He raised his eyebrows at her. "Were you not when he arranged your marriage with Whitstable?"

"I was," she confessed, "but now it has been settled, I don't see why you should be angry, too. He can't help it, you know. It's in his blood, the gambling. Grandpapa was precisely the same."

As though selling his eldest daughter to the highest bidder because he had gambled away the Shrewsbury fortune was not a good enough reason to be angry. Nathanial said nothing as he left her.

He found the Earl of Shrewsbury in his study, a space, he discovered as he entered, that was both cramped and untidy. The Earl himself, glasses perched on the end of his nose, stood by the fireplace and squinted at a bill in his hands. With a curse, he consigned it to the fire.

"Norfolk," he said, glancing up and holding out his hand. "Terrific ball last night."

"I cannot claim credit—my mother was responsible for organising it."

"Pass on my congratulations, and it's good to see you out of mourning." Frowning, as though slightly confused, he gestured to a bottle perched on a small, velvet-topped table. "Care for a drink?"

"Not this time, although you may want to."

The confusion deepened, and the Earl lowered himself into his seat. "What can I do for you, my boy? If you're asking about Henry, we haven't heard anything these past two months, but that's to be expected. You don't win the war by writing letters, you know."

"And Wellington is an exceptional leader," Nathanial said, knowing how much the Earl revered the famed Duke. "I'm certain he will lead us to victory soon."

"Ah yes. No doubt of it, that's what I say." Shrewsbury poured himself a small glass of brandy and swirled the amber liquid. "Now, what was it you came here to discuss?"

"I would like your permission to offer for Theo," Nathanial said, judging it best to jump straight to the point.

Shrewsbury jumped, and his brandy sloshed across his breeches. "You want to marry . . . Theo?"

"I know it must come as somewhat of a surprise, but we have been close for a great many years, and I believe she is precisely the sort of wife I want."

The Earl's lips mouthed the word *duchess*.

"I know how much you value your daughter's happiness, and considering our fondness for each other, and of course the fact that I would take it upon myself to provide for a family I consider already my own, I am certain you would be happy to accept."

"Happy to . . ." Shrewsbury swallowed. "This is a generous offer indeed, but I . . . I regret to inform you it is too late."

Nathanial raised his eyebrows. "Oh?"

"You see, I have already—she has already received an offer."

"And she has accepted?"

"She has."

"I see." Nathanial stretched his long legs out before him. "Considering I already know of her prior attachment to me"—an attachment he hoped Theo would be amenable to agreeing to—"I am inclined to wonder why she might have accepted another man. Who is the gentleman in question?"

Shrewsbury's face reddened. "The Earl of Whitstable."

This time, Nathanial didn't try to hide his disgust. "A man old enough to be her father? I find it hard to believe she accepted his advances."

"I've known you a long time, Norfolk; you should know I don't take insubordination lightly."

"If I'm wrong," Nathanial said coldly, "be so good as to tell me." For the first time, the Earl looked away. "I have it on excellent terms that she wishes to marry me, and I cannot but feel I will be better suited to her than a man almost three times her age." His lip curled. "A man, might I add, who has already been married twice over."

"And what do you propose I do?" Shrewsbury demanded. "Inform him that my word means nothing?"

"You may leave Whitstable to me." Nathanial would take great pleasure in *that* particular meeting. "Consider your daughter," he continued. "I do not pretend to be perfect, but I will make her a better husband—and a longer lived one, God willing—than that buffoon."

"He's a respectable man," the Earl spluttered.

"He is taking advantage of a family in need of financial aid, and a daughter obliged to marry the highest bidder." Reluctantly, Nathanial moderated his tone; much as he wanted to vent his disgust at the situation Theo was in, that was not the best approach. "Whitstable may be a respectable man, but can he make Theo happy? We both know he cannot." He tucked one ankle over his knee. "And if it comes to a question of whose pockets run deeper, Shrewsbury, consider it a done deal."

"I take it you would be willing to offer . . . assistance?"

"I understand the requirements expected of me, and rest assured I shall fulfil them."

The Earl rubbed his face and tossed his drink back. Knowing this was the crucial moment of decision, Nathanial kept quiet. There was something compelling about silence: the strongest place of negotiation came from waiting for the other to cave.

"Very well," the Earl said after a moment. "Although I expect—I would hope—Whitstable offered me quite the sum."

"Consider it doubled."

Shrewsbury choked and smacked his chest with his fist. Nathanial watched him dispassionately. That had been a foolish pledge, considering how fast the money would go, but he would hardly notice the dent. What was more, and considerably more pertinent, he'd already had enough of this interview.

"That is," Shrewsbury said, spluttering, "extremely generous of you, Norfolk."

"To win your daughter's hand, sir, I would be prepared to do anything," Nathanial said, freely perjuring his soul. "Am I to consider the deal done?"

"As long as you are prepared to—to inform Whitstable. I hardly feel—my reputation, you know, my boy. Wouldn't want him to feel as though . . ." Feeling himself inadequate to the task of expressing his, no doubt, complex emotions, Shrewsbury lapsed into silence.

Nathanial rose and offered the beleaguered Earl his hand. "Believe me," he said, a martial light arising in his eyes, "I am more than equal to the task."

Chapter Four

The Earl of Whitstable was a frequent visitor of Brooks, the gentlemen's club on St James's Street, and it was there Nathanial found him partaking of a late lunch. As always, in the middle of the day, there were few patrons, and Nathanial was relieved to find him sitting on a table alone. This entire business was better conducted in private.

Whitstable looked up and regarded him with a rheumy and somewhat confused eye. "Norfolk?"

"Good day."

He grunted and turned his attention to his pheasant, stabbing it with his knife. "A good day indeed."

"It's fortunate I found you here," Nathanial said, leaning forward until he was certain he had Whitstable's attention. "You're just the man I was hoping to speak to."

"I am?"

"You are. You see, I have it on excellent authority you believe yourself engaged to Lady Theodosia Beaumont."

Whitstable blinked, but recovered himself quickly. "Never mind believe myself, Norfolk. I spoke with her father yesterday and it's all settled."

Nathanial couldn't help the curl of his lip as he said, "And the lady?"

"Pardon?"

"Did you speak to the lady herself about her preferences?"

It was clear this question was both unexpected and unwelcome. Whitstable glowered across the table and used his knife with more force than strictly necessary. "It's an eligible match for a lady without a dowry."

"Yes, I thought you might not have considered her thoughts on the matter." This was the part he had been looking forward to, and he braced his hands behind his head as he leant back, observing with grim triumph that the Earl hadn't taken a bite since his arrival. "If you had, you would have known that she is, in fact, promised to me."

Silence settled over the two men as Whitstable's eyes bugged and his face slowly turned a shade of puce that meant nothing good for his heart. Nathanial was quite prepared to wait until the Earl had recovered his faculties, and turned his attention to the smoky room. With detached interest, he noted the velvet curtains that had been drawn to reveal the bustling street, the crystal decanters that were perfectly positioned at every table, and the green-and-white colouring that indicated this was a male-only domain.

"There must be some mistake," Whitstable said at last, his voice strained. "I spoke with her father. We need only make an announcement—"

"And as you have not yet done so, it limits the embarrassment that could otherwise arise from this situation. I have just come from her father, where I informed him of the prior understanding between the lady and I." His smile was cold. "He was more than accommodating once I made my position clear."

The Earl's jowls quivered with indignation. "And what position is that?"

"That I will not allow her to marry a man so much her senior when her affections are engaged elsewhere."

"This is preposterous. I spoke with her father first. The prior claim is mine."

"Unfortunately for you, Lady Theodosia would rather marry me," Nathanial said smoothly, taking particular pleasure from the way the Earl's face reddened. "Which, if you had consulted her prior to speaking with her father, you might have known."

"Her father—"

"Was unaware of her attachment. My father's recent passing meant I was unable to declare myself as I otherwise would have done." Nathanial hoped the Earl would conveniently forget he had been out of mourning for a full month. "I suggest you accept this with the grace that befits your position."

"You may be the Duke of Norfolk, but that title has barely had the time to grow old on your shoulders."

"Was that a threat?" Nathanial asked softly. This man was twice his age, but in wealth, status and health, Nathanial was the superior.

"Not a threat, of course." Whitstable dabbed his napkin against his mouth. "But for you to have engaged in an understanding with the lady without her father's consent. Shady dealings. Shady indeed."

Nathanial raised an eyebrow. "That is a weighty accusation."

"Well, I had not intended . . . I have been duped, sir. Deceived."

"It is regrettable. Yet short of forcing the lady into a marriage she does not want, there is little you can do to rectify the situation. I do not suggest making it public." His eyes were hard. "Any attempt to discredit me will not reflect well on you."

"You—"

"Good day, Whitstable. I hope your disappointment is of short duration." He rose and walked away, leaving the Earl to his impotent rage and cold breakfast.

Nathanial had proposed.

Theo considered her nerves relatively steady, but now she felt as though her entire body was trembling, hot and cold all at once. She wasn't sure if she was more shocked that he had asked her to marry him, or that he had given her such liberties for when they were married.

She, Theodosia Beaumont, was going to marry one of the most eligible men in London. A man she had heard more than one young lady compose sonnets about. And, if she was honest with herself, she could understand why. It was not his features alone that compelled—though he was by no means unhandsome—but the way he held himself. With the confidence that came from a man born to wealth and privilege.

Annabelle shut her bedroom door behind her and turned to face Theo. "Is it true?" she demanded.

"If by that, do you mean am I engaged, then yes." Theo climbed onto the window seat and stared at the condensation still blurring the outside world from her view. "To Nathanial."

"Theo. *Nathanial*." Annabelle's voice was a hushed whisper. "He's the Duke of Norfolk."

"Believe it or not, Anna, that had occurred to me."

"Be serious." Annabelle placed herself in Theo's line of view. "He told Papa of an *existing attachment*."

"Of course he did," Theo said impatiently, although her stomach coiled at the thought. Nerves and perhaps something else. Although she knew she was not, the idea of being the object of Nathanial's affections wasn't totally abhorrent. "He had to say something to convince Papa to relinquish the Earl of Whitstable's claim."

"But you're not attached to him, are you?"

Theo gave a scornful snort. "Lord, no. It's a—a marriage of convenience."

"So you aren't in love with him," Annabelle mused, returning to the bed and curling up on the pillows, legs drawn up before her. She wrapped her arms around them. "And he isn't in love with you."

He was not, as he made more than amply plain in his proposal—if it could be called a proposal. He had outrightly said she could not expect loyalty from him.

It was a fact well known that gentlemen often strayed from their wives; even the happiest of marriages involved infidelity as a matter of course. But hearing his intentions stated so baldly had been a trifle unpleasant. Crude, even.

Nathanial was at liberty to do as he chose, but she did not have to know, or even think, about it.

"I would not expect him to be," Theo said calmly, "considering we have not often seen each other this past year, and even less before then. But Annabelle, you can't tell anyone it's not true."

"Of course not." Annabelle tossed her blonde head before putting her mind to her next consideration.

"You must be happy not to marry the Earl, of course, but what happened to your knight in shining armour?"

Theo sighed. "He wears a waistcoat, I suppose. And he is not so much a romantic figure as an old friend. But when you consider it was Nate or Lord Whitstable, there was no competition. I would have married just about *anyone* who wasn't him."

And, now she had time to think about it, Nathanial's intention of leaving her to her own devices meant she might find her hero in a perhaps less conventional way.

"Did Nathanial . . ." Her sister paused delicately, looking a little wary at the prospect of asking the question. "If he doesn't love you, what reason did he give for marrying you?"

"His mother wants him to marry, and I suppose he would rather marry someone he knows than a stranger." Her stomach swooped with . . . nerves? "And he doesn't want a traditional marriage, I think. With a wife that adores him or wants to use his money."

"*You* want to use his money," Annabelle pointed out.

"No, Papa wants to use his money, which is very different. *And* I warned him in advance. I said the Earl of Whitstable had offered to pay Papa's debts, or at least some of them, and put Oliver through school, and he *still* said he would marry me."

"He *must* love you then."

"No," Theo said, with only the hint of a sigh. She traced her initials on the condensation—as they were, not as they were going to be. "I can say with perfect confidence that he doesn't love me. And," she added hastily, "I don't want him to."

Annabelle gave her a long, considering look, her fingers bunched in her skirts. "What about his mama?" she asked at last, with no little trepidation. "The Duchess is . . . what if she doesn't like you?"

"Oh tosh! She has known me since birth, and what could be better than Nathanial marrying an old friend? I'm sure she'd much rather me than some unknown."

"You cannot be serious!"

Nathanial looked at his mother with resignation. Elinor, present for one of her dutiful visits, stared at him in what he could only presume was mute horror.

"I am perfectly serious," he said. "I asked her to marry me this morning and I have her father's permission."

"But Theo is—" His mother struggled for words. "She's a nice girl, of course, but she's not *duchess* material."

"In what way?" he enquired, his voice hardening. It was perfectly true that Theo was, while not ineligible, not the glittering match his mother had hoped for. Her father was too done-up, and she was not endowed with a fortune of any consideration. But now he was committed, he found he would not tolerate criticism of his intended. At least, not to his face; he was well aware his mother would be vocal enough when he was out of earshot. "She is the daughter of an earl whose estate borders mine."

"The daughter of an earl who is beyond destitute," his mother snapped. "Everyone knows the Beaumonts don't have a feather to fly with. They'll leech you of everything you have."

"It is fortunate, then, that I am rich."

"Hardly fortunate when you will abuse your riches in such a way. Besides, you've hardly seen the girl recently."

"Have I not?" Nathanial raised an eyebrow. "How can you be certain I have not been calling on her?"

"Well—" She stopped, frowned. "*Have* you?"

"I've seen her more than enough for me to be assured she is precisely the woman I wish to marry."

"Nathanial," Elinor said, leaning forward and taking his hand in hers. "Can you look at me and tell me you're being utterly honest?"

"Of course he cannot be!" The Dowager pressed her fingers against her forehead. "He's only saying it to vex us for persuading him to marry."

"I am most certainly not," he said. "I have every intention of marrying Theo, with or without your approval."

"When I suggested you consider matrimony," she said, "I had no thoughts of you choosing a penniless chit of a girl with—is she even in possession of a dowry, Nathanial?"

"It seems rather churlish to care about trifles such as dowries when I have no need of them."

Elinor frowned at him. "Then you *must* love her."

"Of all the ladies I've had the pleasure of meeting, I've only asked one to be my wife. You may draw whatever conclusions from that you will."

Neither his mother nor Elinor seemed overly pleased with that statement, judging by the thinned lips and narrowed eyes they directed at him, but Elinor at least leant back in her chair. "I suppose it could be worse," she said.

"Indeed it could! Theo is a dear girl and I have every expectation she will make me a splendid wife."

His mother sagged in her chair. "She used to run wild in the woods with you at Havercroft, Nathanial."

"Then she is already familiar with the estate," Nathanial said, tired of the proceedings and the opposition he had anticipated but did not enjoy. Unlike Whitstable, whom he had positively enjoyed taking down a notch or two, his mother was a different matter. "I need not remind you, of course, that as my wife and a duchess, she will be deserving of every respect."

His mother bristled, but Elinor laid a hand on her arm. "Theo hasn't yet fully grown out of her tomboy ways," she said soothingly. "I'm certain marrying a duke will lay a sense of what's proper on her head. And consider how handsome their children will be!"

He groaned. "Please, no talk of children."

"You *will* sire heirs, Nathanial," his mother said, sniffing. "As for respect—you may be sure I shall do my duty, and I shall be *civil*, but I don't like it, and that's that."

"Luckily," he said, his tolerance for his family quite exhausted, "the only people required to like it are Theo and myself. As I know you have every intention of informing Cassandra and Penelope of my decision, Elinor, I shall leave my news in your capable hands. Goodbye, Mama."

He did not turn to see his mother's expression as he left the room.

Chapter Five

Mrs Juliet Stanton had been unreluctantly widowed for approximately five years. In that time, she had taken a number of lovers. Not because she had any particular desire for many of them, but because they provided her with comfort and status at very little cost. It left her on the fringe of the *ton*, but there were more important things, such as being able to afford the latest fashions, and having a carriage of her own. Money could buy almost anything, and a gentleman's pocket was directly linked to his breeches—or so she had, in five years of widowhood, concluded.

One of her more esteemed callers, who never failed to leave a token of his appreciation, was His Grace, the Duke of Norfolk.

It had taken Juliet a long time to dig her claws into him, and she had no intention of letting them slip. When the Duke called, she was *always* at home.

"The Duke of Norfolk," her butler said, bowing her guest into her dressing room. He, as did the rest of the staff, knew she would always receive him. As it was, she had been intending to visit the opera, and had a dress already laid out, but that could be easily rectified.

"You may go, Mary," she said to her maid, gesturing for the dress to be taken away. Luckily, she was wearing nothing but a silken dressing gown, and as she turned to the Duke, it slipped off one shoulder. She revelled in the way his gaze marked the movement. "Your Grace," she said. "What a delightful surprise. Business or pleasure?"

"I'm not in the mood for cards tonight."

"Pleasure it is." She motioned to the butler, who closed the door discreetly behind him. Now the Duke was here, she would allow no more visitors tonight. "I shall have wine brought up directly."

He passed through her dressing room into her bedchamber, and she followed, feet bare against the carpet. Unusually, for a man so disposed to talk, he remained silent, leaning against the door and observing her as she toyed with the lace around her bosom.

Still, he would not be like that for long; men weren't complex creatures. A little silence, a little softness, a little of her special sweetness, and they always opened themselves up to her.

"You always keep your rooms in such disarray, my dear," he said, his customary languid tone somewhat edged.

"Why, if I had known you were coming, I might have prepared them a little." She padded forwards to him and laid a hand on his arm. He glanced down at the contact, and at the diamond bracelet clasped around her wrist—a gift from another of her callers. "You may relax here," she said. "When you are with me, the outside world does not exist."

"A fanciful thought." With an impatient movement, he shook her off. "Reality is not so easily dissuaded."

"Then perhaps you should tell me your worries, Your Grace, and I might help."

He laughed. "Help? You are in no position to help me, Juliet, no matter how I might wish it."

"But you do wish it?"

A knock at the door interrupted them, and her man laid a decanter of wine, with two glasses, on the table.

"I have no wish to talk," he said, sitting on the bed and tugging at the buttons of his waistcoat. "Not at present."

"I'll fetch you some wine," she said, not allowing her unease to penetrate her voice. Something was most definitely wrong; the Duke was not a man of purely carnal delights. Her company was, usually, worth more to him.

As she returned to the bedroom, she lingered in the doorway, watching him, the wine loosely clasped in her fingers. He glanced up to see her there and beckoned her impatiently forward. There was a distracted look in his eyes she didn't like, but she sauntered closer anyway, letting a smile curve her lips. "I believe you came here for a distraction?"

"Yes," he said curtly. "So distract me."

They came together with a little less than their usual passion, and when they finished, she handed him a goblet of wine, worry tightening her chest. Had he finally tired of her?

"Are you suitably distracted?" she asked.

"Momentarily." He shook his head and gazed at the burgundy liquid as though it held the answer to his problems. "I suppose I ought to warn you I will be temporarily detained."

Knowing better than to let the Duke see the possessiveness that threatened to grip her, she merely arched a brow. "Oh?"

"I'm getting married, and should take my bride for a brief tour of the country after we wed."

For a moment, the only sound was the spluttering of the candlelight. The Duke of Norfolk was getting married? To *someone else?*

Her hopes had never been properly articulated, not even to herself, but he was her longest standing lover and one of the most generous. She had thought that with enough time, she might encourage him to elevate her so he would not be obliged to lose her.

Instead, *she* was losing *him.*

"Really?" she said with a careless laugh. "I hadn't thought you the marrying kind."

"I'm not."

She trailed her fingers along his arm to his shoulder, savouring the feel of his muscles against her skin. "Then why pledge yourself to a girl you cannot care for?"

"Obligation." He took another sip before putting the goblet to one side. "She understands, I think, the reality of the situation between us."

"And that reality is?"

"That we will be married in name only—at least until I have need for an heir." He turned his gaze back to her and tugged one of her copper curls. "I have no intention of my marriage detracting from my usual life, Juliet, never fear."

Only it would. No longer would he be the carefree Duke that had graced her bed for so long. He would have a wife, whose demands on his time could not be denied. And who, moreover, would be sure to exact such demands. No woman was safe against his charms, and especially not a girlish debutante. She would be jealous and possessive, and he would no doubt appease her.

Juliet hated the girl already.

"And who might this lucky lady be?" she asked throatily, exploring the outline of his mouth with her nail. "The Season has many candidates. Have you chosen from among them?"

"The lady is Lady Theodosia Beaumont."

Juliet's expression darkened. Lady Theodosia was not personally known to her—there had been few occasions they might meet—but she knew of her. A slip of a girl with a pair of arresting blue eyes under a dark head of hair. The precise opposite of Juliet's ethereal charms.

"You surprise me," she said. "I thought her father was impoverished." Her tone was light, but a little of her bitterness seeped through. "Can she really match the great Duke? There are few women who can do that, I fancy."

His smile hardened. "I've known the family for many years. Their estate borders mine, and I have a great deal of respect for them."

"I'm sure I meant no offence."

He sat up, slipping free from her arms and ceaseless caresses. "Then you must learn not to give it."

"I am sorry," she said, pressing a kiss against the back of his shoulder. Every inch of her prickled with the injustice of having to apologise, but she kept the smile on her face. "I spoke in haste and without thought. If you desire to marry Lady Theodosia Beaumont, what right have I to comment on the match? I only wish you to be happy."

"And," he said dryly, "for my visits to continue."

"I would not be flesh and blood if I did not desire that."

"Then let me put your mind at rest—once I've returned from my honeymoon, we will continue the usual way of things."

She pressed another kiss to his back and wrapped her arms around his chest. "I can ask for no more," she said, though she was struck with the urge to cry—or perhaps rage. For now, however, she could do neither, so she merely pressed her chin against his shoulder and closed her eyes.

Later, she would consider what she could do to reclaim her Duke.

The marriage between Lady Theodosia Beaumont and the Duke of Norfolk was an appropriately lavish affair. After the vows, during which Theo's mother wept, they retired to the traditional wedding breakfast, and later to Norfolk House.

The Dowager Duchess had removed from the premises before the wedding, and Theo was now mistress of the great house. The housekeeper gave her a tour where she met all the staff and was regaled with a dizzying number of duties and names, and she did her best not to appear too overwhelmed. Being a duchess was very different from being the eldest daughter of an impoverished Earl, and she was now, for the first time, seeing precisely what would be expected from her. Nerves overset Theo, and she barely said two words to her new husband before they retired for the night. In separate rooms.

It was fortunate, she reflected, that she had no expectations from Nathanial. He had gone through with the wedding and she was safe now from the designs of the likes of Whitstable. That was all the duty required of him.

She stared at her reflection in the mirror as Betsy, her lady's maid, removed the heavy diamond necklace from around her neck—an heirloom from the Dowager—and laid out the nightgown. Her mother had taken her shopping before her marriage and bought a great many things Theo could see no use for. The flimsy nightgown, so very different from her usual cotton affairs, was one of them.

"There, Your Grace," Betsy said, placing the necklace inside its box. "That's everything. Will you require anything more?"

Although she knew her marriage to Nathanial saved her from a far worse fate, she half wished she could turn back time and still be in her childhood bed. Her reflection, too, showed a girl with dark hair curling to her shoulders and flushed cheeks. She did not have the poise expected of a duchess.

"That will be all," she said, flicking her gaze to Betsy's ruddy face. "Thank you."

Betsy bobbed a curtsy. "Your Grace."

Your Grace. That would take some getting used to, as would her marriage. To Nathanial.

Not, of course, that it would change too much. She would attend the same balls and parties, though with a little more freedom, and she would be granted more pin money than she knew what to do with. Nathanial had already outlined what she could expect from being his wife.

Theo turned her attention to the large bed. It was a grand affair, almost terrifyingly so, and she half felt she might lose herself amongst the wide expanse of mattress, tangling sheets, and piled pillows. It was a bed for a princess.

For a duchess.

Before she had a chance to investigate further, there was a knock at the door. Nathanial poked his head through. "I thought I saw your maid go downstairs," he said by way of greeting.

Theo stared at him in horror. The flickering candlelight illuminated his sharp cheekbones and mobile mouth. Now, more than ever, she understood the sonnets dedicated to his face alone.

"What are you doing here?" she asked, resisting the urge to wrap her arms around herself. She may be his wife now, but she was a single layer away from being naked. "I thought we agreed—"

"We did agree," he said, advancing further into the room and shutting the door behind him. "You may relax. I'm not here to steal your innocence."

Theo didn't precisely want to experience the act her mother had, vaguely, explained to her, but an emotion akin to disappointment settled in her gut. To compensate, she rose. His gaze darted down her body, and her hand, braced against the table, tightened. "If you're not here to share my bed," she said, "why *are* you here?"

A slight frown caught his brows as his gaze, once again, dipped, and found its way back to her face. "To talk, but perhaps this isn't the best time."

"Do you think we made the right decision?" she blurted.

He stepped closer, until he captivated her senses. He had no right being so tall—her brother Henry was the larger of the two men, but Henry wasn't here. There was only Nathanial and her, in her bedroom. As man and wife.

Goodness, Betsy had piled the fire far too high; she had not thought it was so hot. Resisting the urge to fan herself, she clasped her hands before her.

"To marry?" he asked. "Don't tell me you're having cold feet now."

"No." Her voice was oddly breathy, and she stepped back to create some space between them—space they needed, because for some unaccountable reason, she was far too aware of *him*. "Not cold feet exactly, but—"

"You fear I regret the match?"

Looking up at him, at the grey eyes that usually held so much amusement, she noted their seriousness. Their steadiness.

"Yes," she whispered.

He reached out and tucked a strand of her hair behind her ear. "Then fear not, my dear—you will prove a charming wife."

"And you a charming husband?"

His hand hesitated. "Do you wish me to be?" he asked at last.

She hardly knew what she wished. All she knew was when he stood in front of her as he did now, she longed for *something*. The air was no longer quite enough; she would suffocate without more.

His thumb brushed her cheekbone and her lips parted as she sucked in a breath. His gaze darted to her mouth. When he glanced up again, there was warmth in his eyes that hadn't been there before. Her knees felt distinctly wobbly.

"I should go," he said, retracting his hand. "Goodnight, Theo."

She ought to move, to clamber onto the large and awe-inspiring bed, but she couldn't quite coax her legs into action. And when Nathanial glanced back from the doorway, hesitating with one hand wrapped around the wood, she thought she saw the same confusion written across his face, as though something had just transpired between them—something as unexpected for him as it was new for her.

But instead of articulating his thoughts and putting a name to the sudden tension in the room, he merely shook his head and closed the door behind him as he left.

Chapter Six

After their honeymoon, during which they rather modestly toured the Lake District, Theo and Nathanial returned to London to take up their position at the front of Society's *ton*. Nathanial had, of course, procured Almack's vouchers, and they reached that hallowed establishment for ten o'clock on the second evening of their return.

Theo had been to Almack's several times over the course of her debut. She had, however, never once entered on the arm of a duke, and it transpired that made the situation entirely different.

For a start, she was announced as Her Grace, The Duchess of Norfolk, a title that seemed altogether too stately for her. Then, as though that in itself wasn't enough, she found herself the subject of every person's stare. Whispers erupted from behind fans and under bobbing curls.

Nathanial, to her relief, steered her across the packed room to his sister, Elinor's, side. She didn't look especially interested in spreading rumours, and instead waved her fan at them. "Theodosia," she said.

"Nathanial, I'm almost surprised you came—I haven't seen you at Almack's in an age."

"I usually find the entertainment somewhat wanting," he said languidly. "But I thought I ought to accompany my wife, seeing as we are so recently back from our honeymoon."

"How generous of you," Theo muttered.

"And because," Elinor said, a little too pointedly, "you are so madly in love, of course."

"Ah." Nathanial's voice was quiet, and Theo pinched his arm for having made such a stupid, infernal claim to *both* their families. By the scepticism in Elinor's voice, she didn't believe it for a moment, anyway. "Yes. Of course."

"I suppose you can hardly bear to be apart," Elinor continued, an eyebrow slightly raised. The resemblance between her and Nathanial was even greater when she did that. "I remember when I married my dear Robert, I was the same."

"Absolutely," Nathanial said dryly. "As you can see, we are joined at the hip. Theo, dance with me?"

If any other man had asked her with such abruptness, she would have been tempted to refuse, but Nathanial was her husband and they were supposed to be in love. It was extremely irritating.

Sometimes, at moments like these, she remembered the moment between them on their wedding night. The thickness of the air, and the way he had looked at her. But since then, nothing out of the ordinary had happened. They had dined together, travelled together, and Nathanial had not so much as alluded to it.

Theo was starting to believe it was a dream.

"You are rude," she scolded as he led her to the forming couples.

His lips twitched. "It is becoming abundantly clear I am destined to be a great disappointment to you."

"You're laughing at me."

"I wouldn't dream of it. I have an excellent sense of self-preservation."

"You're abominable," she informed him.

"That's right." He steered her expertly through the dance, his hand ghosting over hers, the touch so delicate she might have almost imagined it. "No, don't tuck in your lip. You're exceptionally charming when you jut it at me."

"I hate you."

74

"Quite so."

The amusement lurking in his eyes drew a laugh from her. "As payback, I must dance with several *extremely* personable gentlemen to make you jealous."

"A jealous husband?" he said with a lopsided smile. "Surely not."

"You must pretend to be, you know. Otherwise how else will people believe we're in love?"

His smile widened. "Of course. How else?"

"And, to be sure, I will flirt with them *shockingly*."

"I should expect nothing less," he said, and although she knew he was teasing—their entire conversation had been in jest—she felt just the flicker of disappointment as the dance ended and he bowed over her hand.

He did not kiss it as a true romantic gentleman ought to have done.

Of course, he was not a true romantic gentleman; he was her husband. The two were, in her mind, entirely different. What she needed to do was find a gentleman who might be persuaded to fill that role.

With that thought in mind, she went in search of her next partner.

And thus the evening passed. She danced with any number of young men, but to her disappointment, none were up to snuff. Most, aside from the truly awkward, were amenable to light flirtation, but that was not enough for Theo. Nathanial, when he was in the mood for it, could flirt; she knew from him how little flirtation meant. Besides, none quite fit her idea of what a true hero should be.

As night turned into early morning, Theo resigned herself to failure once again.

That was, until she beheld the gentleman that emerged from the card room.

He was tall—taller than Nathanial and indeed most other gentlemen in the ballroom—with dark hair swept with careless grace across his forehead. The lighting wasn't bright enough to see the precise colour of his eyes, but she felt certain they would be a dreamy dark; a colour she could sink her entire soul into.

What's more, he was dressed in the height of fashion. Not as a dandy, whose aspirations towards fashion she held in the deepest contempt, but as a Corinthian. His coat was perfectly fitted across his broad shoulders, his buttons were highly polished, and his breeches clasped shapely calves.

He was, in short, her every romantic ideal.

She fluttered her fan, hardly listening to Lady Tabitha, who stood beside her and jabbered about beaus. Perhaps, if she was lucky, the strange man would approach her.

He glanced up and met her gaze from across the room. The world stilled and her sense of being shifted, as though gravity drew her towards him. This was what love should feel like: an undeniable connection that almost shimmered in the air between them.

Heavens, she ought to have met him before she married Nathanial.

Suddenly aware she'd been holding his gaze for far too long, she glanced away.

"And so I told him that I couldn't *possibly* consider his suit," Lady Tabitha continued beside her, oblivious to the fact Theo's attention was fixed on the man who strolled deliberately towards them.

Oh, he was so close now he could probably hear what Lady Tabitha was saying.

Theo's heart in her mouth, she did her best to attend the final part of Tabitha's monologue. "After all," Tabitha said triumphantly, "he is merely the son of the local squire, and *I* am the daughter of a Viscount."

"Yes," Theo murmured, glancing over her fan to where the man had stopped, one group from her. Men were such odious creatures—after walking towards her with such deliberation, he ought to have found an excuse to be introduced. Instead, he was talking with Lady Bolton with every appearance of absorption.

"Come," she said to Tabitha, linking that lady's arm firmly with hers. "Penelope is not dancing and I've yet to speak with her."

"Lady Peterborough?" Tabitha clarified, her earlier superiority dissolving. "You're on first-name terms with Lady Peterborough?"

"We grew up on neighbouring estates." Theo dragged Tabitha through the crowd towards Penelope, her path coincidentally taking her past the man. "She *is* ten years older than me, to be sure, but I know her well. Besides, now I've married the Duke, she's my sister-in-law."

"Theo," Penelope said affectionately when they arrived, kissing Theo's cheek. "How nice to see you." Her voice, unlike Elinor's, was sincere. Elinor had married before Theo was out of leading strings, but Penelope had been a fixture of Theo's early childhood, and the only one of Nathanial's sisters who approved of the match. "What a crush! I declare I've never seen Almack's so crowded."

The man, who had looked up as Theo passed, now stared at her with a look of calculating surprise. Perhaps *now* he would approach.

"I've not seen so many gentlemen here all Season," Lady Tabitha gushed. "Which is just as well—I find nothing is quite as much fun without gentlemen, don't you?"

"Tabitha," Theo said in exasperation, "do you think of nothing but beaus?"

"You're *married*," Tabitha said as though it were obvious. "Of course you don't have to consider how many gentlemen are present, or how many you dance with."

"I've not been married long."

"But you snagged a duke." Tabitha sighed dreamily. "There are so few unattached dukes, you know—and none so handsome as the Duke of Norfolk."

Theo started to dispute that, before stopping. As far as Penelope—in fact, as far as the *ton*—was concerned, she was in love with Nathanial, and was no doubt obligated to think him the most handsome man in the room.

Starved of that option, she looked at Penelope, in the hopes Penelope might support her, but she found Penelope staring over her shoulder with a look of disgust and—was that fear?

"Lady Penelope," a smooth voice said from behind them. It reminded her of honey, with a bite of pepper underneath. "What a pleasure to see you here."

"I'm Lady Peterborough now," Penelope said, pinching her lips together.

"Then allow me to present my congratulations."

Theo turned, already knowing who she would see. And there he was: the man she'd seen from across the room in all his dark-haired beauty. Up close, he was perhaps more handsome than she'd imagined, with a straight nose and green flecks in his brown eyes. She judged him to be perhaps thirty, and his smile, when he turned it on her, was enough to melt her knees.

"I do not believe we've been introduced," he said, raising his eyebrows at Penelope. "I find you to be keeping excellent company this time we meet, Cousin."

Cousin? A frown puckered Theo's brow. She hadn't been aware of any cousins in Nathanial's family—and certainly none of this calibre. All *she* had were female cousins, and she had never felt the deprivation so keenly.

"This is the Duchess of Norfolk," Penelope said pointedly. "Nathanial's bride."

"Then it appears I have two sets of congratulations to offer." He raised her hand and pressed it to his lips. "Duchess."

"Theo, meet Sir Montague Radcliffe," Penelope said. "Our cousin."

"It appears I arrived back in England at the right time," he said, his eyes never leaving Theo's.

"This is Lady Tabitha," Theo said. Her voice was slightly breathless.

"A pleasure," Sir Montague said, bowing over Lady Tabitha's hand. He glanced back up and his gaze found Theo's again. "Might I have the pleasure of this dance, Duchess?"

She glanced at Penelope, but Penelope was too engaged in looking across the room at her sisters and Nathanial, and so she accepted with a smile.

"I see you have the fortune to have married into the family," he said as he led her out onto the dancefloor. "Once again, allow me to offer my congratulations. I shall be certain to congratulate my cousin—I had not thought him capable of so dazzling a match."

"I'm not dazzling at all," Theo told him bluntly, drawing a surprised, genuine smile from him. "Quite the contrary, in fact. I'm surprised no one has mentioned it."

"They have not, and if they did so, I would tell them how wrong they are."

He really was an *excellent* flirt. How fortunate she had met him. "I'm much obliged."

"Lady Peterborough called you Theo," he said, his hand fitting into hers. She had never noticed how charged a touch could be, tingling through her body from the point of contact. "What must I do to gain such familiarity?"

A dangerous question. "I was unaware they had a cousin," she said instead.

To her relief, he laughed, unconcerned by her clumsy redirection. "Keeping me a secret, are they? The truth is, I'm the black sheep of the family."

Theo had suspected that from the look on Penelope's face. "Is it for good reason?"

"Your Nathanial would say so."

"He's not my Nathanial," she retorted before she could help herself. She coloured. "That is to say . . . We are not joined at the hip."

"It appears not—to my benefit."

She looked up at his captivating, slightly mocking smile. Nathanial smiled like that, sometimes, when he thought she was being particularly amusing or silly. "Are you so pleased to dance with me?"

"I resolved to ask you to dance the moment I laid eyes on you."

Oh, he *was* charming, and far more so than Nathanial. It would have been all too easy to release her inhibitions and allow herself to enjoy the pleasure of his company, but Penelope's expression stuck with her.

"Sir Montague," she said, cocking her head. "May I ask you a question?"

"With pleasure."

"Will I get into trouble for dancing with you?"

"Why?" He laughed, but his eyes were curious. "Is the Duke such a fearsome husband?"

"Oh no," she reassured him. "We have a comfortable arrangement, he and I. But I wondered if—you see, I am fond of Penelope, and she doesn't like you."

His eyes hardened for an instant before he laughed again. "You are amazingly direct, Duchess. No, don't blush—you are quite right: Penelope does *not* like me."

"But why?"

"There are several reasons, and now I have returned to town, I expect you will be regaled with them." He considered her. "Have you been married long?"

"Not long."

"Then perhaps you will remember what it is to hold someone in affection. I confess, I behaved badly towards Penelope when I was younger, and I see she has not yet forgiven me—despite a husband." He smiled. "I have been away from London a great many years, you see."

"Did you leave because of Penelope?" she pressed.

"Heavens no. I left because I took part in an ill-conceived duel."

Not only was he a rake—her suspicions of that were confirmed by his admission he had treated Penelope badly—but he was a man inclined to duelling. "Was the other man killed?"

"Sadly, yes."

She blinked in shock. She had never encountered a murderer before, no matter how accidental it may or may not have been. Did he suffer from guilt? He certainly didn't seem to—his skin was lightly bronzed and he regarded her with a mocking smile, as though he sensed the thoughts that passed through her head.

"Well," she said, struggling to find the right thing to say, if there *was* a right thing to say. "I'm sure you must be very sorry."

"I beg you would not attempt to attribute any morals to me. As my family will no doubt inform you, I am irredeemable and my character is sadly flawed."

"Well, perhaps you have not killed any more men since you left," she ventured.

Another surprised laugh left him. "No, I have not killed any men since then."

Ought she congratulate him on his forbearance? That didn't quite seem right, but then, neither did suggesting that his lack of recent murderous tendencies made him an upstanding member of society.

In truth, the frisson of danger that accompanied him intrigued her.

The music ended and the gong rang for the evening's supper. Sir Montague offered her his arm, which she would have taken if it were not for the cold voice behind her.

"Duchess," Nathanial said. His eyes glittered with an emotion she couldn't place. "I believe the honour is mine."

"Nathanial." Blushing, confused by both his expression and the commanding note in his voice, Theo accepted his arm. "I believe you are already acquainted with your cousin, Sir Montague."

Excellent work stating the obvious.

She blushed, wishing her shame did not creep so high up her neck to her cheeks. Nathanial glanced at her, taking in her blush, before returning his gaze to Sir Montague. "I am," Nathanial said curtly.

Sir Montague bowed, his gaze never leaving Nathanial's face. "And so we meet again, cousin."

Nathanial inclined his head and glanced down at Theo. "Shall we go in, my love?"

He only called her 'my love' when he was pretending they were affectionately married, but for the strangest reason, she didn't *want* to pretend in front of Sir Montague.

"Really, Nathanial," she scolded under her breath as they entered the dining room. "When I said you should play the jealous husband, this was *not* what I meant."

"What better time than when you were flirting so brazenly with another man?"

There was a hard note in his voice that compelled her to snap, "I was not flirting so very much. Certainly no more than with any other gentleman."

"I would beg to disagree. And so, I would surmise, would the entire ballroom."

So this was to be their first argument, and over a man she had met but once and very briefly. In a place, moreover, where anyone could see them. Theo's stomach roiled and she felt too hot. Her smile slipped.

"This conversation should not take place here," she said.

"Then you shall be certain I shall address it at home."

Home. That cavernous place in which she now lived, its halls filled with servants waiting for her command. It felt no more like home than this ballroom, where instead of a mistress, she was a glittering ornament.

To her relief, Nathanial appeared to relax as he greeted a mutual acquaintance. She allowed him to lead her to her seat and the rest of the night passed in a blur. Nathanial played the role of young husband with his customary careless charm, and if Theo noticed the fury in his eyes that surfaced whenever he glanced at Sir Montague, no one else appeared to.

He did not leave her side for the remainder of the evening.

Chapter Seven

By the time they arrived home in the early hours of the morning, Theo had a headache and little inclination to confront Nathanial. Judging by his silence and his frown like a gathering storm, he did not share her inhibitions.

"That will be all," he said to the butler as they walked into the house. "The Duchess will ring for her maid when she retires."

"Very good, sir."

Theo's head throbbed. "Really, Nathanial," she said as she followed him into the drawing room. "You're being ridiculous."

He stopped in the centre of the room and swung around to face her. "When I said we could come to an arrangement, I did not mean that you could flirt with my cousin in front of the entire ballroom."

"I was flirting no more than any other young lady there."

"Any other young lady," he said grimly, "is not married to me."

"You are being ridiculous!" The words left her mouth too fast, but she could not bring herself to regret them. "What is it about Sir Montague that you dislike? For you know it is not my *flirting*, or you would have approached me far earlier." Angry tears sparkled at the corners of her eyes, and she brushed them aside impatiently. "You told me we would not change our lifestyles when we were married."

"And yet I accompanied you to Almack's."

"If that is the problem, to be sure I absolve you of all responsibility."

His jaw snapped and his mouth thinned. She had never seen him this angry, and certainly never at her. The sight made her chest hurt. "Sir Montague is not a gentleman you should associate with," he said.

"Why?"

"He was on the Continent for killing a man."

"And *that*, he had the goodness to tell me himself."

Nathanial hesitated. In the darkness, he seemed tall and silent as a god, his wrath just as terrible and unending. His presence swamped her, and she wanted nothing more than to escape this room and him.

But he was not one of her unfortunate suitors she could chase away with a well-timed smile and strongly expressed opinions. Nathanial met her opinions head-on, just as he was doing now.

Perhaps, if she was obliged to embark on a marriage of convenience, she ought to have done so with a less stubborn man.

"If you gave me a reason—" she began.

"Is my request not to ally yourself with him not enough?"

She put her hands on her hips. "No, and you know that as well as I do. I will listen to reason, Nathanial, but I refuse to blindly obey."

"I am your husband—"

"And you're behaving like a child," she said. He stiffened. "If you thought you could order me around in this overbearing fashion, you chose the wrong bride."

His nostrils flared and she gripped her reticule with both hands, preparing herself for the inevitable. They had been married less than two weeks and already he regretted it.

What an inglorious end to what had been an unpromising beginning.

"You should go to bed," he said, his voice quiet. "Before either of us say anything more we might regret."

Part of her—a rather foolish part, under the circumstances—wanted to push him still further. But no matter how tempting it might be, it was akin to picking the scab off a wound, and Theo hated blood.

"Goodnight, Your Grace," she said.

The sound of his title made him jerk, and it briefly occurred to her that she had never used it before. Previously, he had been the Marquess of Rotherham, but even then, she had referred to him by his first name.

So be it. He deserved the formality as punishment for being obnoxious.

With a curtsy, she swept past him, hoping that for once he saw a duchess before him rather than little Theo Beaumont, dress smeared with mud.

Nathanial did not come to bed for another hour. She knew that because she lay awake wondering whether he would come in and apologise. But when he finally came upstairs, although his footsteps hesitated outside her door for a moment or two, he made no move to enter, and eventually his bedroom door clicked.

Well! Odious man. Theo slammed her book shut and blew out the candle, glowering into the darkness.

For all Nathanial thought he knew about women, he still had a lot to learn. He must have seen the light underneath her door and *known* she was awake waiting for him, yet still didn't come in.

She rolled over and pressed her face into the pillow. Very well—her sweetest revenge would be sleeping peacefully without an apology.

But although she slept as she'd intended, her dreams brought with them visions of Nathanial and Montague until they merged into one.

Theo awoke the next day with a newfound determination to avoid Nathanial at all costs. If he was going to refuse to apologise, she would merely not burden herself with his presence.

Perhaps she might in fact find Sir Montague while walking with Annabelle. Her sister was right that heroes did not usually lurk in bushes, but anything was better than staying here.

First, however, she would have to rise earlier than Nathanial. Not usually a difficult task, but if she dallied, she might miss her window of opportunity; and that truly would be disastrous.

To Betsy's obvious surprise, she flung back her covers. "I would like to dress and breakfast immediately."

Betsy frowned, though her bun pulled her forehead so tight it was a wonder she could form any expression at all. "You haven't finished your drinking chocolate, Your Grace."

"I can finish it at breakfast. But I must rise quickly."

Betsy had come with her from her parents' house and no doubt recognised the expression on Theo's face, but they had been together too long for her to attempt arguing. "Yes, ma'am."

Impatiently, Theo entered her dressing room and rifled through her wardrobe until she found a blue walking dress that suited her purpose. It brought out the colour of her eyes and, so she thought, flattered her figure admirably. Now she was a duchess, she could commission more dresses than she knew what to do with, but this remained her favourite.

As soon as she was dressed, she hurried downstairs and into the breakfast room—only to pull up short at the sight of Nathanial already seated with a newspaper open before him.

"Nate," she said in shock. "What are you doing here?"

He gestured to his tea. "Eating breakfast, as you can see."

"Yes, but—it's before eleven."

"I agree, it's dreadfully early. Yet here you are."

She swallowed, the words of their argument hanging between them. This was precisely the awkwardness she had hoped to avoid. "Forgive me, Your Grace, but—"

"If you call me *Your Grace* once more, I will throw this tea at you," he warned. "Now why don't you sit down?"

A reluctant smile touched her mouth. "You *are* obnoxious, Nate, coming downstairs to prevent me from sneaking away."

"I thought that might be your plan, but I didn't want you to leave before I'd had a chance to speak with you."

"Another scolding?" she asked, folding her arms. "Because if it is, you know I won't stay and listen."

"Wretch," he said, but an answering smile lit his eyes, and he held out his hand to her. "Come here, you abominable brat, and stop looking at me like I'm about to bite."

Cautiously, she placed her hand in his and his fingers curled around hers. His gaze travelled across her face for a long moment, dropping from her eyes to her mouth in a way that, for an unaccountable reason, made her heart pound. The trace of a frown appeared between his eyes and he released her hand a little too fast. "Can you forgive me?" he asked.

He was impossible. She scowled. "Will you not allow me to be angry at you?"

"Ideally not."

Finally, she took a seat beside him. "I suppose I ought not to have said some of the things I did, either."

"And I suppose I should be content with that as your apology."

"You *were* being unreasonable," she reminded him.

"If I was, it was not without provocation. But," he added, sobering, "my anger was not at you and I should have directed it to its proper place."

"Why do you hate Sir Montague so much?"

"Aside from the fact he tried to steal my wife from me?"

She bit her lip, but could not hide her smile. "Don't be absurd."

"Very well. Let us just say there is bad blood between us, and while I'm sure he was charming— Penelope could tell you, indeed, how very charming he can be—his motives are unlikely to be pure."

"I can handle myself, Nathanial."

"Can you? You don't know what he's capable of, Theo."

"And what?" she challenged, meeting his gaze, "is he capable of?"

His smile was grim. "Everything you could possibly imagine."

At around midday, the butler knocked on Nathanial's study door. "Sir Montague to see you," he said. The butler, having been a loyal devotee of the family for a number of years, did not attempt to hide the disapproving ring to his voice. Sir Montague was well known to the retainers, and not for anything good.

Nathanial glanced up with a frown. He'd expected this visit, but it didn't displease him any less for having been anticipated. "Send him in."

"Very good, Your Grace."

Montague, in a blue coat and tan buckskins, entered the room with a hand outstretched. "Nathanial, glad to see you've finally come into your title."

Nathanial declined the hand. "Is that right?"

"And to hear you've married." Montague laughed with his customary, and irritating, charm. "I must congratulate you. The Duchess is a remarkably pretty woman."

"I noticed you found her so."

He laughed again and sat, though Nathanial had neglected to offer him the seat. "You can glare at me all you like, but I wasn't the only one entranced. She is remarkably refreshing."

Nathanial had known she would have no shortage of gentlemen interested in her charms now her status had been elevated; and he had meant it when he had said he would not mind if she took a lover.

He had not, however, anticipated his cousin taking an interest.

"Tell me why you're back in London," he said abruptly. "I was under the impression you were planning on staying on the Continent."

"Not forever. Paris is charming, but nothing can compare to London."

"If you even consider—"

"As enjoyable as your righteous anger is," Montague interrupted, "I did not come here to discuss your wife."

Nathanial raised an eyebrow. "Why, then? Are your pockets to let?"

"Do you think I have no shame?" Montague spread his hands wide. "You are my cousin. I'm calling to pay my respects to the new Duke."

"You had better stayed away."

"You wound me."

"I rather think you can bear it," Nathanial said dryly.

For the first time, Montague tilted his head, his smile fading. "Is seven years not enough time to soften your grudge, Hardinge?"

No amount of time would persuade Nathanial to soften his grudge. He no longer cared for Lucy— indeed, now he was older, he suspected he never had—but that did not absolve Montague of responsibility. Not only had he compromised the girl, but he had pursued her despite knowing Nathanial had taken an interest—or perhaps solely for that reason. He had taken her and he had ruined her, and while Nathanial was in general an even-tempered man, there was nothing he detested more than betrayal.

His father's title could never go to Montague. He would do everything in his power to prevent it.

"It is not," Nathanial said, leaning back in his chair. "Nor should it be. I have no doubt you are here to prevent my marriage, but I'm afraid you were too late."

"I would never dream of doing such a thing."

Nathanial almost snorted. Montague's interest in Theo may partly be due to her sweetness, her blunt charm, but the main reason was no doubt because she was his wife.

An odd possessiveness gripped him. He had lost Lucy to a man who did not care for her; he would not lose Theo.

"Let me make myself plain," he said. "You may trifle with every other girl in London. Do what you will, live how you choose. But my wife is out of bounds. Do you understand?"

Montague's smile was amused and cruel. "So the rumours are true. You did make a love match."

If Nathanial agreed, Montague would hound Theo still more securely. If he denied it, Montague would be tempted to test the theory. Although they had known each other a long time ago, they had been close, once. Montague could read him the way few people could.

Nathanial stood abruptly. "Thank you for calling, but this conversation is over. Do not visit my house again."

"Seven years is too long to hold onto grudges," Montague said as he, too, rose. "You would find me more pleasant company if you remembered our friendship."

"Our friendship was over the moment you pursued Lucy."

"Still hung up on her?"

"Seven years is a long time," Nathanial returned, a guilty feeling arising at the thought he had not considered Lucy, or her fate, in almost that long. He pushed it aside. "Stay away from Theo."

Montague gave a sardonic bow and left the room. Nathanial remained standing, staring at the ajar door.

It was damned bad luck that Theo had taken a shine to the one man who could turn her out of the house if Nathanial died. Of all the gentlemen in the world, Theo had chosen to allow his cousin and heir to charm her. If Montague had stayed away, or if she had taken him in violent dislike, Nathanial might not have needed to interfere or keep an eye on her.

But he did not trust Montague, and especially not when he, at present, stood to inherit.

A sure way to prevent that was to produce heirs of his own. A boy. Yet that was not a given, and the process was hardly a quick one. And it would involve—

Nathanial did not let himself think about what it would involve. He had made a pledge to her that he would not visit her bed any time soon, and the hesitancy with which she had looked at him that first night had assured him she was not expecting his advances.

He would merely have to ensure that she was not taken in by Montague, through whatever means possible. That would prove a challenge given their

102

arrangement allowed them to take lovers, provided they were discreet.

But Theo would not be taking Montague as a lover if he could help it. Even if that meant taking a more active role in his marriage than he had intended.

He poured himself a glass of claret. He had a feeling he was going to need it.

Chapter Eight

There were few pleasures in London that Montague, over the course of his thirty-two years, had not sought. He'd had his fill of opera singers and dancers; now he was older, his tastes ran a little differently.

Which was why, when he found himself at the residence of Juliet Stanton, he had every intention of accepting the offer she presented.

The card party, held only for a select few, was conducted in a lavishly furnished drawing room; a parlour, similarly furnished, held the few that wanted to play deep. Juliet Stanton catered to all.

Montague did not play deep—he did not have the pockets for it, and although as a young blade he had gambled heavily, as all young men did, it wasn't in his blood. Instead, he played whist with a small party of like-minded gentlemen while Juliet Stanton held the bank. She courted interest with smiles and batted eyelashes and quiet murmurs of appreciation and encouragement. Montague had been playing the game long enough to know an expert player. She was not young, Mrs Stanton, but she played off her charms to perfection; her forest green dress brought out the copper in her hair, and her shoulders were bare to expose her elegant neck. Her smile, too, was practised, and when she leant forwards, it was to reveal the swell of her breasts.

Juliet Stanton was a woman, Montague mused, who was accustomed to dealing with men's desires.

She glanced up, blue-green eyes holding a hint of amusement. "It is your turn to play, Sir Montague."

He placed his card on the table with deliberation. "Do you consider yourself a gamester, Mrs Stanton?"

"Why, not particularly."

"A shame." He paused, letting her lean into the silence, and glanced away, to a single table lying unused. "I thought perhaps I might challenge you to a game."

"I fear I may not be a worthy opponent."

"On the contrary, I assure you. I think you can provide me with everything I need." He let his gaze drop across her body. There were other men here, but judging from the smiles she occasionally flashed them, like bait to the fish, they were already enjoying her charms.

Indeed, this entire affair was not just to boost her income—as he knew it would be doing with her playing bank—it was to advertise herself. And she was an appealing prospect.

She met his gaze with a boldness he appreciated. "Perhaps, then, we should play."

The process of setting up a table was a quick one, and he challenged her to a game of piquet. She dealt, retaining the honour of holding bank. He didn't care; this entire endeavour was not about the cards and both of them knew it.

"I had no notion you were planning on returning to London," she said, glancing at her hand. "It was my understanding you intended to be away for a long while."

"Seven years is a long while by my estimation, Mrs Stanton." He glanced around. "You have a tidy establishment here. Might you have room for another patron?"

A smile touched her mouth as she glanced at her cards. "Perhaps. I should warn you, I have exquisite tastes."

"I should expect nothing less from such an exquisite lady."

Once again, she held his gaze as she looked at him. "I've heard of you, Sir Montague," she said.

"Rumours fly in London, especially when your cousin is a duke."

A burst of anger tightened his hold on his cards, but he merely said, "Has my cousin been spreading these rumours?"

"What makes you think I run with such exalted company?"

It was Montague's turn to smile. "Rumours fly in London," he said. "It's your turn to declare."

"I have nothing to declare," she said, holding her cards to her chest. He considered her, and the cautiousness that lurked in her eyes. Although the playful smile was still on her mouth, the atmosphere had changed at his reference to her arrangement with Nathanial. He would have to play this carefully if he was to succeed.

"Perhaps we can come to an understanding."

Her eyebrow twitched; the only sign she gave that she was interested. "What could you have to offer me?"

"I am the Duke's cousin. We are not close now, but only four years separate us, and I knew him once. Suffice to say I am as pleased about the Duke's marriage as you are." There—he had scored a hit. Her mouth tightened. "I believe we may have more in common than you might think."

"I believe you win, sir," she said, placing her cards on the table and standing. "You may see me later to settle the score."

Excellent. He nodded as she walked away, back to her party of sycophants who clung to her every word and smile as though it were manna from the heavens.

Montague had never understood that level of mindless devotion. Calf love, that was what it was. Aside from a fleeting fancy for Penelope long ago, he had never been subject to such an emotion, and he could hardly conceive how troublesome it would be.

The party continued until the late hours. Montague accepted Juliet's invitation upstairs to her boudoir—a luscious room draped in red silk and heavy with perfume.

"So," she said, removing her earrings and dropping them onto her dressing table. "You claim we have something in common."

"Are you always so abrupt?"

She sent him a glance through her eyelashes. "I rarely engage in business that doesn't benefit me."

"I hardly expected otherwise. I'm a generous man." With a flourish, he produced a sapphire necklace from his waistcoat pocket. "I believe in both parties being satisfied."

She strolled towards him and picked up the necklace, examining the gold to check it was real. Fair enough; he did have a reputation, after all.

"Very well," she said, turning and showing him her back. Knowing what was expected of him, he deftly unlaced her. She shrugged her shoulders, and in a practised wiggle, let the dress pool on the ground beneath her. She wasn't wearing a chemise or stays.

"Now," she purred, stepping closer—close enough that he could count the freckles that lightly dusted her chest. "Show me what you would like."

Their lovemaking was less about the love and more about the making, which was precisely how Montague preferred to conduct his liaisons. They ended up on the floor, tangled in a silk sheet, and he pulled on his shirt.

"Now," he said, "we may discuss business."

She propped herself up on her elbow, an auburn curl falling across her breast. "A man after my own heart."

"As I'm sure you're aware, I returned to London as soon as I heard my cousin was married." He examined his fingernails with a slight frown. He had not intended on returning to England until such time as he might contrive to dispose of Nathanial without suspicion, but the marriage had forced his hand. A wife would mean children—and if he were the husband of that pretty chit, he would be more than happy to sire a great many children.

A great many children that impeded Montague's chances of inheriting the title. And, more importantly, one of England's largest fortunes.

"I suspected that was the reason," Juliet said, yawning. "Why else would a banished heir return?"

"I won't be the heir for much longer now he's married to that girl." Montague moderated his tone. "What I need is assurance that there will be no children."

"What you *need* is to get rid of the wife," Juliet said, no emotion in her voice. "Do you have a plan?"

"I need you to keep the Duke occupied while I target the Duchess. It shouldn't be difficult—she seemed amenable to my advances when I saw her last."

Juliet pulled the last of her pins from her hair. Her face remained expressionless. "You intend to seduce her?"

"A separation will ensure no heirs."

"And you think a mere flirtation will achieve this?"

Montague smiled as he recalled Nathanial's possessiveness. Rumours of a love match were probably unsubstantiated—at the ball, he had seemed unconcerned with her whereabouts or behaviour until she encountered him—but he was still her husband and subject to that age-old vice. Jealousy. "Perhaps not if it is a mere flirtation, but if I can induce her to fall in love with me, and perhaps make her preference for me clear, I believe he will be angry enough to not want involvement with her."

"A bold supposition," she mused. "But you may be right—Nathanial does have his pride."

"And that is where you come in, my dear. Dig your claws in deep. You are more experienced than she could ever be, and you know him better."

"And if he wishes for a child?"

Montague gave a thin, humourless smile. "We shall have to ensure he does not."

Chapter Nine

Of all things that came with being a duchess, Theo's favourite was the box at the theatre. Her father had never been able to afford one, and there was such ignominy in sitting in the stalls that they had never been.

Nathanial had a box.

And it was the grandest box she had ever seen, with an unparalleled view of the stage. For the first time in her life, she was able to sit at the front of her box and wave to her acquaintances, knowing that she—*she*—was a source of envy.

It was extremely satisfying.

Annabelle, her eyes equally wide, stared at the view. "You can see so much from up here," she breathed.

Theo waved at Lady Tabitha and grinned, dispelling any impression of a great lady. "Isn't it fun?" she asked, glancing at Nathanial who offered them both a quietly amused smile.

Out of the corner of her eye, she spotted Sir Montague, sitting in the stalls with two gentlemen and a lady. The lady, with auburn hair coiled elegantly at the back of her head, was one of the most beautiful she'd seen. If she'd been sitting with anyone but Sir Montague, Theo might have been tempted to ask her name. But although she and Nathanial were friends again, she suspected his opinion on Sir Montague hadn't changed.

"And the stage," Annabelle gasped, pressing a hand to her mouth. "Theo, *look*."

Before Annabelle could comment on any more, the curtains rose, and a whispering silence fell across the crowd. The opera began, a beautiful lady taking centre stage, and Theo couldn't resist leaning towards Nathanial, her voice concealed by the swell of music.

"Is your opera dancer performing tonight?" she whispered.

He blinked. "Excuse me?"

"Only, I know men have opera dancers, or perhaps an opera singer, and I wondered if one of those ladies was yours." She placed a hand on his knee and his eyes flicked down to the contact. "Don't worry—I don't mind."

"It's not a question of whether you mind, Theo." He stopped and glanced at the stage, and the beautiful ladies standing upon it. One in particular was especially striking, with a head full of blonde curls and red lips. Theo felt a pang at the idea Nathanial could be in love with her. "As it happens, I don't have an opera dancer, and if I did have one—" He groaned and rubbed a hand across his face. "This is not something we should be discussing. Not here, and not like this."

"Don't worry, Annabelle is not attending to a word we're saying."

"That's not the point." He took the hand on his knee and gently removed it, as though its presence there bothered him. Theo glanced up at him, surprised to find a trace of redness across his cheekbones. "We are still in public. And this isn't something well-bred ladies discuss."

"I'm not a well-bred lady, I'm your wife."

"Even *more* reason you shouldn't be asking those sorts of questions."

"But you would confess it, if she was?"

He groaned again. "Lord, Theo. Yes, you wretch."

Satisfied, she turned back to the stage. The scene had changed now; a man and a woman stood opposite each other and sang, their voices soaring above the orchestra, winding and twisting together in harmony that spoke of loss and love and grief. The words were in Italian, but Theo didn't need to understand them to feel the heart of the music. It tugged at her, beckoning emotions she didn't know she was capable of feeling as the woman pressed a hand to her chest.

Unexpected tears stung her eyes, and she blinked, pressing her mouth together so her face didn't betray her.

Wordlessly, Nathanial took her hand once more, his thumb smoothing circles across her skin. His fingers laced between hers, and she held on tight, letting him anchor her. There was something reassuring about the warmth of his hand; it lit something in her chest that the music drew out and cultivated.

He didn't look at her, and she didn't glance at him, either. Despite this, she was somehow aware of his proximity in a way she hadn't been before. Perhaps it was the way the on-stage lovers embraced, but for the flicker of a moment, she wondered what it would feel like for a lover to embrace her in that way.

What it would feel like for *Nathanial* to embrace her in that way.

The curtains dropped. For a heartbeat, she thought Nathanial might not release her—that perhaps he felt the same reassurance and comfort and newly budding awareness from the way their fingers locked together—but his hand loosened.

She snatched hers back and held it to her chest.

Annabelle wiped away tears. "That was wonderful. I didn't know music could . . ."

Theo pulled off her dratted glove, where Nathanial's warmth still lingered, and fixed her attention on anything but his face. Hers was a little warm. "Yes," she said, distracted. "It was spectacular."

"I'll get us some refreshments," Nathanial said, and Theo nodded without looking at him. As soon as he left, she peered over the edge of her box into the milling crowd below. The beautiful, auburn woman was still seated, exchanging smiles with a gentleman Theo didn't recognise, but Sir Montague was nowhere to be seen. Perhaps they were not together after all.

"Who are you looking for?" Annabelle asked.

Theo did not know how to explain she was searching for a distraction from her husband's presence.

"I'm not looking for anyone," she said. "I'm just looking. In the box, you can see everyone."

Everyone, that was, save the elusive Sir Montague. He would have been the ideal distraction.

Just as she was thinking how pleasant it would be to exit the box and find someone to converse with, Sir Montague himself bowed in the doorway. "Forgive me," he said as he looked directly at her, his dark eyes intense. In a rush, Theo remembered the power over her those eyes had. "I could not resist presenting myself to you as soon as I knew you were here."

Theo tapped Annabelle on the leg so she would stop gawking. "Sir Montague! I believe we have not met since Almack's."

"We have not. Are you enjoying the theatre, Your Grace?" He advanced further into the box at her motion.

"Exquisitely," she said. "Sir Montague, please allow me to present my sister, Lady Annabelle Beaumont."

"Lady Annabelle." Montague's dark eyes scanned Annabelle, whose cheeks, unusually, flushed. "A pleasure. You share your sister's beauty."

Annabelle was complimented into silence. Since Theo's marriage, she'd received far more attention from gentlemen, but she did not seem to relish it the way Theo had. Sometimes, Theo thought her sister would rather read than attend balls.

Yet Sir Montague made her bite her lip and glance down at her hands.

Theo fixed Sir Montague with a stern glance. "You are forbidden from flirting with my sister, if you please."

"My apologies. The compliment was meant equally for you."

"I am an old, married woman now," she said, trying and failing to hide her pleasure at the lazy smile Sir Montague sent her.

"Married you may be, but I will not allow you to be old." His smile sharpened, and Theo could not stop looking at the blade of his mouth. "If you are, I must be decrepit."

Theo laughed, surprised. "You can hardly be so very old."

"I am past thirty."

There were more than ten years between them, and at least in terms of experience, Theo felt the difference keenly. The thought brought a pang with it—why would a man so much older and experienced want someone as young as her?—and she cast a cursory glance into the stalls. And frowned. There was Nathanial, undeniably Nathanial, speaking with the auburn-haired lady she'd noticed before.

The same one she could have sworn Sir Montague had been seated beside.

Coincidence, she was certain.

Yet there was something about the way the lady smiled, with razor intent, that put Theo's teeth on edge. "Who is that lady?" she asked lightly.

Sir Montague glanced where she indicated. "Mrs Stanton," he said, though there was something reserved about his tone, and he sent her a hesitant glance. "Though you must not credit me with giving you her name—I doubt hers is a society the Duke would want you to keep."

As Theo watched, this Mrs Stanton laughed and put her hand on Nathanial's arm—a possessive gesture that he did nothing to shake off. As Theo watched, she leant up and whispered something in his ear, her body uncomfortably close to his.

And Nathanial, to Theo's horror, smiled.

To think he had the gall to tell her off for dancing and flirting with Sir Montague.

"This Mrs Stanton does not appear to be someone of whom my husband disapproves," she said, the lightness of her tone failing her. "In fact, it seems quite the opposite."

Annabelle sent her a helpless look that she ignored; instead, she turned back to Sir Montague. He was handsome, all right, with that thin mouth and hard jaw—and eyes that spoke of danger and hardship and something else she couldn't identify. Perhaps it was a *good* thing Nathanial was currently preoccupied with another woman; it gave her the luxury of more time with Sir Montague.

And if her husband was so taken with red-headed beauties that he forgot to get his wife a drink? Well then, perhaps his wife would be so preoccupied with Sir Montague that she forgot her thirst.

To her disappointment, there was very little time left in the interval, and Sir Montague only stayed a few more minutes, offering a teasing commentary on their mutual acquaintances—many of whom he had known for far longer than she—before departing. Annabelle only had time to splutter "*That* was Sir

Montague?" before Nathanial arrived in their box with two glasses of lemonade.

"You took longer than I expected," Theo could not help saying as she accepted her drink.

"My apologies." It may have been her imagination, but he did not seem as easy-going as he had been before he left. "I met an acquaintance in the stalls."

Annabelle watched the conversation unfold with equal parts horror and dread, but Theo ignored her. "Which acquaintance?" she asked.

"Merely an old friend. I'm sorry I kept you waiting."

An old *friend*, was it? Theo didn't believe that for a second. Aside from the fact the lady in question was distressingly beautiful, she had seen the way this Mrs Stanton had laid her hand on Nathanial's arm, and *that* spoke of proprietorial intent.

Knowing she was behaving irrationally, but with the irrepressible urge to exact some sort of revenge, Theo tossed her head. "No matter," she said as the curtains rose. "Sir Montague was good enough to come and entertain us in your absence, and I can assure you we had an excellent time. Did we not, Annabelle?"

Annabelle made an inarticulate comment.

"Did he, indeed?" Nathanial asked quietly.

"Oh, yes—and he was excessively charming. I do not think I've met a man as charming in my life. But you can be assured, Nathanial, we were perfectly discreet."

"In a box where everyone can see you?" His nostrils flared. "Yes, perfectly discreet."

Though she smiled, Theo was aware of an urge to cry. "At least I did not whisper in his ear before everyone," she said, and he glanced at her sharply. She didn't dare look at him. "I would not go *that* far, I assure you."

"Theo—"

"It's beginning." She leant forward, holding her opera glasses before her eyes though she saw nothing through them. For the entirety of the second half, she watched the performance with every appearance of avid interest. But even though when the on-stage lover died, she allowed a tear or two to slip down her cheek, Nathanial did not take her hand again.

To Nathanial's surprise, when he went downstairs the next morning at eleven, it was to see Theo hadn't yet risen. After waiting for some time, and having read the morning paper in unusual detail, he made his way to her dressing room. He found her there as he'd predicted, dabbing perfume on her wrists and for all intents and purposes perfectly ready to go down.

She glanced up and saw him in the mirror as he entered without knocking, and he noted with chagrin that the expression on her face was momentarily stricken.

"You may go, Betsy," she said coolly.

"Yes, ma'am." Betsy glanced at him before she left, her rather round face betraying a hint of anger.

"You have loyal servants," he commented, brushing an invisible fleck of dust from his cuffs. "I congratulate you."

She turned back to her reflection in the mirror and the two red spots that gathered there. The dress she'd chosen today was a frothy concoction in pale green that dipped daringly low.

"If you came here to congratulate me, you could have done so downstairs," she said.

"I might have done if you'd deigned to appear. But I believe one of the privileges of having a wife is the liberty of entering her dressing room without condemnation."

Her eyes—eyes he now noticed looked a little red-rimmed—flashed to him. "And are you much in the habit of entering dressing rooms?"

"There are certain questions ladies ought not to ask," he said, strolling forwards and examining the jewellery that lay on her dressing table. "And before you protest that you are no lady, you are my wife and a duchess."

"I shall take that as a yes."

"You may take it any way you please." He brushed his fingers across a familiar diamond-encrusted necklace. "You haven't worn this since our wedding day. I'm surprised—it looked well on you."

"They are more your mother's jewels than mine."

As he glanced down at her bare neck, he found himself tempted to run his fingers along it, to see if she would shiver the way he imagined she would. Ever since that first night, when he had looked down at her in that flimsy nightgown, he had been aware of something he hadn't before.

Attraction.

He hadn't known, until that moment, how soft and lush her body was, and what her hair looked like when it fell over her shoulders. He hadn't known how tempting it would be to kiss lips that had parted for him almost as an invitation.

But they had agreed their relationship would not be along those lines; she was his friend, not his lover, and she was very clearly looking elsewhere for entertainment. He could not force himself on her now.

Yet as he met her gaze in her reflection, his fingers itched with the urge to touch her and explore just how responsive she could be.

"Those jewels belong to the Duchess of Norfolk," he said, tucking his hands behind his back to remove all temptation. "As that is now your title, they belong to you. And they would go delightfully with your dress."

She didn't so much as glance at them. "They're a little heavy."

"I see."

Her throat tightened as she swallowed, but she merely continued rubbing her wrists together.

"I have made my opinion about Sir Montague plain," he said, watching her face in the mirror. Her lips parted in a sharp, soundless gasp, but she otherwise didn't move. "Will you not trust my judgement on this?"

For the first time, she twisted to face him fully, and although he had every intention of focusing on the matter at hand, the dipped neckline of the dress was particularly enticing, and there was a becoming flush on her face.

"Your judgement?" she asked, her voice tight. "And why should I trust your judgement on Sir Montague when you were *consorting* with another lady right before my eyes?"

"Mrs Stanton—"

"Is also associated with Sir Montague. If she is allowed to make his acquaintance, I hardly see why I should not."

He had seen Juliet and Montague together—that was part of the reason he had consented to speak with her in a way he would not usually have done. But if anything, that was another reason why Theo *shouldn't* associate with Sir Montague.

"Because Mrs Stanton is not a lady," he said. "And Sir Montague is not, as I can verify from experience, a gentleman."

"And what?" she enquired, arching a brow, "makes a gentleman, if Sir Montague is not and you are?"

He bit back his anger. "If you must ask that question, you wouldn't understand."

"Don't speak to me as if I were a child."

"Would you rather I treated you as my wife?" A dangerous question; a wife sitting before him with such mingled hurt and defiance in her eyes called for more than he could give.

Even if, at that moment, he would have very much liked to give it.

"I would rather you treated me as an equal."

They *were* equals. They were friends. Or at least, they had been before this maddening interlude. Was this another thing he risked losing to this sham of a marriage? Frustrated, he turned and paced the room as she continued to powder her little nose, her back tight. When he next glanced at her, however, he sighed and slowed, coming to stand behind her once more. "I didn't come here to argue with you, Theo."

"No, you merely came here to order me about." She put both hands on her lap and kept her gaze steadfastly on her reflection. "When you asked me to marry you, we agreed we would not intrude on each other's private lives. You showed no interest in me before, and there is no need to start now."

"The difference is now you are my wife."

Her gaze snapped to his. "I did not think that was going to change things so much."

Neither had he, but that was before. Before Montague had made his way back to London, before he had known what it might feel like to want the lady he was bound to forever more. Those factors complicated matters, and he wasn't certain precisely how he would navigate them. What he *wanted* was an uncomplicated marriage and a cousin far, far away. Neither of those things had come to pass; now, it felt as though he was fighting for a sliver of his wife's attention.

But, if he did not, Montague would be sure to claim it. She was ready, in fact, for him to claim it. Nathanial could not let that happen.

Further discussion would be fruitless, however, so he merely said, "You should wear the diamonds," and left the room.

Theo spent the day avoiding Nathanial. She went for a drive past Hyde Park in the phaeton Nathanial had given her on her marriage, flirted with every young gentleman she saw, and met her mother and sister. Then, she went shopping and spent an obscene amount of money on shoes and a hat with a large feather. Nathanial would hate it, which was her primary reason for its purchase.

Once she returned home that evening, she fully intended to unexpectedly leave for a soiree. That had not initially been her plan, and she was rather tired, but anything would be better than spending time with her husband. That would teach him for lecturing her and telling her to wear diamonds she didn't like.

Except, she concluded reluctantly, she *did* like the diamonds. And they would go beautifully with her evening dress. She touched them, thinking about the way Nathanial had touched them, and the way he had looked at her in the mirror. Her stomach did an odd little leap at the memory.

Perhaps, though she hated to admit it, the situation was not wholly his fault.

She would wear the diamonds. Then, if he chose to apologise, they would right things between them and all would be well again.

Betsy said nothing as she clasped the diamonds around Theo's neck, and when finally Theo descended downstairs, a few scant minutes before she needed to leave, she was conscious of an odd feeling. Butterflies writhed uncomfortably in her gut, and she had to take several deep breaths before she pushed open the door to the library.

Nathanial, as she had known he would be, was sitting in an armchair before the fire, a book in his hands and his ankle propped against his knee. He was the picture of domestic comfort, and the sight almost compelled her to leave. She would have done, if he had not looked up at her entrance, and if an expression of surprise and pleasure had not crossed his face.

"Theo." He put his book down, and she tried not to be aware of the way his gaze took in every inch, lingering on her neck. On the diamonds she now wore, tying herself publicly to him even when he wasn't escorting her. "You look remarkably dashing. Are you off out?"

She toyed with the hem of her gloves. "Lady Finchley is throwing a soiree."

"I had not known you had thought to attend."

"I had not until recently."

Silence settled between them, but Theo was determined not to break it first. She had come to him, and now the ball was in his court; he could choose to accept her peace offering, or he could reject it and she would leave.

He rose, and she inhaled sharply as he approached her, pausing only when he was a scant few inches away. "Theo," he said, his voice low, and sighed. He took her hand, his thumb tracing patterns across her glove. "I have no wish to argue with you."

"Then don't," she said hastily.

His voice was dry as he countered, "Don't provoke me." But the constant movement of his thumb was both distracting and reassured her that his anger, like hers, had burned itself out. "Shall we call a truce, my dear?"

"It depends," she said, tipping her head back as she looked at him with a slight smile he returned. "Will you come barging into my dressing room to lecture me if I ever displease you?"

"That entirely depends on whether you remain in your dressing room, delaying breakfast, so you can avoid me."

She was betrayed into smiling fully, and his mouth twitched even as he stepped back. Absurdly, she felt almost bereft without his hand around hers. "A truce," she agreed, absently massaging the place his thumb had been.

As though he could not help himself, he leant forward and kissed her cheek. "There is little chance I can match your style, but I shall try. Allow me five minutes to change."

Five minutes would not be long enough for him to change from his day clothes to evening wear. "Nathanial, you cannot think of coming with me."

"Why should I not? You should have a male escort."

"That is not so very important," she said shyly. "It is an informal affair, and I *am* married."

"Five minutes," he repeated, tweaking one of her curls. "And Theo? The diamonds look good on you."

Chapter Ten

February squalled into March, and Theo's marriage with Nathanial continued along the course they had established. He escorted her everywhere, danced with her more often than not, and prevented Sir Montague from so much as approaching her. That did not mean she was unable to speak with him at all, but infrequently, and never alone.

Sometimes, she wished Nathanial would take a step back and allow her a little more freedom. She had not met any other gentlemen—Nathanial did not appear to mind *them*—that sparked her interest the way Sir Montague had and continued to do. But there was something pleasing about Nathanial's attentions, no matter the lack of romance.

Now, all she had to do was navigate those and find a way to speak with Sir Montague.

Her opportunity came in a late March snowfall. Nathanial had taken a night off from his escorting duties, claiming fatigue, and Theo had attended ab ball with Lady Seymour, Tabitha's mother. There, she had danced with Sir Montague twice, and talked with him for a pleasingly long time.

Moreover, when she emerged from the ball into thick snow, her carriage nowhere in sight, he was kind enough to offer her a ride home. Lady Seymour's carriage was also nowhere in sight, and Theo, not one to look a gift horse in the mouth, was only too happy to accept.

Finally, she had a chance to be with her hero. Alone. Her stomach twisted with nerves and anticipation. No one had ever kissed her before. Would he kiss her, in the privacy of his carriage? Did she *want* him to kiss her?

The answer to that question, of course, was yes. She thought. She was almost entirely certain that she wanted Sir Montague to take her hand, announce his devotion to her, and kiss her. Those words would look wonderful coming from his mouth.

Sir Montague's name was called, and he helped her down the steps to the road, where his carriage was waiting. It was not as fine as one of Nathanial's carriages, but it was perfectly sturdy, and she settled back on the seats with a nervous glance at Sir Montague, who had taken the seat opposite. His knee nudged hers, and her heart gave an uncomfortable lurch.

This was it. The moment she had been waiting for. But she was so very cold, and the rocking motion of the carriage was not, she felt, conducive to kissing. She rather feared for her teeth.

The lamp swung from above the door as they moved onwards, and Theo wrapped her hands more firmly in her cloak.

"Are you cold, Duchess?" he asked.

"A little. I had not expected the snow."

"No, I think no one had."

For a moment, Theo wondered about her own carriage's lack of appearance. Had they run into some trouble? Then she dismissed the thought; it was snowy. Perhaps they were just delayed. As soon as she was home, she would send word that she was safe and that they should bring the carriage back. All would be well.

"Here," Sir Montague said, moving to her side of the carriage as he draped his coat across her shoulders. "Is this better?"

"Oh, it is so warm!" She looked up at him with a shy smile, though the swinging light made his eyes look black. The thought made her feel uncomfortable. "And it is so large on me."

"And do you like that, Duchess?"

"Well, yes." Were they flirting? She was certainly blushing. But the carriage rocked again, and she gripped onto the seat with both hands to stop herself swaying. "I think it is quite nice to feel small, sometimes."

"I can do that for you," he said, leaning in, his eyes intent on hers. Her stomach clenched with anticipation and fear. He looked at her as though he wished to eat her. "What would you like, little mouse? Of what do you dream? I can provide that for you."

He looked just as handsome saying these things as she had imagined, but her knees still trembled with wretched nervousness.

"I just like—conversation."

He leaned back, amused. "Conversation?"

"Yes, if you please. As we did at the soiree."

"You see no difference between the soiree and now?" His leg pressed against hers again. "I have been searching for ways to get you to myself for weeks. Your husband has been assiduous indeed in his attentions." Sir Montague's breath tickled her face. He smelt of wine, and she wondered if he was inebriated. That would certainly explain a few things. "But tonight, you are mine."

"I beg you would not kiss me," she blurted. "Not *here*."

"But we are alone." He was even closer now, and the fear prickled over her skin. He was so very much *larger* than she was; if he should choose to kiss her, she would be helpless to stop him. "And who knows how long that shall last for."

Theo threw up a hand to stop him getting closer. "But it is not romantic for you to kiss me now, in a moving carriage."

"You dream of romance, then, little mouse?"

"Do you not?"

"Few men do," he said, and laughed, finally leaning back and giving her space to breathe. "Very well, Duchess. If it is romance you look for, I shall do my best."

Hesitantly, she glanced up at him. "First kisses should not happen in moving carriages," she confided.

A rare smile, free from mockery, spread across his face. "First kisses? No, they ought to be special."

The womanly heart in Theo knew that if she had not stopped him, Sir Montague would have kissed her then. But, as they arrived at Norfolk House, she found herself unable to regret having turned him down. She had thought this evening would be wildly romantic, but something about it had not lived true to her expectations, whether it was the man or the situation. The snow was too cold to be comfortable; the carriage's movement too violent to encourage lovemaking.

And Sir Montague, despite his many charms, and the flash in his eyes that made Theo's breath catch with nervousness, was not quite right.

She did not let herself think about that overmuch as she shrugged off Sir Montague's coat and handed it back to him. "Thank you for a lovely evening, Sir Montague."

He possessed himself of her hand and kissed it with a flourish. "For you, Duchess, anything."

Conscious of the fact her heart should be fluttering more than he seemed capable of making it, she accepted his hand down from the carriage and into the house. Its lights were still blazing, which Theo thought unusual; Nathanial had begged for a night in because he was fatigued and wanted to retire early.

The carriage rattled away along the street as Nathanial himself, dressed in informal buckskins and a coat over his arm, hurried down the stairs. "Theo," he said, in such obvious relief, she stared at him.

"Nathanial? What is the matter?"

"The carriage returned without you." He reached her and, as though it was the most normal thing in the world, pulled her into his embrace. One arm snaked around her waist and anchored him to her. She pressed her cheek against his shoulder, nose almost touching his neck, and breathed in his familiar scent. Over the course of the past two months, she had grown accustomed to it.

"My carriage returned without me?" she asked with a frown. "How odd. Was Hawkins himself?"

"He said he was given instructions from you that you no longer had need of his assistance."

Theo glanced up into his face, Sir Montague's words finally becoming clear. He had orchestrated the carriage ride she shared with him by sending her carriage home.

Nathanial appeared to read the truth in her face; his grey eyes shuttered and his mouth pressed into a thin line, as though he was holding back everything he wanted to say. "I see."

"Don't be angry," Theo said, placing a hand on his chest and wishing, though she hardly knew why, that he would hold her again. They had passed two months without incident, and she was used to their easy friendship. Being with Nathanial, when they were not fighting, was the easiest thing in the world, and it gave her a pang that she thought she might lose it.

"I shall ask no more questions of you," he said curtly. "I suspect I should not like the answer."

Without thinking, she reached up and traced the harsh lines of his face until they softened. "You may put your mind at rest on that point."

"Which point?" he asked, eyes searching hers.

"Nothing of that nature occurred."

He nodded slowly, still watching her closely. A strange consciousness unfurled within her at the sight of his perusal. Her heart, so silent when she had been in the carriage with Sir Montague, chose now to give an almighty thud. Sir Montague had her hero's dark

142

beauty, but Nathanial was familiar and warm, and Theo could not recall how she had ever supposed he was the less handsome of the two.

"I thought you were retiring early," she said in the yawning silence.

"I intended to, before I heard news that our carriage had returned. I was coming to look for you."

"Oh!"

He took hold of her wrist, pulling her still closer, until their bodies were flush. "What's that surprise for, wretch?"

"I had not thought you would be so worried." She peered up at him, relieved to find his frown was gone. "You know we are not husband and wife in that way."

"Are we not?" he said speculatively, a spark of amusement and—yes, there was something else there, igniting like a candlewick, as he placed his finger under her chin. "No, perhaps not. And yet . . ." That expression in his eyes sparked. "I am glad you did not kiss Montague tonight." Slowly, his eyes still on hers, he bent his head. Theo could have moved away, she could have denied him the way she had denied Sir Montague, but she was frozen in place as Nathanial brushed his lips against hers. Lightly, his mouth soft. It was the merest whisper of a kiss; a promise, not a delivery. It was, perhaps, the perfect maidenly first kiss, and come at such a moment that Theo could not argue it was unromantic.

It was distinctly not enough.

She moved as he pulled back. Just a fraction, just enough that he caught the instinctual lean of her body towards his. A low chuckle escaped his throat as he slid a hand along her cheek, into her hair, and down to cup the back of her neck. His mouth returned to her with more pressure this time. Gentle, yet unyielding enough that Theo could say with authority that *this* was a kiss. Her husband, her friend, was kissing her, and—

Theo kissed him back.

She had not, strictly, intended to. Perhaps she would not have done if heat had not flooded her body, or if his hand had not skated up her arm and across the back of her shoulder blades, holding her to him. If her thoughts had not been suspended, if she had not been aflame with the same spark that had been in his eyes, if he had not consumed her so utterly. The world narrowed to Nathanial and the way his mouth moved against hers with teasing pressure.

This was how heroes should kiss.

Only she wasn't kissing a hero, she was kissing *Nathanial*.

She broke away, stepping back from his embrace. Dazed, confused, flustered. A blush spread from her chest, up her neck, to her cheeks. She truly was on fire.

He had kissed her. She had kissed him back. This was not the marriage they had promised one another, and if she allowed herself to be lost in him, what would happen then? He was her husband and he was not in love with her.

The thing she had been most determined to do was to find a man who *would* love her. To find, in short, her hero.

That man was not Nathanial, no matter how he was looking at her now, his eyes dark, his mouth pinned tightly together.

"It's late," she said, stumbling back. Her hands were shaking—goodness, why were her hands shaking? She felt as though her entire body might shudder apart at the seams and spill all her hidden thoughts and feelings onto the ground for Nathanial to sort through.

Nathanial's brows creased, and he swallowed. "Theo—"

"Goodnight, Nathanial," she said, fleeing upstairs. Her heart pounded like a freed beast, trampling over her feelings until she was at a loss to know what she was feeling at all. With trembling fingers, she touched her bottom lip, where she could still feel the ghost of his kiss, light as butterfly wings. If she closed her eyes, she could imagine him before her now.

These were not the terms of their relationship. He should have known better than to kiss her. She was not an opera dancer or Mrs Stanton. She was his *wife*. There were rules in place. He should not—

She should not—

She buried her head in the pillow and did her best not to listen for Nathanial's footsteps outside her bedroom. When they paused, just outside her door, her heart contracted, but after a breathless few seconds, they moved on.

Theo closed her eyes and crushed the disappointment in her chest until the only thing she could feel was the relentless pressure against her lips that clung to her like a curse.

Chapter Eleven

Nathanial didn't see his bride at breakfast the next morning. Nor, though he waited in the library for quite some time and even ventured up to her dressing room, did he so much as see her leave the house. When he inquired about her whereabouts, however, it was to discover that she had left to visit her family.

"Thank you, Jarvis," he said. "If the Duchess arrives home tonight, please let her know I would like to speak with her."

"Yes, Your Grace."

Left alone once again, Nathanial paced the floor. Although he was aware of a pressing need to speak with her, he hardly knew what he wanted to say. To tell her it was an isolated event and he had no intention of it happening again? To *reassure* her that as her husband, he had no designs on her?

The truth was, he hadn't intended on kissing her then. The thought had not been further from his mind when he had set off to find her. Not there, not then, and not, necessarily, at all. But she had returned his embrace, a flush on her cheeks, and she had touched his face with such sweetness.

And she *hadn't* kissed Montague.

Nathanial didn't usually consider himself a jealous man, but if his wife was going to kiss anyone for the first time, he would much rather it be him.

And then she had run away.

He had never kissed a woman who had run away.

Frustrated, and well aware Theo had no intention of returning any time soon, Nathanial took a walk he had not made in some time. Since his marriage, in fact. He might have done, if he had not been so busy with Theo, and if Juliet had not made their connection rather more public than he liked at the theatre.

Staying away had been easy. Today, however, he wanted a distraction, and he knew that if nothing else, Juliet knew how to distract him.

He found her in her drawing room, brow furrowed as she stared at a piece of paper on her writing desk. For a moment, he merely observed her. She was clearly expecting no visitors; although her dress was expensive, she wore her hair loose. It made her look younger.

He leaned against the doorframe and rapped on the half-open door. Juliet glanced up and her eyes widened. "Nathanial," she said, forgetting his title in her surprise. "You—you came."

"As you can see."

"I thought you might not." She left the paper on the desk, apparently forgotten, as she hurried towards him, arms outstretched. "What can be the reason for you staying away from me so long?"

"Why, don't tell me you missed me," he said, glancing across at the missive. From this distance, he couldn't read it, but it was clearly a letter. "You have enough to keep you entertained."

"I do not have another duke," she said coyly, moving to kiss his cheek. For no reason he could articulate, he avoided her caress. "And you know, dukes are hard to come by, Your Grace."

Now he was here, he felt unsettled, as though the walls were too close and the air too stale. He strode to the sofa and sat, his hands loose in his lap. "Do you merely value me for my title?"

"Not at all," she said, sitting beside him and trailing a finger up his arm. "I find many things appealing about you, as you well know."

"Such as the depths of my pockets." He shrugged off her restless fingers. "Would you have encouraged me if I were a Mr Hardinge of indifferent wealth?"

She paused, and he knew the answer; he had known the answer since their relationship had begun. His value to her lay in his title, his wealth, the many things he could offer her. Theirs was a mutually beneficial relationship.

At least, it had been.

She tilted her head. "What of me?" she asked, but although her tone strove to be carefree, it drooped at the end like a flower deprived of light. "Would you continue to see me if I were plain, or if I didn't offer you what I do?"

"I think we both know the answer to that."

"Then we are in a similar position, Your Grace." Her gaze sharpened. "Except you have a wife and are less inclined to share my bed."

"I am busier than I'd intended, certainly."

"I remember a man who assured me in no uncertain terms that his wife would not change his life."

Nathanial also remembered that man, in the same way one recalls a particularly distant dream. "It appears matrimony is a rather consuming state." He

151

looked again at Juliet. There were fine lines around her eyes and she was looking at him with more possessiveness than he liked.

She was no Theo. And the prospect of being with her now was not an appealing one.

"This was a mistake," he said, standing abruptly. "Excuse me."

"Your Grace—"

Without another word, he strode from the room.

Juliet tucked her muff more tightly against the chilly breeze. An iron sky glowered down at her, and not for the first time, she concluded this had been a mistake. Meeting Montague at her home was one thing; there, they could speak in private and no one would see them together.

Here, in Hyde Park with the Serpentine River glinting away in the distance, they were exposed in a way she didn't appreciate. Montague added nothing to her status or reputation, unlike Nathanial, and *he* had never consented to walk out with her.

Finally, Montague strolled towards her in a dark coat and elegant navy gloves. "Juliet," he said, a secretive smile curling his lips. That was a smile that would make many a young girl's heart flutter, if they were susceptible to such things. Juliet was not. "You are looking especially well today."

"I know," she said, accepting his arm. "I always look well. You're late."

He pulled out a pocket watch and examined it. "Only by ten minutes or so."

"Ten minutes in the cold may as well be half an hour." With Montague, Juliet didn't bother with her usual politeness; they had a mutual purpose that depended little on her personal charms. "Did you not get my note?"

"I'm here, aren't I?"

"I said it was urgent."

"I'm here," he repeated, smiling at a young lady as they passed. "I had not taken you for a shrew, my dear."

"The Duke visited me this morning for the first time in a long while," she snapped. "And he was distant. Said something about being occupied with his wife. He looked at me and he didn't *see* me,

Montague." And she had tried everything she knew of; nothing had erased that distant look in his eyes like faraway stars. "He was thinking of her—I know it."

"It appears you are having less luck with the Duke than we had hoped."

"Thank you for identifying the obvious." The cold had penetrated her gloves and the tips of her fingers were numb. She was not built for the cold; the sooner spring arrived, the better. "How are you faring with her?"

"She's willing but shy. When I find the right place, if I make it romantic enough, I have no doubt she'll be amenable. Then all I'll have to do is allow Nathanial to see our intimacy. I know women, and he's not had her yet. I'm certain of it."

"What's taking you so long?" Juliet demanded. "She's a blushing girl and you an experienced man— if you cannot lure her to bed, there will be few who can."

"Patience, my dear," he murmured. "She needs time."

"We do not have time, Montague. The longer we dally, the more likely the Duke is to fall in love with her pretty face." A pretty face Juliet could not compete with; despite her best efforts, she could not ward away time forever. "I have known Nathanial well over these past five years and he is falling for her. I can feel it."

"That will matter little if she does not fall for him."

"And you are certain of that?" Juliet pulled her hand from Montague's arm and turned to face him. "He is her husband; she may not deny him."

"Was that your experience with your husband?" Montague's voice was gently mocking, and she turned her head away. He gripped her chin with strong fingers. "You may choose not to trust me, but the Duke's pretty little wife is within my grasp. If I bide my time, she will lift her skirts for me, and we will both get what we want."

"Only if the Duke knows about it."

Montague smiled cruelly. "Oh, he will know about it, my dear. I'll make sure of that."

Juliet caught his arm and wrenched it from her face. "You had better act quickly before there is an heir and your chance at consequence is lost forever."

"And you," he said, allowing her to draw his hand away, "had better find a way to lure your Duke back to you before you lose him forever. A pretty game you tried to play in the theatre, and so publicly. If I know my cousin—and believe me, I do—he hasn't just neglected you because of his wife."

That had been a mistake, but she would never admit it to Montague. "Leave the Duke to me and you will not be disappointed."

"You have many charms," he said, his gaze raking her up and down. Later, she knew, he would visit her, and she would accept his advances, because the web they had woven was too tangled for her to risk rejecting him. "Play your cards well, and you will yet win him back. And you know how to do that?"

"How?" she asked, unable to help herself.

Montague placed his lips by her ear. "By pretending he doesn't exist." Smiling, he leant back and offered her his arm again. "There is nothing so guaranteed to drive a man wild with longing—we are all dogs with bones, and we protect what's ours."

"What will prevent him from protecting his wife?"

"Why, I will." With a practised air, he smiled at yet another woman who passed. "I shall be taking little Theodosia to a masquerade tomorrow night, and we shall see what comes of it."

Juliet raised a brow. "That little mouse at a masquerade? Does she know?"

"She will." With that, he dropped her arm, offered her a sardonic bow, and left her standing alone in the middle of the path. Careful not to let a hint of displeasure escape onto her face, she tucked her hands back into her muff and tightened her numb fingers into a ball.

Theo successfully avoided Nathanial.

It had not been an easy feat; when she knew he was waiting for her downstairs, she slipped down the stairs and out of a side door, leaving a message with Jarvis that she was visiting her family. And when she returned home that afternoon, with a cold nose, it was to an invitation from Montague to a masked ball. He made no mention of Nathanial's name, and she could not but feel it was an excuse to see her again.

An excuse she . . .

Well, frankly, she didn't know if she relished it or not. It was flattering, to be sure, and Theo enjoyed the flattery, but she couldn't deny the fact something had changed the moment Nathanial had kissed her.

Or rather, the moment she had kissed him back.

She bashed out some scales on the pianoforte in the drawing room, the notes hard and angry and often irregular. This was the first time since their marriage that she had bothered to sit down and practise, but the cold had dissuaded her from venturing outside, and she had no engagements.

Except this masked ball tonight.

With Montague, her every romantic ideal.

Or so she had thought until Nathanial had kissed her.

She played a clashing chord and glared at the keys. If Nathanial hadn't kissed her, she wouldn't need to feel as though she owed him something—owed him, specifically, not to go with Sir Montague.

But this masked ball provided her with an excuse *not* to be with Nathanial, which was very tempting. If they spent any time together, they would have to discuss the kiss, and no amount of friendship could prepare one for that conversation. She had been thinking about it all day and still had no idea what to say.

"Theo?" Nathanial said from the doorway of the drawing room.

"I'm practising," she informed him, in case the evidence before his eyes, and ears, was not enough. To ensure she drove the point home, she played another few runs of inaccurate chords.

"I thought perhaps you could spare a few moments for your husband," he said, taking the seat directly behind her. "Or had you forgotten that in your attempts to ignore me?"

"I'm not ignoring you."

"Oh? Then perhaps we could talk."

Perhaps, perhaps, perhaps. Her life was made up of perhaps—of maybes and coulds and shoulds. There were no certainties on which she could depend; the only certainty she had was that Nathanial was her husband. And although they had been married for almost two months now, the kiss had proved she knew so little about him. She did not know how his hands felt, or the way her name would sound if he whispered it to her.

She did not know what it would be like to be truly married to him.

But heavens, thinking about *that* helped no one.

"Very well," she said, turning on the seat and placing her hands neatly on her lap. "About what do you wish to talk?"

A bleak smile touched his lips. "So formal, Theo. Is spending time with me so unappealing?"

Oh, she could not hate him when he looked at her like that. "Of course not," she said, and when he held out a hand to her, she took it. "I'm just—I'm very busy."

He looked at her intently, but he merely said, "I appear to have the misfortune to have married a social butterfly."

"Is that not a duchess's role?" she teased, but her tone fell flat. She fiddled with her dress. "That reminds me. I have a-an engagement tonight."

"Tonight?"

"Yes. I had not thought you would mind."

"Of course not, if that is what you wish." His gaze searched hers. "Would you like me to attend?"

With Sir Montague? She almost laughed. "Oh, you should find it boring." She couldn't seem to still her nervous hands. "Why, did you have plans?"

"It appears I don't any longer," he said, still looking at her with eyes that pierced straight through her. "Perhaps another time."

"Yes," she said, rising. "Perhaps another time."

Perhaps, perhaps, perhaps.

"We should talk about that kiss," Nathanial said as she reached the door, and she froze. "I would not like you to think I am forcing my advances on you."

"Of course not," she managed.

"And it will not happen again if you don't want it to."

Theo mumbled something incomprehensible and flew from the room, covering her burning face with her hands. Of course he would think she did not want him to kiss her—she had run from him. Twice now.

But, of course, she *didn't* want him to kiss her. That would be absurd. They were friends, and friends did not kiss. Friends did not circle each other like moths to a flame; they did not wake up dreaming about the look in his grey eyes.

For him, it had probably been nothing. A dalliance with a woman he, in the eyes of the law, owned. And for her, too, it would be nothing. She would suppress any other things until they *were* nothing.

After all, there could be nothing as terrible as discovering feelings for one's husband. They had married for convenience and she would not let herself forget it.

Chapter Twelve

When evening came and Theo descended the stairs, a mask dangling from her fingertips, Nathanial was luckily absent from the hallway. Thankful, but almost a little disappointed, she fled out of the front door and into the carriage Sir Montague had sent for her.

The masquerade was held at the house of a Mrs Chichester, and as Theo alighted from the carriage, she wondered if her dress was a little too modest. Women strutted like peacocks, dressed as Roman empresses, shepherdesses, peasant girls, and other costumes she could hardly imagine. She had dressed as a Greek muse, but her mask looked sorrowfully plain beside all the others, and she hardly knew how she would recognise anyone.

This issue was compounded when she entered the house. Masquerades were occasionally held at the Opera House and the Pantheon, and she had heard talk of them, but she suspected they were very different affairs. Here, nymphs and shepherds exchanged kisses by the pillars that framed the room, and dancers, in dresses short enough to expose almost their entire legs, clustered before the musicians.

She should not be here.

She barely had time to articulate the thought when a man approached. Tall, dressed almost entirely in black, and with a horned mask on, the only identifiable part of him were his dark eyes—eyes that in this flickering light looked positively wicked.

"Duchess," he said, taking her hand and bowing over it. "You look exquisite."

"Sir Montague, you recognised me so easily," she said with a breathy laugh.

"Only because you gave me word of your costume. I should never have found you otherwise."

"Good," she said before she could help herself, and followed the thought with, "I have never been to such an event as this."

"There are always those who choose to embrace anonymity for an evening," he said, taking her hand and leading her away, to the side of the room where it was less crowded. There were plenty of darkened corners, she noticed, that many people were taking advantage of.

In one particular corner, she noticed the ruddy hair and porcelain face of Juliet Stanton. Theo looked away before she could see more.

"What is your costume?" she asked, taking a seat to watch the proceedings. Although some couples had taken it upon themselves to dance whatever they pleased, she was relieved to see a minuet forming in the centre of the room. "You recognised mine, but I do not recognise yours."

"Is it not obvious?" He gestured to the horns. "I come as the devil."

Not for the first time, Theo wished she were anywhere but there. "You said once you intended to cause mischief," she said. "Is that your intention here?"

His eyes gleamed at her. "Why, would you be amenable to causing mischief with me?"

She glanced away, to the smaller room where refreshments were served. "I'm thirsty. Would you be so good as to get me a drink?"

"Certainly," he said, taking her hand and pressing a kiss to her knuckles. The look in his eyes would have made another woman swoon—Annabelle, certainly, would have swooned, and Lady Tabitha would have been positively incoherent.

A week ago, she might have also swooned. Now, thoughts of Nathanial were marring her very own romantic hero.

When Montague came back, he handed her the glass with a knowing look in his eyes. "No one will recognise you. You're safe."

Safe from Nathanial knowing I'm here. But she did not bother articulating the thought, and merely took a sip. The wine was rather stronger than she was used to, and she made a mental note to limit her consumption. The last thing she wanted was to compromise her wits.

Still, now she *was* here, she may as well make the best of it. "You should ask me to dance," she said, putting her glass down. "A masked ball is still a ball, after all."

He offered her his hand, and she took it. As his fingers curled around hers—his hand so much larger, his fingers so much stronger—she was reminded of that feeling in the carriage. A feeling that if he should choose, she would be unable to resist him.

"The world is not watching," Montague said as he pulled her closer. "You don't have to fear, little mouse."

She had been this close to Nathanial when she had kissed him. If she were to reach up, she could kiss Montague. And, despite the conflicting feelings and the uncomfortable sensation that lingered in her stomach, she wanted to.

How were his kisses different from Nathanial's? She had no doubt both men were experienced.

Who wanted to kiss her more? Which one did *she* want to kiss more?

It was a terrible conundrum. One she loved and hated in equal measure.

"Why did you invite me here?" she asked.

"Is not the excuse of spending time with you enough reason?"

She had only had a little wine, but already it made the lights a little too bright, the music a little too loud. The world took on a glassy air as she allowed Montague to guide her through the dances, his hand on her waist and his gaze fixed on hers. It was easier to give in, to allow the stars to sink until they scattered around her as the music swirled and they continued to dance.

Theo had gone to a masquerade.

Nathanial scribbled a quick note to his friend, Lord Walters, and handed it to his valet. "See that this is delivered," he said. "There's been a change of plan."

"Yes, Your Grace."

She might have thought she'd outsmarted him, accepting Montague's invitation to Mrs Chichester's masquerade, but he still had friends. The missive he had received just ten minutes previously was still crumpled on the desk. Its writer had been correct about one thing: he did indeed care to know that his wife was attending a masquerade in the company of a certain gentleman.

The girl had no idea what she was letting herself in for, he thought grimly as he donned his costume for the evening: King Charles II. Once he had his mask, which covered all of his face but his mouth and eyes, he summoned the carriage and journeyed to Mrs Chichester's house. All the way, he planned what he would say to Theo to make her understand what she was risking.

He did not allow himself to think about what he would do if he walked in to find her kissing another man. Or worse, kissing Montague.

The masquerade was as extravagant as Mrs Chichester's events tended to be, crammed with milkmaids, servant girls, princesses, and historical figures. He scanned the lines of dancers, refusing to believe Theo would be anywhere but dancing, and eventually found her in a toga that revealed a slip of shoulder, and a diamond-studded white mask. If he had not known her so well—the black hair, braided and pinned to the back of her head, the way she moved with such unconscious grace, her smile—he would never have recognised her.

The man opposite her was undoubtedly Montague. They danced together, but although Montague's hands lingered on her arms and shoulder blades, and although his gaze never left her face, she made no physical gesture of encouragement.

That was something, at least.

He found a woman sitting by herself and offered out a hand. "Dance with me?" he asked. Here, no one need know anyone's name; identities were not the order of the day. She rose with a smile, accepted his hand, and he led her out onto the dancefloor. Not beside Theo, but close enough he could watch her.

"Are you enjoying the evening thus far?" she asked, looking up at him with her plump lips slightly parted. Perhaps she was expecting him to kiss her.

She would be disappointed.

His Theo, just feet from him, smiled up into Montague's face. The sight made him almost lose his composure.

"Tolerably," he said, glancing down at his partner. "I anticipate enjoying it more shortly."

A smug smile widened on her mouth. "I have no doubt you will, my lord."

He would not be enjoying it with her, but she did not need to know that, and as the dance progressed, he flirted with her all while keeping an eye on Theo. Montague pressed a glass into her hand when the music ended, but she shook her head, said something Nathanial couldn't catch.

"Will you not come into the gardens with me?" his partner asked. "I've heard they're quite something this time of year."

"March?" He couldn't suppress a smile at her attempt to interest him. "I'm afraid I'm not what you're looking for."

"And what are *you* looking for?"

Nathanial nodded at Theo. "Her."

His partner's eyes widened, then narrowed. Head held high, she stalked off, and Nathanial watched her go with no great sense of loss. She had served his purpose, and he had more important things to focus on.

He watched as Theo sat, fanning herself with her hand as Montague said something to her that made her smile. From the way her head lolled against the wall, she wasn't entirely sober.

Black rage threatened to swell at the thought, but he wasn't a man who gave into such emotions, so he merely paced through the throng towards them and pushed his anger into a white-hot ball in his chest.

"If you could fetch me some water, I would be most grateful," Theo said. "It's so very warm in here."

"It's a lot cooler outside," Montague said, and Nathanial could have called him out there and then. "We could have a walk through the gardens."

"And miss another dance?" she teased, glancing up at him. Nathanial couldn't see her face under her mask, but he knew there would be a dimple in one cheek. That damned lopsided dimple that captivated him every time it made an appearance.

"What the lady desires, she shall receive," Montague said, his gaze lingering on her before he strode away.

Now was Nathanial's moment. He sidled up beside her. "A lucky lady indeed," he said, looking down at her and meeting her shocked gaze, "if she can receive everything she desires."

Chapter Thirteen

If Theo could have contrived to drop through the floor into whatever lay below, she would have done. As it was, she could do nothing but stare into the face of the man standing before her. His mask concealed all but his grey eyes and mouth, but she had spent enough time thinking about both to know them immediately.

Nathanial.

He gave a bow, his eyes glittering half with anger, half with razor interest.

He had never looked at her like that.

She was aware of a sinking feeling. It appeared, either due to the wine's potent effects or the surprise of Nathanial's arrival, that she wanted him to kiss her a lot more than she wanted Sir Montague to kiss her.

This was perhaps her moment for it. He clearly did not recognise her, or he would have scolded her and taken her home, so she might act as she pleased. She could flirt with him, perhaps kiss him again, and he would never know it was her.

Anticipation, low and heated, unfurled in her stomach.

She glanced up at him, her eyelids low. "And what do you know about a lady's desires?" she asked, her voice low and husky. She had never sounded like that before, and it was liberating to think she could do so here without judgement.

Maybe she *had* had a little too much to drink.

Nathanial hesitated for a moment, as though he had expected a different response, before leaning forward and tucking a stray curl behind her ear. His face was too close to hers as he murmured, "Perhaps you might be good enough to show me."

Her face heated under the mask, and she was relieved to think he couldn't see her. An experienced lady, no doubt, did not do anything as foolish as *blush*. "Surely first you should invite me to dance with you," she said, holding out her hand. "I love to dance."

"That I know well." He accepted her hand. "I've been watching you for quite some time. Will your friend mind you dancing with me?"

Theo tossed her head, the wine making her bold. "No one can command me."

The music began—a waltz—and he placed his hand on her waist. Though they had danced before, this was different; he guided her body to slot against his like two puzzle pieces, and even through her dress, she could feel the heat of his hand.

Her flush extended down her neck in a rush of warmth she could do nothing to hide.

"Are you all right, my muse?" he asked, clasping her hand in his. When she met his gaze, there was unexpected softness there. "We don't have to do this."

If Nathanial had been any other man, she would have asked to return to the side, knowing Sir Montague would find her. She would have chosen Sir Montague over every other gentleman in this place *except* Nathanial. And he had told her, when they married, they would not behave as husband and wife.

This might be her only chance.

"I love to dance," she said, resting her hand along his arm. In response, he pulled her even closer.

"Then let us dance."

He had never treated her with this reckless abandon, with such a want of propriety. For a moment, she wished they were not masked, and they were in the privacy of their home; that he knew it was her and was holding her close regardless.

She wanted him to look into her eyes and see *her*.

For now, though, she would settle for this dance.

"I've never been to a masquerade before," she said, hoping the confession wouldn't give her away.

His eyes were magnetic. "And what do you think of them now?"

"I think they are something I could grow accustomed to," she said as he guided her across the ballroom. Each step was sure, each movement precise. Dancing with him was like flowing; she followed where he led, losing herself in the intricacies of his touch. She had not known so much could be conveyed through subtle presses and pushes. She had not known that her body could match another's so perfectly.

She was blind even to the way Sir Montague prowled around the edges of the ballroom, his black figure towering over everyone.

All there was, all there ever could be, was Nathanial.

The music stopped.

There was a hush, a pause, a space where the spell hadn't broken and reality hadn't yet intruded. Nathanial looked at her with that same spark in his eyes, and his hand still pressed against the small of her back—not that she knew precisely when it had moved to that position—bowing her body to his.

The other couples laughed, moved, changed positions, but Theo kept staring at Nathanial. He looked at her now, like . . . like he was hungry.

Answering heat moved in her, an ache low in her body that she had never experienced before. Nathanial could ease it for her, she knew. All she had to do was give in to him. Here, where her identity was safe, and he would never know he was consorting with his wife, she could be as wanton as she dared.

The thought made her shiver, and she blinked. The spell broke, and Nathanial straightened. He didn't move the hand on her back.

"I've heard the garden is especially beautiful this time of year," he said.

"March?" She swallowed a laugh, because she knew what he was asking, and she knew what her answer would be. "I would love to see it."

"Then please, my love," he said, the endearment dropping from his tongue with the sweetness of honey, "follow me."

The world took on the blurred quality of a dream as she accepted Nathanial's hand and allowed him to lead her outside. At first, the coldness in the air made her shudder, but the heat from under her skin—heat that seemed to emanate from her very core—burned away any lingering chill.

The gardens were just as grand as she had imagined. Flaming lights illuminated the vast lawn and the gravel path along which couples wandered. In the distance, a fountain glinted in the lights, and further away there was a maze. With the statues pressing against the hedges, and the small walls that separated the gardens and walkways, there were ample places a couple might find privacy.

"Are you cold?" he asked. "No matter; we shall warm you soon enough."

This couldn't be happening. Nerves jittered in her stomach. She must be out of her mind, allowing any man to compromise her like this, never mind her husband.

"Or," he said, raising an eyebrow, "are you wishing to remain inside?"

Looking at him now, it almost seemed as though he *wanted* her to return inside; as though, despite the fact he'd brought her out here to—well, do something—he wasn't certain he wanted to.

Except, that spark in his eyes told her he *did* want her. And she so desperately craved being wanted, even if this was just tonight. Even if he didn't know whom it was he wanted.

They took a path through the gardens, past giggling couples and quiet rendezvous, until they reached the centre of the maze. It was barely lit, and in the darkness, Theo felt as though she was somewhere far more scandalous than on a walk with her husband. She had to remind herself that no one knew it was them.

A statue of a nymph poured water into a fountain, and Theo looked at it, gilded in moonlight.

What am I doing?

The nymph, unsurprisingly, had no answer.

Nathanial touched her arm, drawing her attention back to him. "Now, my muse," he said, running his fingers along her jaw. "Do you want to know what you inspire in me?"

This was her point of no return. If she asked to return to the ballroom, he would take her.

If she asked for more, he would give it.

Her breath caught in her throat as she nodded. "Perhaps you might show me, my lord," she whispered.

His gaze darkened. "I'm not a lord," he said, and kissed her.

Before, their kiss had been soft, gentle, delicate.

There was nothing soft about this; his mouth crushed hers, one hand possessive at the back of her neck, angling her head so he could open her mouth. He consumed her, demanding everything she could give. And she offered it freely, melting against the forcefulness of his kiss, letting her chest press against his. There was so much to a male body she hadn't explored before. She ran her hands along the line of his shoulders, marvelling at the way he allowed her to touch him so brazenly. The back of his neck was warm and soft, tiny curls clustered on his neck. They were silken against her fingers.

He broke away from the kiss and turned his attention to her neck. She tilted her head back and looked at the diamond-encrusted sky. Clouds concealed the moon, but the stars were still there, twinkling down at her. The world was so big, and she so small—she felt suddenly the absurdness of allowing one person to consume her so utterly.

"What's the matter?" he asked, in a voice that was both gently mocking and heavy with desire. "Would you like to stop?"

The stars could not draw such a precious moment from her.

"No." The word was breathless. "I want . . ." She did not know how to answer, but that didn't matter; Nathanial understood her request and kissed her again. His mouth was hard and angry, lust and rage combined, but his knuckles grazed her lower cheek, the space left bare by her mask, in a soft gesture that melted her heart.

In return, she slid her hands through his hair, cupping his head to hers, offering herself up to him like a goblet of wine. His eyes were dark, intoxicated, and she had no doubt hers were the same.

He was everything. More than everything.

She skimmed her fingers down his spine and around to his chest. His hands stilled on her as she explored, dipping under his waistcoat until only a thin layer separated her questing fingers from his hot skin and the muscles that tightened with her touch.

As she dug her fingers into his side, he grunted and moved again, running his palm up her stomach until he reached her breast. His thumb brushed her nipple, and she gasped.

"You are delectable," he murmured, licking down her neck. She shuddered. "You are sweet. You are irresistible." He breathed the last word as though he could hardly believe he was saying it. Her fingers tightened in his shirt, pulling him inexorably closer, and he pressed her against the statue's white base. Above her, the nymph continued to pour, the sound of trickling water unceasing, offset only by their panting breaths. She was *panting*. Each breath was a gasp, coaxed from her by his ceaseless hands. First, they explored her breasts criminally slowly. Then, when she was concerned she might catch alight, he slid his hands down her waist, past the flare of her hips and down her thighs. Heat pooled between her legs.

"This dress seems somewhat in the way," he said against her neck, drawing up her skirts so he could access her bare skin. "This is better."

This was, in Theo's opinion, entirely too much. As his fingers skated closer to the apex of her legs, she gripped his arms until it must have hurt. "Uh," she managed.

He paused seconds before touching her *there*, in the place she most needed—and most dreaded—him to be. "Yes, my muse?"

What could she say? If she intended to go back to the house, she should have said so long before they reached this point.

And his fingers were so close. The terrible ache inside her longed to be appeased, and she knew that Nathanial, who had no doubt experienced this with countless ladies, knew precisely how to satiate it.

The thought sent a weight to the base of her stomach, but she merely shifted against him, searching for those fingers.

"I see," he said, and kissed her again. He removed that hand, to her disappointment, and instead lifted her bodily in the air. Her skirts were around her thighs and her legs were bare, which meant she could wrap them around his waist, locking her ankles and holding him against her. He laughed—a hard, edged sound—and pressed her more firmly against the statue. With one hand, he removed the skirts that piled between them, so the sensitive flesh at the apex of her thighs rubbed against his breeches.

And, more pertinently, a hard, thick ridge that pressed against her core. His breath was harsh as she shifted her hips, searching for the place that might offer the most pleasure.

Theo no longer cared if someone were to find them. If this was what it meant to be wanton, perhaps she should have indulged some time ago. Every brush of his hands—across her breasts, her buttocks, her back—wrought more sensation from her, and she ground against him. He groaned.

"You will be my undoing," he muttered.

With every gyration of her hips, the heat pooling at her core built. She was liquid, heat, blazing light, and he seemed to know, thrusting against her until her gasps became moans and the flesh between her legs was almost unbearably sensitive. The friction he offered was everything, it was more than everything, it was too much.

"That's right, love," he said, his voice rough but the hand now cupping her cheek infinitely gentle. "Don't hold back."

Theo did not have the breath to tell him she had already given everything to him; he owned every part of her. She was utterly, irrevocably, his.

He moved to allow some space between them, but before she could protest, he ran a hand to her slick core. She stilled, shocked by the intimacy of it, the vividness of the pleasure that slid through her.

"Trust me," Nathanial said, his eyes so dark she couldn't see where his pupils ended and his irises began. "I won't hurt you."

She didn't even have to think about it. "I trust you."

He kissed her again, urgent and needy as he touched her. They were wildfire, burning everything they touched. Theo wrapped her arms around his neck, holding him close to her, as her body grew hotter and lighter and she thought she might implode from the intensity of it.

Finally, as she quivered right on the edge, he eased back. "Well, my muse?" he asked. "Do you understand now?"

She raised her gaze to his, and whatever he saw there made him groan and pull her back against him once more. That simple pressure was enough; she shattered, the heat catapulting through her. Nathanial held her as she shuddered, his lips capturing her moans, his arms tight around her. He had broken her into a thousand pieces and now, as her body slowed and she came back into herself, he was fitting every shard back together.

Perhaps if she had wanted him less, she might have been happy with just this. Perhaps, if she was a better person, she would not hate the fact he thought she was someone else. The dark emotion that swept through her made her eyes burn. She tried to force her breathing to steady.

But Nathanial, so alert to every movement of her body, stopped stroking her hair and tipped her chin up so she met his gaze in a haze of swimming tears. One broke free and he brushed his thumb across the mask under her eye, smoothing it away.

"My muse," he said, so gentle it almost broke her all over again. "Are you sad?"

"I—" Her voice cracked and she swallowed. It was too late, now, to reveal to him who she really was.

She did not think she could bear to see his horror. She could not endure his regret.

"We should return to the ball," she said.

Even in the moonlight, she could see the way his face tightened. "Back to your friend?"

Sir Montague. Her heart gave another lurch. The night could not get worse. "I doubt he will be waiting for me."

"If you believe that, you are a fool."

How quickly the tenderness had left him. She backed away, and to her relief, he let her. "Pray excuse me, sir. Goodnight." As fast as she dared, she hurried back towards the house.

Chapter Fourteen

Nathanial watched Theo go, fury warring with the lust that still rampaged through his veins. He had not meant to take things so far, but he had not known she would be so innocently enticing. He had been entranced by her. If she had not cried or backed away from him, he might have taken her there and then.

He hated her for it.

Yet he could not stop himself wondering what her reaction would have been if he had revealed his identity. Would she have been horrified or pleased? Would she have been relieved that this experience, so new to her, had been with the man she had married? Or would she have panicked at having been discovered?

He rather suspected the latter would have been true, and the thought brought new weight to bear on his chest.

The ball held no more pleasure for him now. The only reason he had come in the first place was to retrieve his errant wife, and now that would prove impossible without revealing his identity.

Nathanial swore, tasting the ugly word on the frigid night air, before turning home. After this, he needed a long walk to clear his head.

Theo slipped along the edge of the room, relieved Sir Montague was nowhere to be seen. Her head spun and her hands trembled. Going out into the garden had been a terrible, wonderful, awful mistake.

She closed her eyes.

"Your Grace," a sultry voice said. Theo opened her eyes to see Mrs Stanton standing before her, burnished hair piled on her head and a particularly flimsy black mask against her alabaster skin. "What a pleasure to see you here."

Shocked, Theo stumbled back. "How do you recognise me?"

Mrs Stanton smiled. "I know of no one else Sir Montague would accompany."

Fresh shame welled in Theo and she could have cried at the reminder of Sir Montague. "Excuse me," she said, maintaining her composure by strength of will she had not known she possessed. "I must go."

"Already? Sir Montague has been quite concerned." Mrs Stanton's fingers squeezed Theo's arm painfully. "After all, you disappeared outside for such a long while." Although her mouth smiled under her mask, her eyes glittered with anger and jealousy and all the feelings Theo had experienced at the thought Nathanial had been prepared to entertain a nameless, faceless young woman in the garden.

Mrs Stanton, she was sure, knew whom Nathanial had been. She had known, or suspected, what they had done in the garden.

The thought ought not to have made her feel better, but it was a bitter kind of triumph, to know she had been the means of making this beautiful woman jealous. To know that Nathanial, at least, had not sought her out.

Perhaps Mrs Stanton thought Nathanial knew who Theo was. For a moment, Theo ached with the hope it might have been true—but then, why had he called her 'my muse'? Why had he not revealed his identity and revealed he knew who she was?

No, it was a foolish hope too far, and Theo sucked in a breath to counter the sting of disappointment. All she wanted in the world was to go back home and climb under the sheets of her bed so she could have a good cry.

"I confess I quite enjoyed myself," she said pettishly, and inclined her head. "Excuse me." While Mrs Stanton watched with controlled fury, Theo tossed her head and headed once more for the exit. She would walk if only that would take her home faster.

But before she reached the door, Sir Montague stepped out from the darkness.

"Please," she said, holding out a hand. "I don't want to talk."

"What *do* you want?" he asked in a quiet voice that sounded almost . . . hurt. She looked up into his face, and the darkness of his eyes that hid all emotions behind them. Once, she felt she could have drowned in those eyes, but tonight she was unmoved.

Neither he nor Nathanial had behaved like a hero tonight.

"I want to go home."

His mouth tightened, and for a moment, she wondered if he would refuse to let her pass. Nathanial had warned her of the consequences of trifling with

Sir Montague—perhaps she was about to find out how terrible they could be.

But his gaze travelled once more across her face, and whatever he saw there inspired him to step back and usher her through the doorway. "Allow me to escort you home, Duchess. My carriage is waiting."

Reluctantly, but with little choice unless she wanted to walk the dark streets alone, she accepted his hand and allowed him to hand her up into his carriage.

The journey to Norfolk House was thankfully short, and although Theo had half expected Sir Montague to make some reference to what happened, or indeed what he had hoped for when he had brought her to the masquerade, he said nothing. He merely loomed in the darkened corner of the carriage, watching as she worried at her gloves. When they arrived, he leaned over her and opened the door.

"I hope you will not mind that I do not escort you to the house itself," he said. "I hardly think my presence will be welcome."

There was nothing Theo could say to that; he was right. His presence would not be welcome. "Thank you," she said eventually. "For tonight."

"I believe the custom is to tell you it was my pleasure," Sir Montague said, his dark, magnetic gaze holding her hostage. "But as I'm sure you're aware, it was nothing but a disappointment."

Theo caught her breath as, with a bitterly sardonic smile, he offered her his hand and handed her down onto the street. At this time of night, even the lamps did little to stave off the darkness, and she felt utterly alone. As Sir Montague watched from the carriage, she went up to the house and let herself in. Nathanial was not yet home, and she fled upstairs to her bedroom, only realising, when she got there, that she had never heard the carriage pull away.

Montague glowered at the spot Theo had been sitting in just minutes before. He had seen her arrive safely, and had behaved in all ways like a gentleman, but it would have been so easy to abandon the shackles of society and manners and expectations and take her against the seat.

Had Nathanial taken her the same way? He had not thought his cousin capable of it, but Theo's face when she returned—afraid, hurt, worried—bore the markings of a lady who had not enjoyed the proceedings. And although his natural instincts were not to cherish or protect, he had found himself wanting to ease the sting somewhat.

A foolish notion. Fanciful. It made little difference to him whether she had voluntarily engaged in the activities Nathanial had no doubt taken her there for. All that mattered was whether their relationship would survive, and whether she would be borne an heir. Unlikely, if they had only come together once.

But the thought he had missed his chance, that *Nathanial* had beaten him to it, made his fists clench. He laughed humourlessly before directing his groom to take him home. The masquerade had lost its appeal, and he knew that for better or worse, he would be thinking of Theo, little Theo, and what might have happened in the gardens.

Montague drummed his fingers restlessly against his thigh. All in all, this had played excellently into his hand. Nathanial had been angry and jealous, tipped off as Montague had directed, and he had behaved rashly. This was precisely the kind of response he had hoped for. And yet, for a reason he could not quite decipher, he was dissatisfied with the events of the evening.

It had been his expectation that he would be the one to kiss her sweet lips and take her into the velvet night. He had hoped to learn all the secrets her body might have to offer.

Yet Nathanial had got there first.

Montague could not recall the last time he had felt jealous over a lady, and the emotion was distinctly unwelcome. As they arrived at his house, he dismissed the thought and alighted onto the street.

A shadow outside detached itself from the wall and approached. "Sir Montague," the figure said. Juliet. Here, at his home. Montague bit back his irritation. "I suspected you would not return to the party."

"How very astute of you."

She tossed her hood back to reveal her pale face and narrowed eyes. "I presume you saw the Duchess disappear into the gardens with the Duke."

"I had no idea you were at the masquerade."

"Nonsense." She put her hands on her hips. "I know you saw me there."

She was fast presenting herself as more of a hindrance than a help. "Then why did you not flirt more with the Duke? Keep him entertained so he did not take the Duchess into the gardens?"

"What else could I do? He came in search of her."

"Of course he did. I arranged for him to discover her whereabouts." He raised an eyebrow at Juliet. "But I had thought more highly of your feminine wiles."

"My wiles don't compare to a jealous husband," she snapped. "And you know as well as I do that the Duke was jealous."

"Then console yourself with the thought that we succeeded here tonight," he said, keeping his tongue languid. With one hand, he grabbed her wrist and squeezed hard enough to hurt. She glanced down at the contact, and her eyes widened. "Tell me, Juliet, what did you expect to gain by coming here?"

"Release me."

"Answer the question."

"You're a brute," she told him instead, her eyes flashing. "The Duke would never accost me in such a manner."

"The Duke is a gentleman," he said, using his other hand to take her chin. She was fragile under his touch, like a bird. He could snap her at any moment. "Don't make the mistake of thinking the same of me."

She stared at him, anger and fear warring in her eyes. Good—she should be afraid. There were few things he wouldn't do, and he was tired of playing the long game.

There were now two things he wanted. The title and the wife. He would ensure he got both.

"Now," he said, releasing her chin. "Tell me for what purpose you came here."

"Making Nathanial jealous was a mistake. You saw how he was. He will only want her more."

"Perhaps," Montague murmured, staring down at Juliet. She had rouged her cheeks and reddened her lips, giving her the look of a doll, if dolls possessed eyes with such sharp, calculating gleams. "I imagine he wanted her a great deal tonight."

"Can you not see why this is a problem?"

He pulled Juliet closer, his fingers tight around her elbow. "Jealousy is the most unproductive of emotions. Consider, Juliet, if you will. Nathanial, lost in jealousy, takes advantage of the Duchess. Will that induce her to love him? Or will she fear him and he bury himself in regret?"

"But that leaves chance for an heir."

"A chance," Montague conceded. "But a small one."

Juliet tossed her head impatiently. "I hardly know why you're talking of love now. Love matters little— it is desire we must temper."

"Nothing tempers desire like regret," Montague said, and kissed her. If he could, he would have kissed Theo's swollen lips at the ballroom, when she had reappeared. He had wanted to tangle his fingers in her mussed hair and tell her his name until she was not likely to forget. But she had not looked at him as though she wanted him, and he cared—cofound it, he *cared*—whether she wanted his advances.

He pulled at Juliet's hair, tugging her head back and exposing the long line of her throat. She swatted at his hands. "We agreed you would tempt the Duchess away from her husband."

"And so I will. Helped, of course, by Nathanial chasing her away."

Juliet glowered at him, and he almost laughed at the pettish hurt in her face. It appeared he was not the only one consumed by thoughts of what had occurred in that garden, though he fancied he hid it better.

"You should stop scowling," he said, stroking her face with the pretence of affection. "Jealousy doesn't look good on you."

"Whereas cruelty is the only thing you know how to wear," she retorted, drawing back from his caress. "Lure the Duchess into your bed, Montague, or there will be consequences."

"Was that a threat?"

"Not to you."

He doubted that, but he also didn't care. There were greater things on his mind than Juliet Stanton.

Chapter Fifteen

Theo woke to a stiff face and a tightness in her chest she couldn't account for until she remembered the happenings of the previous night.

The way Nathanial had touched her—reverently, gently.

Furiously.

As though his caresses were beyond his control.

She dressed in a daze, her heart aching as she looked into the mirror to behold a face she barely recognised. Yesterday, she had come home with bee-stung lips and eyes that were brighter, glassier than they had ever been. Now, that brightness had dimmed.

Her plan, as it had been so often recently, was to leave the house without Nathanial seeing, but before she could do more than make her way downstairs, there was a morning caller.

"I'm so glad we've found you at home," the Dowager Duchess of Norfolk said, sweeping into the drawing room and pressing a perfumed kiss on Theo's cheek. "You look a little pale, my dear. Are you quite well?"

"Perfectly," Theo said, unable to help casting a glance at the door in the fear Nathanial might arrive. Even in the company of his mother, she did not want to see him. "This is an early call, ma'am."

"I wanted to bring you the news myself." The Dowager straightened, a proud smile on her face. "Cassandra was delivered of a healthy baby boy in the night. Another boy in the family." She looked proudly at Theo, though she'd had no hand in it. "We have almost all girls, you know."

"Oh!" To her chagrin, Theo realised she had forgotten entirely that Cassandra was due. "How wonderful. What is his name?"

"William, after his grandfather."

"A lovely name." Knowing it was her duty, no matter how she hated it, she rang the bell for Jarvis. When he appeared, she said, "Please be so good as to fetch the Duke. His mother has some news for him." To the Dowager, she added, "We'll visit as soon as Cassandra is receiving visitors."

"I believe that to be in the next day or so." The Dowager beamed around the room, happy enough that she was warm even to Theo. Elinor had five children, Penelope had two, and Cassandra already had one, but the arrival of another grandchild was a joyous occasion.

Perhaps she would also expect grandchildren from Theo.

Theo dipped her head. The thought of grandchildren made her feel a little ill. Nathanial touching her knowing it was her; would he perform his duties with resignation and little enthusiasm. Could she bear it?

Could she refuse, when children and heirs were a condition of their marriage?

"Well, Mama?" Nathanial asked from the doorway. "I hear you have news for me?"

Theo started at the sound of his voice, but she didn't dare look at him. Instead, she glanced across at the Dowager, a false smile on her face.

The Dowager held her hands out to him. "The best news! Cassandra has a boy. A little boy named William."

"Congratulations." Nathanial took her hands and Theo glanced up at him in time for her to see him look at her, something hard in his eyes. Or rather, it was the *absence* of everything she'd been so used to seeing; an expression that had never been directed at her before. As though she were nothing.

There was no way he could have discovered she had been at the masquerade, but there could be no other reason for that coldness. Had Mrs Stanton told him?

Yes, that must have been it. Except . . . if she had told Nathanial about Theo being there, she would also have mentioned the garden. Did . . . Did Nathanial know that the mysterious stranger he had seduced was her?

Did he think that, because she had not acknowledged him, she had allowed herself to be seduced by a stranger?

No, surely not. *Surely* not. If he did think that, everything was over.

"Cassandra must be pleased," Nathanial continued smoothly, giving no sign he had seen Theo's start, her flush, or the stricken expression that crossed her face. "It's time there was a son in the family."

"And you?" the Dowager asked, patting the seat beside her, which was, coincidentally, also beside Theo. "It would be advantageous for there to be a son and heir."

Theo gripped her knees hard enough that her knuckles whitened.

"Two months into a marriage and you're already anticipating grandchildren?" Nathanial raised a brow. "A little precipitous, Mama."

"For a love match such as this, I would not have said so," the Dowager said.

A love match. Theo had never hated three words the way she hated those.

"Come now," the Dowager chided as Nathanial took his seat, "you are in safe company here. You are not obliged to sit stiffly beside one another."

Perhaps, if she tried very hard, the ground would open up and swallow her whole. She cast around for a reason to leave the room—leave and possibly never return.

Nathanial stretched out his legs, looking for all the world as though he was perfectly comfortable where he was, his elbow almost brushing Theo's. "My wife is feeling somewhat under the weather today," he said blandly. "Are you not, my dear?"

"Only a little," she said, summoning her courage and smiling at the Dowager. If Nathanial could play this game, so could she. "Nate has been so good as to care for me." Fingers trembling, she placed a hand on his leg. He flinched under her touch. Just slightly, but enough for the shock to ricochet through her.

"Of course he has," the Dowager said, sending her son an approving glance. "Well, I must be off. I have a great many calls to make."

"We shall see Cassandra as soon as we can," Theo promised as they stood. "Thank you for taking the time to call."

"Goodbye," the Dowager said, exiting the room much as she had entered: with a dramatic swirl of her skirts and a sense of indomitable force.

"Well," Nathanial said coldly, as Theo rubbed nervous hands down her front. "I've been caring for you, have I?"

"You told your family that we were a love match—"

"I know where you were last night," he said suddenly. "That little adventure you did not see fit to tell me, that you attended in the company of Sir Montague."

So he did know she had gone. She waited for him to mention her activities in the garden, but he merely glared at her, waiting for her response. Perhaps he did not know after all. Relief felt thick against her tongue as she tucked her hands behind her back and cast her gaze to the floor. "Oh," she managed.

"Have you nothing more to say for yourself?"

"I wish I had not gone," she said, and thought she saw him stiffen. "It was a mistake. Is that what you would like me to say?"

Nathanial's scorching gaze fixed on her for such a long time, she felt as though he was peeling aside every one of her layers to reveal her innermost thoughts. When he spoke, his voice was low. "The next time you see fit to go somewhere with Montague, you will inform me first."

Theo was not entirely sure how it had happened, but they were now close enough that they could kiss. He was leaning down and her face tipped up to his. Warm breath flowered across her face and danced along her lips. If she wanted, she could reach up and bridge the distance between them, and that awareness washed over his face as clearly as it washed over hers. For a dizzying moment, she thought he would initiate.

"Do you understand me?" he demanded, leaning away. "That is the last time you go somewhere without my permission."

"Permission?" Theo folded her arms. "I was under the impression that our arrangement didn't require any form of permission."

"Our *arrangement* was not so you could degrade yourself where anyone could have recognised you."

"If you knew where I was," she flashed, though she hardly knew what she was saying, "you must have known it was a masked event."

"Montague—"

"Sir Montague is not your concern."

"He is precisely my concern," Nathanial said through gritted teeth. "If he had not taken you there, you would not have . . ." His throat worked. "You would have never thought to have gone without his influence."

"You seem to think you know a lot about me," she said, the tightness in her chest soaking through her until every muscle ached with tension. "I wonder if you know everything you think you do."

"I know enough."

Theo took a long breath, retreating into the formality that acted as a shield between them. "As you say, Your Grace."

"Then we can have nothing more to say to one another."

At that, she looked at him, really looked at him, at the way his mouth quivered at the corners, the way something burned alongside the fury in his eyes, the way his skin seemed drawn tight across his forehead and cheekbones. The tips of his eyelashes were pale and invisible from a distance. She knew that. She knew how soft the back of his neck felt under her fingertips, and the low sound he'd made when she wrapped her legs around him.

She knew so much, and yet so little, of the man she had married.

"I suppose there is not," she said, not allowing herself the luxury of regret as she brushed past him. They had been such good friends before their marriage, before the intricacies of emotion had interrupted their friendship.

But to tell him that she had craved his every touch, that even now she longed to tell him it had been her in the gardens, that she had known it was him, would be impossible. They had agreed, from the offset, that this would not be a union troubled by undue affection or love. She would not be the one to break that, even if everything else had changed.

Nathanial went out of his way to avoid Theo over the next few days. He dined out when she dined in, and endeavoured only to leave his dressing room when he was sure she had left the house.

Three days after their argument, however, he could no longer avoid her. Cassandra had written, inviting them to visit little William Haddington, and duty awaited.

Theo waited for him in a fetching blue pelisse that made her look especially well, if a little pale. Then again, she had been pale ever since the damn masquerade. Occasionally, he wondered if he had gone too far, or taken out too much of his anger on her. After all, this was their agreement: she could do what she liked with whom she pleased.

He had just not supposed she would do it, and especially not after he had kissed her. Yet she had. It was not, logically, a choice she was obligated to regret, but he hated that she had made it.

And she had accompanied Montague to the masquerade. If he had been the one to take her into the gardens, no doubt she would have gone.

It was clear now she was miserable. But Nathanial, no matter how much he tried to convince himself that he should not care, could not move past it.

"Smile," he said as he handed her into the carriage. "Or do you want my sister to believe we're fighting?"

"Is that to be our fate every time we appear together?" she asked, her voice dull.

"That is the fate of most couples, Theo, little as you might like to think it."

She glanced away to her gloves, which she worried. He hadn't noticed before how she plucked at the stitching when she was nervous, how when her mind was occupied, her fingers fluttered, and she remained oblivious.

"We will not find the process too arduous, I am sure," Nathanial said, as though he, too, was oblivious.

Theo said nothing more, and all too soon, they arrived. He helped her down from the carriage, fingers tightening around hers when she tried to pull away, as he'd known she would. If appearances were all they had left, by God he would not let them go now.

"Come, my dear," he said, tucking her hand into his arm. She glanced up at him once then, a frightened glance that made his chest squeeze in irritation and repentance, but once again said nothing as the butler showed them inside.

Cassandra lay reclined on a sofa in the Yellow Saloon, her face pale but her hair pinned neatly behind her back. As always, she wore a pretty, muslin gown, and Nathanial reflected that not even the indignities of childbirth could keep his sister from fashion. A wetnurse in the corner cradled baby William, who appeared to be sleeping.

Cassandra placed a finger to her lips and beckoned them forwards. "Brother," she said, her gaze flicking to Theo's face and away. "How good of you to come."

Theo pulled her hand from his arm. "You look well. And baby William is very sweet."

"He's a darling," Cassandra said, "and about time we had a boy. I merely hope there are more to come."

Nathanial kept quiet. Montague's presence irked him enough that he would keep Theo on a leash, if he must, to ensure her safety, but he did not appreciate the thought that the only way to control Montague was by providing heirs.

William chose that moment to awaken, and he was passed to his mother, who showed him off with a proud face. Nathanial considered his nephew to look much as babies tended: small, red-faced, and oddly wrinkled. Theo was effusive in her praise, however, and Cassandra slowly started to unbend as Theo gushed over William's tiny, waving fists and delicate features.

Cassandra slid him a meaningful look as Theo took the baby into her arms and held him against her chest. And for a moment—just a moment, before she glanced up at him, her face stricken—her expression dissolved into such gentle joy he could hardly bear looking at her.

"Well, Nathanial?" Cassandra asked, nodding at Theo. "Does not your bride look well with a child in her arms?"

"Theo always looks well," he said shortly, prompting another quick glance from Theo, this time one of surprise.

"He cries so very quietly," Theo said, half in awe as she stroked William's cheek.

"Yes, he truly is a dear," Cassandra said, reaching for William back. "And I believe he takes after his father."

In Nathanial's opinion, this squirming infant resembled no adult human.

"I am surprised, however," Cassandra said, "that you took the time to visit, Nathanial. When was the last time you visited your nieces or nephews?"

"Considering he is the only nephew, never before," Nathanial said.

"And your nieces?"

Nathanial waved a careless hand. "I have so many of those, it would be unfair of me to favour one above the other."

Cassandra raised an eyebrow, but she struggled to hide her obvious pleasure as she looked back at William, her son. The only male in the Hardinge line, save Nathanial.

"You must visit often," she said, a tinge of command in her voice. Being The Lady Haddington, wife of the Viscount Haddington, she was used to commanding, though she infrequently attempted to command him. Perhaps because she knew the futility of such an attempt.

He gave a gentle smile. "Perhaps, when it doesn't interfere with our other plans."

"What other plans?" she demanded pettishly. "What could be more important than seeing your nephew?"

"Many things, my dear sister. I had thought Theo and I might retire to Havercroft."

Theo flashed an edged, angry look at him, but there was nothing she could say in front of Cassandra. Something he had counted on.

"So soon?" Cassandra asked. "It's hardly April."

"We will wait until the end of the Season, of course," Theo interjected. "We wouldn't want to miss too much of dear William's early life."

"Unless, of course, there is a reason for you to retire." Cassandra's eyes gleamed as they darted to Theo's stomach. "You may tell me, even if you do not wish to tell Society. I can be quite discreet, you know."

Unlike Theo. A glance at her told him her face had flamed.

"There is no reason other than my preference for a quiet life with my wife," Nathanial said. A quiet life he intended to participate little in, but his sister did not need to know that. "Think—we would not wish to draw attention away from you and William."

Satisfied again, Cassandra looked away, but Theo did not; she held his gaze, that hard, angry look in her eyes not dimming for a moment.

He had not thought, before their marriage, that she would rise against him. He'd known she was stubborn, of course, because their childhood together had done plenty to illuminate that particular trait, but there was more to this defiance than pure stubbornness.

And if he reflected that his anger was unjustified, given the particulars of their arrangement and marriage, he did not allow himself to dwell on it.

Eventually, Cassandra motioned that she was tired and William needed to feed. The child was handed back to his wetnurse and Theo and Nathanial left, her hand once more tucked in his arm.

She jerked it free as soon as they reached the privacy of their carriage. "You do not have the right to order me around," she said, her voice tight. "To *command* me as though I were little more than your servant."

He had always presumed he would marry an equal, a woman whom he had no need to command.

"When you are wilful enough—" he began through gritted teeth.

"Wilful?" She raised her eyebrows. "You offered me marriage, Nathanial, and I was grateful. You offered me a bond that was not to be a shackle, and I was even more so. Do you retract your word now?"

He had never seen such boldness in her.

He had never thought her more beautiful.

"I made a vow to protect you," he said, controlling his voice. "That is the bond to which you agreed."

"Then perhaps you might consider I am capable of protecting myself."

"Are you?" Nathanial could not help but think of the way she had accepted his hand at the masquerade.

The way she had followed him to the darkness of the garden and let him have his way with her.

The fact she did not know who he was, and still allowed these things.

"I will be remaining in London for the foreseeable future," she said coldly, folding her hands in her lap. Gone was the nervous fidgeting from earlier. "If you wish to leave, you have my blessing. Perhaps you wish to take Mrs Stanton to visit the country; I'm sure she has little experience outside London." With that entirely unjust passing blow, she turned her attention to the streets outside the window.

Chapter Sixteen

The secret to a—well, if not *happy*, then quiet—marriage was, it transpired, avoidance. After the blazing argument Nathanial's pre-emptive move to the country had occasioned, they both contrived not to see each other.

And Theo, naturally, was very pleased at this turn of events. *Extremely* happy, in fact.

Unfortunately, this extremely felicitous state of affairs only lasted two weeks, until Theo attended Mrs Selfridge's ball. The ball was widely proclaimed to be one of *the* major events of the Season, and when Theo arrived with her mother and Annabelle, she felt as though everyone who was anyone was there.

Including, to her chagrin, Nathanial, who was standing beside his mother.

They had not spoken about their plans for the evening, or, indeed, any plans, so there was no good reason that she should feel as though she had been deceived. Yet, as she watched him, emotion swelling in her chest, she could not but feel as though this choice was a direct snub. Nathanial, as she well knew, actively *avoided* attending on his mother, and would rather have stayed home than escort his mother to a ball.

Yet here he was. Not even pretending to offer her any attention.

Which was, of course, fine. Theo turned her attention to the rest of the room in search of a distraction and found Sir Montague walking towards her. Her stomach jumped.

Annabelle clung to her arm. "Is that Sir Montague?" she asked in an oddly breathless voice. "He is extremely handsome, is he not?"

"You should not be noticing these things," she said severely. Sir Montague was *not* a proper companion for her sister. "And you should stay away from him."

Annabelle peered at her, raising an eyebrow. "Why? You have not done. And that is despite Mama saying he is a bad man."

"I think he *is* a bad man."

"That does not seem to have dissuaded you."

"I," Theo said through gritted teeth, "am a married woman, and before you ask, that makes things extremely different."

"He's coming." Annabelle gripped Theo's arm, and Theo had the sinking feeling that finally her sister had discovered a preference. She had fallen foul of Sir Montague's charm and dark eyes and way of making every lady he spoke to feel like the only one in the room. "Do you think he will ask you to dance?"

Theo didn't have time to answer before Sir Montague was upon them, bowing over first Theo's hand, then Annabelle's. "Duchess," he said. "Lady Annabelle. You both look radiant tonight."

Theo tried not to look too pleased, but she had been especially proud of her red gown, stitched with hundreds of tiny white roses. And Annabelle, dreamlike in pale blue with her blonde hair and blue eyes, was also looking her best.

"Thank you," Theo said, accepting the compliment so Annabelle would not have to. She contemplated dancing with Sir Montague, and decided she would when she had forgiven him for taking her to a masquerade. In short, after she had made him suffer a little.

His gaze met hers, not inconsiderable amusement in their depths, and he turned to Annabelle. "Lady Annabelle, would you do me the honour of granting me a dance?"

Theo's jaw dropped. If she had not been so sure it was firmly attached, she would have expected it to clatter against the floor. Sir Montague was asking *her sister* to dance?

Oh, this was the outside of enough. This was—

"Certainly, sir," Annabelle said, smiling shyly up at him.

Theo collected her jaw and tried to find something to say, but the dance was already forming, and with a wink, Sir Montague whisked her sister away.

Yes, this was bad. It was *terrible*. If Theo had thought herself half in love with him due to his eyes alone, she could only imagine what effect he was having on Annabelle. At the sight of Annabelle smiling up at him—and worse, Sir Montague smiling back—Theo set her jaw. To have them all there like this was unbearable.

With a pang, she wondered if this was how Nathanial felt when watching *her* dance with Sir Montague.

Not to be outdone, she immediately procured herself a partner, entering the dance and vying to be as close to Annabelle and Sir Montague as she could. It wasn't because she was jealous, she told herself. It was just that . . . Annabelle was her *sister*. And she was laughing, which was unlike her in the presence of a gentleman. Sir Montague wasn't flirting, precisely—Theo had seen enough of his flirting to know that—but he was being pleasant. Charming, even. And her sister, poor innocent Annabelle, was enjoying the dance far too much.

Theo hoped he would fall and break a leg. Or, better, become paralysed without any hope of walking again. Annabelle would be disappointed, no doubt, but she was eighteen. There was plenty of time to find a more suitable lover than Sir Montague.

A glance across the room told her that Nathanial was dancing with a pretty blonde, and had the audacity to smile at her.

There would be no more enjoyment for Theo tonight.

"You are charming," her partner told her, trying in vain to capture her attention.

"Oh hush," she told the poor boy.

The dance seemed to last an inordinately long time, far longer than *she* had ever spent dancing with Sir Montague, and when at last it was over, he was still unfortunately in possession of all his limbs.

"Thank you," she told young Lord Bailey, who lingered around her as though he hoped she might pay him some more heed. "I must speak with my sister."

He wilted, deflated, and Theo waited as Sir Montague procured some lemonade and Annabelle took her arm once more. "Theo!" she said with touching and naïve enthusiasm. "Did you see me dancing? I declare I had so many compliments."

The prevailing fashion was for fair, and with her flushed cheeks and sparkling eyes, Theo had to concede her sister looked extremely pretty. Usually, she wouldn't have minded—she'd have been happy, even—but today she wished Annabelle had been in terrible looks. Or better yet, stayed home.

The amusement reappeared in Sir Montague's eyes when he glanced at Theo. "She made a charming partner."

"Mama wishes to speak with you," Theo said pointedly to Annabelle. It was only partially true; once her mother saw Annabelle approaching, she would be more than happy to scold her for dancing with a known rake.

And Theo had a bone to pick with said rake.

Sir Montague looked as though he was enjoying himself immensely as Annabelle left and he took a sip of his drink. "Oh dear," he said, not sounding troubled in the slightest. "I appear to have upset you."

"Not at all," Theo said stiffly.

"I see. Perhaps you wish to dance, then?"

"You are mistaken." Theo glanced around in search of Nathanial, but he was nowhere to be seen. The girl he had been dancing with, however, was safely back with her friends. Theo felt a wave of unreasonable relief. "I am not in the mood to dance, and especially not with a man who favours my sister."

"Ah, so I *have* offended you?"

"She is my *sister*," she hissed. "And we both know what kind of man you are."

The amusement drained from his face. "What man am I, then, Duchess?"

"Don't speak to me as though you are not aware of your reputation." She needed to slow her tongue, but the events of the past few weeks had worn her thin; she was a threadbare rug left in the sun, tired and worn. "You took me to the masquerade hoping that by showing me favour, I would show you favour in return."

His brows lowered over his eyes, which were so dark as to be almost black. "You mistake me," he said, so low she almost could not hear him. "It is not your favour I was hoping to encourage."

"Then what?"

"Can you not guess?"

"If that is the case, why dance with my sister?"

"I danced with your sister because I knew if I asked you, you would deny me. And I confess, I had hoped to make you jealous. Did I succeed, little mouse?"

Theo opened her mouth to tell him *yes*, but the words were trapped in her throat. "If you want my good opinion," she managed, "do not make my sister fall for you."

"Do you wish to be the only lady I seek?" His eyes were intense, boring into hers. "You have that honour, Duchess. You have had it since I first saw you, and if I have offended you, I sincerely apologise."

"I—" Theo had not expected sincerity, not from Sir Montague. Dimly, she was aware she ought to be blushing, but all she could do was stare at him, suspended in disbelief and the creeping awareness that he appeared to mean everything he was saying. "You cannot be serious."

"I have never been more so. Of everyone in the room, your opinion is the one that means the most to me."

"More so than your family?" All of whom, save Cassandra, were in this room.

"I have no family," he said, an odd, twisted smile on his mouth when she looked up in pity. "Does that surprise you? I suppose I must have had a mother once, but I don't remember her, and my father denounced me when I fled to the Continent. I believe he has died since. So unless you include my cousin Nathanial and his siblings, whom I think you'll agree would rather I were *not* related, I am adrift in the world."

In perhaps the strangest twist of the evening, Theo's heart ached for Sir Montague. There was something behind his words, a loneliness, that spoke right to her heart. She had a family, but she knew what it was like to feel alone in a room full of people.

"Perhaps if you found a wife," she suggested, "you might not be so lonely."

Good idea, Theo. Look how well that turned out for you.

Sir Montague looked down at her with an odd expression in his eyes. The mockery was gone. "Ah, but for that, I would have to marry for love."

"It is not"—she struggled to get the words out—"so very difficult."

"And yet, nevertheless, unlikely. Something great would have to induce me into matrimony. Excuse me, Duchess." With a slight bow, he left, moving towards the card room and not stopping to greet anyone on his way.

Theo barely had time to watch him leave before Nathanial accosted her, one hand on her arm, fingers a little too tight. "Don't pine too obviously," he said, something hard in his voice. "Someone might notice."

Theo blinked and tried to pull her arm free. "I am not pining, Nathanial. Let me go."

"The next dance is about to begin. Come."

If she pulled away now, there would be talk—even more talk—and Theo could not bear that. But nothing could stop her glare as he led her to where other couples were forming. "You could have *asked* me."

"And given you a chance to refuse?"

Theo's head ached. Her heart ached. Nothing about this evening had gone right.

Nathanial's brow pinched, and the hand around hers tightened. "Are you all right?"

"We don't have to do this," she said wearily. "Put aside your concern, Nate. I know you do not mean it."

His jaw worked and she looked away before she could see anything more in his face. "Fear not," he said, something cold in his voice. "This is the only dance I will solicit your hand for."

Theo tried to be glad, she really did. But she was tired and all she wanted, all she had ever wanted, was Nathanial's good opinion. And, with his hand warm on her arm, their bodies close like this, it was impossible not to remember the last time they had been this close.

For a moment, she was tempted to tell him that she had been the one in the garden, to give voice to this last secret that haunted the space between them. For a moment, she wanted to use this final moment of physical intimacy to break down the last barriers they had erected around themselves.

But to do so would be to bare her heart, and she could not face his disappointment. Or worse, his horror.

"It pains me I must ask this," Nathanial said, "but for the sake of onlookers, I feel a smile might be appropriate."

If Theo forced a smile now, she might burst into tears. She pressed her mouth more firmly together and concentrated on keeping her breathing even. "Is it not enough that I am dancing with you?"

"If it were, I would not have asked." He paused for a beat, and when she did not look or smile, added, "You accepted the role of Duchess when we married, and this is what it entails."

"And you promised to do everything in your power to make me happy. Instead, you—" Now she truly was going to cry. She turned her face away, blindly staring at the wall. Nathanial stopped, leading her to one side, but he did not let go.

"I am trying to *protect* you," he said, taking her chin and turning her face back to his. "Sir Montague is not entertaining you because he holds you in affection. He's using you to hurt me."

Theo thought this night might be the worst of her entire life. "I am all astonishment," she said, forcing the words out past a throat that closed around them. "I thought for him to be able to hurt you, you would have to care about me."

The look that leapt into his eyes made her stomach clench. "You are my wife."

"A mistake," she said thickly. "As I'm sure you will agree by now."

His arms tightened around her. "By God, Theo, mistake or not, you are still married to me, and you will not forget it."

"I hate you."

"I'm gratified to hear I have inspired such strong emotions."

If they were not in a ballroom, she would have pulled away long ago, and fled. Nathanial would not have been able to see how deeply he could wound her, and she would have had space to vent her emotions. Instead, as he pulled her back into the dance, tears shimmered across her eyes, though none fell, and she did not dare look at him again. His arms held her close, and occasionally she thought she felt his thumb swipe across her arm, or her back, or occasionally her hand, as though he could not help himself.

As though, despite how much he clearly despised her, he hated to see her distress almost as much as she hated letting him see.

"The dance is almost over," he said after several long minutes of their silence. "Before you escape, I will kiss your hand."

Theo shook her head, feeling the tears wash across her eyes and threaten to break down her cheeks. "You do not need to. That is a—an archaic formality."

"Nevertheless, I will do so." His eyes were so very dark tonight; the grey of the moon shrouded in clouds. "After all, we are in love."

A single tear broke free and Theo scrubbed it away, hating Nathanial for hurting her; hating herself for caring. When the dance ended, Nathanial took that same hand in both of his, fingers warm, thumb soothing as he brought her knuckles to his lips. When he released her, a frown lowering his brows, he opened his mouth as if to say something, but Theo cupped her hand against her chest and fled, leaving him standing motionless in the centre of the room.

Chapter Seventeen

Juliet Stanton was not a woman who lacked connections, and her acquaintance was varied in its depth and breadth. Largely, she consorted with the *ton*, or those who would tolerate and accept her presence, but when occasion demanded, she had many friends who came from the torrid and muddy gutters of the East End.

The man who stood before her now was a member of that society, and his grimy boots had left marks across her carpets. His voluminous overcoat was shabby, patched in places, and the hair that fell over his forehead was lank and greasy. She'd already had opportunity to note his fingernails were ingrained with dirt.

"Well?" she asked, every inch the indolent lady. Her dress, as she ensured, was both expensive and provocative, and she lounged across her sofa with careless grace. Just in case this man didn't know who he was dealing with. "Do you have it?"

"I do, m'lady," he said, his cap clutched between his hands. His gaze slid across the rich furnishings of her drawing room, but although he behaved with every obsequiousness, he didn't seem intimidated by the wealth she had taken such pains to display.

Juliet motioned to a small walnut table inlaid with gold. "Place it there."

"And my payment?"

She dangled a small bag between her fingers, allowing it to chink. "I have it here."

In response, the man reached into his large pockets and withdrew a small vial, placing it on the table. "Three drops is all you need," he said. "More than do the trick."

"Very well." Juliet eyed the clear liquid with suspicion, but tossed the bag across. "No word of this to anyone, you understand?"

"No, m'lady."

She didn't bother correcting his mistake. If he thought her a lady, all the better; he may never be able to identify her if this ever came out.

Not that it would, of course. If there was one thing she had learnt since becoming widowed, it was how to be discreet.

"Take the money and go," she said.

The man needed no further encouragement.

Chapter Eighteen

After Mrs Selfridge's ball, and as the Season was coming to a close, the *ton* fell into a slump that only a picnic on the bank of the river Thames could assuage. Lady Tabitha and Lord Thorpe conceived the happy scheme, and in the space of a week, the idea had grown enough that half of London's society vowed to join. By the time Theo arrived with Nathanial, the elected picnic spot was crowded and busy.

"Duchess!" Lady Tabitha said in excitement, and Nathanial took that opportunity to drop her arm. "How *delightful* you could join us. And Your Grace! I'm so glad to see you both."

Nathanial gave her a brief bow, murmured pleasantries, and at the beckoning of one of his friends, left them. Lady Tabitha tucked her arm through Theo's. "Now, my dear," she chattered, "let us see who is in attendance. I declare it's so very warm!"

It was an unseasonably hot July day, and Theo found herself wishing she had stayed home. Keeping up this endless charade was exhausting; as Duchess, she was often one of the most highly ranked people in any room; everyone vied for her attention, her good will, her favour. And everyone watched her eagerly, waiting for a mistake. A woman's reputation was a fragile thing, long cultivated and easily broken. It would take very little to cut the strings by which it was attached. A mistake like she had made at the masquerade, an indiscretion that was made public, and it would all come tumbling down.

"Sir Montague!" Lady Tabitha trilled, dragging Theo across to where Sir Montague stood. "How wonderful to have found you here! I declare, I had not expected you to come."

If Tabitha was looking for a husband here, Theo could have told her she was wasting her time. *Something great would have to induce me into matrimony.* That something great was unlikely to be Tabitha and her modest fortune.

Sir Montague raised a brow. "Indeed?"

"Oh, well, yes." Tabitha batted her eyelashes at him in what Theo suspected was supposed to be coquettishness. "Does not the water look especially warm today?"

Theo glanced at the silvery water of the Thames, which in her opinion did *not* look warm, and wondered how, when she felt so wretched, the sun could keep smiling.

Sir Montague's gaze was on her, and his dark brows drew together. "You are hot, Duchess," he said.

Lady Tabitha snapped open her fan and turned it on Theo with such force, her eyes watered. "Is this better?" she asked solicitously.

As had happened frequently of late, Theo wished to go home. "I'm perfectly well."

"There is a blanket to our left in the shade," Sir Montague said. "Come, ladies, join me and we shall sit together."

"What an excellent idea," Tabitha tittered. "You think of all the best ideas, Sir Montague."

Sir Montague, a lady on both arms, led them slowly to the blanket and sat them down. "Allow me to procure you both something to drink," he said. "It really is extremely hot."

Theo searched for Nathanial in the crowd, and was just in time to see Mrs Stanton, copper curls bouncing, approaching him with a smile on her face. The lump in Theo's throat grew, and her mouth dried.

"Don't you think Sir Montague favours me?" Tabitha asked in a whisper as soon as he had left. "He was so assiduous in showing us to the shade, and you know, I am inclined to freckle if I am in the sun too long."

Theo blinked, surprised that Tabitha could have deceived herself so utterly. "Oh," she managed.

"Have you noticed? I have my maid bathe my face in lemon juice every night, and I'm sure that's made a difference in fading them." Tabitha motioned to her complexion, which was robust, with no freckle in sight. Theo wondered if the contrast was intentional, given *she* had a smattering of freckles across her nose. "Can you believe two months ago we had snow?" Tabitha asked with a little laugh. "I declare . . ."

Theo tuned out Tabitha and her comments about the weather and looked again in search of Nathanial and Mrs Stanton. It would be like sipping poison, she knew, but she couldn't help herself. Was Mrs Stanton placing another possessive hand on his arm? Did he accept affection from her when he wanted nothing to do with Theo?

But Mrs Stanton was not with Nathanial after all. She was standing with Sir Montague by the refreshments, their body language taut and defensive. After a few seconds, Mrs Stanton broke away, her head held high, and Sir Montague walked back towards them, two glasses in his hands.

"Wine for Lady Tabitha," he said, handing her a glass partially filled with red liquid that made Theo's stomach lurch to see it. "I thought you may enjoy it."

Lady Tabitha looked as though she had been handed the moon itself. "Oh, you are *so* considerate," she twittered.

"And lemonade for the Duchess." Sir Montague's dark eyes lingered on Theo's a fraction too long. "You looked as though you might favour something a little lighter and more refreshing."

Theo smiled and took a sip. The bitter sourness of the lemonade almost overpowered her, and she wished they had thought to add some more sugar.

"The Duchess is feeling the heat," Tabitha said suddenly. "Perhaps it would be sensible to leave her for a spell until she's feeling better. Here, Duchess, have my fan."

"You are too kind," Theo said dryly.

"If we take a turn along the shore, I'm sure by the time we've returned, the Duchess will be feeling quite the thing." Tabitha sat up straighter, clearly delighted by the plan that had resulted in her claiming Sir Montague's time for herself. "What say you, Sir Montague?"

"An excellent plan," he said smoothly. "We shall be back for you soon, Duchess."

"Enjoy your walk," Theo said, not finding she minded. Their absence would give her ample time to think about Nathanial and the way he was steadfastly ignoring her. Perhaps he really had given up caring after all.

Sir Montague's dark gaze was on her again, but after a moment he offered his arm to Tabitha and they left. Theo turned her attention to the party around her. There were boats pulled up on the shoreline, a few commandeered by small groups. Laughter hung on the air, as bright and warm as the sunlight.

It was a beautiful picture, and one Theo should have enjoyed. She might have enjoyed it had she been with Nathanial. Had Nathanial *wanted* to be with *her*.

She contemplated her lemonade, but it really *had* been too sour, and the thought of consuming more made her stomach turn. She poured it in the grass. Perhaps they would make a fresh batch with the appropriate amount of sugar soon.

To her surprise, she had not been sitting alone more than five minutes before Sir Montague sauntered back to take his place beside her, sprawling across the blanket as though he had been born there. "I'm surprised I haven't already been superseded," he said. "Are your hordes of admirers absent today?"

"I suspect I'm less admired than you think."

"A beautiful duchess who has Society at her feet?" He tilted his head to look at her, a calculating expression in his eyes. "Or perhaps they don't dare approach you when you look so forbidding."

Theo had to laugh. "Forbidding? Me? You must be mistaken."

"I'm never mistaken, little mouse, and you are indeed forbidding. If I did not know you so well, if we were not such old friends, I would never have dared approach you."

"Liar," she said, prompting a bark of laughter from him. His edged charm and mocking laughter were so far removed from Nathanial's curls and grey eyes, but although Sir Montague looked the part of the hero, she was no longer sure he could sweep her off her feet.

How could he, when her every first thought went to another man?

"I am very glad I know you, Duchess," he said.

A wave of dizziness came over her, and she pushed it aside, forcing a smile for his benefit. "You are an incorrigible flirt."

"Perhaps," he admitted, "but that does not make me untruthful."

"Where is Lady Tabitha?"

"We were fortunate enough to—er—discover a mutual acquaintance."

"You mean you foisted her onto some poor, unsuspecting soul," Theo said, then shook her head. "No, that was cruel of me."

"Yet not unjust. But as pleasant as she may be on closer acquaintance—though I pray I am not blessed with *that*—she is no Theodosia."

Theo knew she should feel something at the sound of her name on his lips. Novels had taught her that hearts ought to flutter at moments such as these, but hers remained obstinately still. In fact, the way he looked at her—as though he was a man starving, and she the feast he intended to devour—merely left her with a shimmer of fear, transient as the clouds across the sky.

"I suppose I ought to be flattered," Theo said, the world losing a little of its clarity. She folded her hands on her lap and concentrated on breathing through her nose.

"I never used to believe flattery to be beyond my powers, but now I wonder." The predatory light in his eyes faded as he searched her face. "You look a little pale. Perhaps a trip on the river might soothe you a little?"

There would be a breeze on the river rather than this insufferable heat, and Theo was prepared to sacrifice far more than propriety to feel a little of that breeze on her sweaty face.

"Yes," she said, accepting his hand as he pulled her gently to her feet. "That would be . . . lovely. I trust you are an able rower."

"You have nothing to fear from me, Duchess."

Perhaps that was not strictly true, but she believed she knew enough of his character to know he wouldn't try ravishing her against her will, especially not in public.

And *especially* not on a boat. There could be nothing less conducive to ravishing than a boat.

Her stomach cramped, and she was conscious of a wish for the shade again. Preferably the shade and the coolness of water. Perhaps she could throw herself into the Thames, propriety be damned.

She did not dare look at Nathanial, if he had even noticed her.

The boat dipped alarmingly as she clambered inside, her legs a little shaky now. The stomach cramps were becoming more pressing, and she was in imminent danger of expelling everything she'd ever eaten.

Breathe.

She had not thought such a simple command could be so difficult.

Her fingers wrapped around the rough wood of the seat, and if it were not for her gloves, it might have given her a splinter. She squeezed, gritting her teeth against the pain and roiling sickness.

"Hold still," Sir Montague said as he pushed the boat off into the water, gathered the oars, and sat opposite her. "There we go."

Cold shivers racked through her, despite the overbearing heat of the sun. She closed her eyes.

"Duchess?" Sir Montague's voice sounded as though it came from a distance. "Are you well?"

The world was not in its proper place. If she reached out to touch it, she would miss. And oh, her stomach hurt unbearably.

"Theo?" He put his oars down and reached towards her. "What's wrong?"

The world tilted on its axis as she leaned over the side of the boat and vomited so hard her body convulsed and everything went dark.

Chapter Nineteen

Nathanial was a damn fool. He knew it as well as Theo, although she had yet to come out and say it to him. He half wished she would. If she had given him the opening, he would have apologised for the way he'd treated her at Mrs Selfridge's ball.

Her tears then had nearly been his undoing. He had almost held her close and told her that he would forgive her every transgression if only she would stop crying.

Instead, they had returned home and ignored each other just as before.

"Norfolk, old boy?" Lord Stapleton said. His florid face was full of rare concern. "Never seen you so distracted. You quite well?"

"Perfectly." Nathanial racked his brains to think of what they had been discussing before he had, once again, let his mind drift to Theo. Hunting. Yes. "The fox hunting in Merton is extremely good, of course, but I know less about shooting potential elsewhere."

Stapleton nodded, setting his chins shuddering. "Caddington Hall, my estate, is in Yorkshire, and I must assure you, the shooting is excellent. We have plenty of grouse. The shooting season begins soon—you must visit sometime, to try out the land. You would be welcome, you know, any time."

"Thank you, Stapleton. A kind offer."

"Not at all, Your Grace, it would be an honour." He almost appeared to stumble over his words before remembering that dignity was his best approach. "We could arrange quite the party. Only think what fun that would be."

Nathanial glanced at the river in time to see Montague pushing a boat containing Theo away from the shore. "Yes," he said distractedly. "Such fun."

"My wife would be delighted to host." Lord Stapleton took the idea in stride and beamed. "I can think of nothing more ideal for the summer, perhaps."

Nathanial spared him a glance. He knew no harm of Stapleton, except that he had made a foolish marriage in his youth and had regretted it ever since. If he joined a hunting party, would Theo accompany him? Or would she remain in the company of gentlemen whose companionship she preferred.

When he next looked in the direction of the boat, Theo was nowhere in sight. Montague, oars forgotten, was standing precariously and bending over something.

His body put the pieces together before his mind could, and he brushed past Stapleton as though in a daze. On the boat, Montague sat back down and rowed to the shore.

Nathanial could not see Theo.

There was a whining in his ears that only grew louder as he strode towards the shore. A hush followed him and all eyes turned to Montague, who lifted Theo from the boat. Limp, helpless Theo, who looked nothing like the lady he'd married. Her body convulsed periodically, brown liquid dribbling from her mouth.

This couldn't be happening. Not his Theo. Not his *wife*.

Montague laid her gently on the ground and Nathanial fell to his knees beside her. His heartbeat resounded in his ears as he wiped away the liquid and held her close to his chest. "What did you do?" he demanded of Montague, his voice not his own.

"I don't know."

"For God's sake, man!" Nathanial cupped Theo's cheeks, willing more air into her lungs, willing her to open her eyes and look at him.

Elinor pushed her way through the crowd to his side. "Robert," she said to her husband. "Fetch a physician. *Now.*"

Theo lay utterly, terribly still. Nathanial was half afraid to move closer in case the delicate movement of her chest proved to be an illusion—but to remain where he was, poised by her side without helping, would be infinitely worse.

One of her hands, limp and pale, lay near him, and he took it in both of his. Her heartbeat fluttered anxiously in her wrist. Too fast.

His father had once told him that all creatures were only afforded a certain number of heartbeats; once they passed, the creature must die. That was why birds and mice, their heart thrumming like a purr, had such short lives.

"Please allow the Duke and Duchess room," Elinor said, cold authority in her voice as she ushered the crowd away. Nathanial barely noticed. "They must have space."

What good would space achieve? That would not bring colour back into Theo's lips, or compel her eyes to open. It would not banish the foam from her mouth, or the jerky convulsions that still racked her body from time to time.

She couldn't die. He would not allow it. She could not die believing he despised her.

Yet no matter how much he willed it, she did not open   her   eyes.

Chapter Twenty

Theo's stomach ached. In fact, every inch of her ached; a deep, heavy ache that sank her further into the mattress. Sweat stuck her hair to her head. In the corner of the room, Nathanial and another man spoke in tones too low for her to hear.

The next time she woke, Annabelle sat beside her. "Oh, sister," she said, clasping Theo's hand and pressing it to her shaking lips. "Theo."

The third time she woke, she was alone.

This time, the nausea had subsided a little. Cramps still racked her body, but she could think around them. The room was dark, but the moon's cool light brushed the far wall. For a moment, she lay still, acclimatising herself to her position. She was back in her room at Norfolk House, and—

Nathanial. Sir Montague. The boat.

She sat up too abruptly and her head throbbed. Her stomach heaved, and she thought she might expel what little was there onto the sheets. Cold sweat prickled her skin. The last thing she could remember was being in the boat and feeling as though she was going to die. In fact, dying had felt like a positively pleasant option in comparison to the nausea that had gripped her.

She sucked in another deep breath and swung her legs off the side of the bed. Her mouth felt dry and her tongue was like sandpaper. Once she had a drink, maybe she would be able to remember. As her traitorous legs took her weight, however, they buckled, and she flung out a hand to steady herself, knocking the nightstand. Something—a book, perhaps—fell to the floor with a soft thud, and she cursed, borrowing a word from Henry's vocabulary.

There was a sound behind her; the unmistakable sound of someone waking. "Really, Theo," Nathanial said sleepily. "That is not an appropriate term for young ladies to use."

Theo fell over. Her knee slammed against the carpet and her legs buckled, sending her face colliding with the floor. Now she had new aches to add to the old.

"Theo, Theo." Nathanial was beside her now, faster than she could have accounted for, and he lifted her up as though she was a child, without so much as a grunt of effort. He was fully clothed, she noticed, the rougher material scraping against her nightdress.

Carefully, he laid her on the bed and she scrabbled to get back under the covers, pulling the sheets back over herself. It was impossible to see his expression in the darkness, but she thought she saw his mouth turn down.

"Now," he said, "what were you trying to kill yourself to find?"

"Water," she croaked.

"You might have said." He lit a candle, placing it on the table beside a large jug. A glass, it transpired, was the object that had fallen, and after retrieving it, he poured her a drink. "Here. Don't drink it too fast."

She clutched the cool glass and tipped it clumsily into her mouth, not caring that she spilt some down her front. The water tasted heavenly—she hadn't known it was possible for anything to taste so good. It soothed the sourness of her tongue, the dryness of her mouth. She felt as though she could finally breathe. The nausea receded slightly.

"There," Nathanial said, taking the glass from her. "Do you feel better?"

"Yes."

"Liar." His voice was soft and affectionate in a way she hadn't thought she would hear again. "Why would I be spending my nights in that devil-made chair if you weren't ill?"

Theo cast a look at the chair in question, an armchair pulled close to the bed. In her eyes, although admittedly there was little light, it looked perfectly comfortable. She had sat in it several times herself and not suffered any ill effects.

As though he could sense the direction of her thoughts, he said, "Let me assure you that after three nights in that chair, I have come to hate it body and soul."

"Three nights?" Theo's mouth dried again. "I have been here for three nights?"

He took hold of her hand and turned it over, caressing her palm with the tips of his fingers. Her entire body warmed. "You have."

"Why?"

"That is a matter better saved for another time."

"I hardly think so," she said, doing her best to imbue her voice with a little sternness. Where had the brooding, angry Nathanial from her memories disappeared to? He had not touched her in this way, or spoken so kindly to her, in so long.

"Do you want more water?" he asked.

"Nathanial. Stop changing the subject." She took a deep breath. "And why are you being so kind to me?"

The fingers on her hand stilled. "Do you truly think so badly of me?"

"You were so angry—"

"You nearly died, Theo." His voice was a hiss in the darkness, the words even more stark because of it. Her heart lurched, tumbling in her chest over and over at the sound of them. She had nearly died. Nearly *died*.

The illness on the boat had been a symptom of something worse. Something so terrible she could hardly breathe past it.

She had almost died.

He cursed under his breath and tightened his hold on her hand. "Forgive me. I should not have said—"

"How? Was it . . ." She remembered the sun, the way she had felt as soon as she had stepped into the cloying heat. "Heatstroke?"

His laugh was harsh. "No."

"Then what?"

"It appears you were . . . poisoned." The words seemed to cost him, and he paused, gazing at the moonlit wall as though he could bore a hole through it. "The how and why I have yet to discover, but the physician was quite sure as to the what."

"Poisoned," Theo repeated. The words bounced around her head, making less sense with each iteration. "But—I did not think I had anyone who wished to poison me."

Nathanial looked down at her then, his thumb moving back across her hand reassuringly. "We know nothing yet. You should sleep."

Theo had been doing, by the sounds of it, altogether too much sleeping over the past few days. She wanted answers. "Who did this?"

"I don't know, love. But I'll find out. I promise."

Without thinking, Theo curled her fingers around Nathanial's hand. "Will you stay with me?"

By all accounts, he had been doing so for the past three days, but they had reached a kind of truce in the darkness, and she had an irrational fear that if he left her now, they would go back to how things had been.

His hand flexed in hers before he squeezed it. "Yes. I will stay with you." He rose as if to leave, but Theo did not relinquish his hand.

"Not in the armchair. You hate the armchair."

"Then where—" He broke off as he understood her intention. She expected him to argue, or give some reason why he could not. After all, their arrangement had not included this. But, as she shuffled to make room for him, he stretched out beside her, on top of the blankets, hands folded on his chest. That glimpse was all she allowed herself before she closed her eyes.

He blew out the candle. This time, the darkness felt friendly. She let out a small sigh.

"Sleep," he told her again. The silence settled around them like a thick blanket.

"Nate?"

"I regret to inform you that you are terrible at following instructions."

She laughed, before saying, "Are we friends again?"

There was a pause, and his weight shifted as though he was looking at her. When he spoke again, his voice was low. "That is what you want? To be friends?"

"Only if you do, too," she said hastily, wishing she hadn't said anything at all.

A hand brushed her hair, the gesture so light she might have believed it was a stray breeze. "Whatever may happen," he promised, "you shall always have my friendship. Now sleep."

Reluctantly, she decided to obey him, if only because the sound of his steady breaths was dragging her into unconsciousness.

Chapter Twenty-One

Now the worst of his fears had been assuaged, Nathanial had a few arrangements to make. First was a trip into town to clarify the terms of his will. There was little he could do about his estate, which would pass on to Montague if he died without issue, but he ensured that if he died unexpectedly, Theo would be provided for.

Montague was his next target, and after he finished with his lawyer, he left for his cousin's house. Perhaps it was a stretch to presume Montague had poisoned Theo, but he was capable of far worse things. The only thing that puzzled Nathanial was the means. Poison was not, he fancied, Montague's favoured method of incapacitation.

Still, this visit had been long overdue.

Ignoring the butler's protestations, Nathanial strode through to the well-appointed, if small dining room. Montague sat at the table in an Indian robe and slippers, clearly not expecting guests.

"The Duke of Norfolk, sir," the butler said belatedly, hurrying after Nathanial.

Shock crossed Montague's face, but it soon passed, and he gave a bland smile. "Thank you, Perry. That will be all."

The butler gave Nathanial a look of deep dislike and shut the door behind him with more force than strictly necessary.

"An old retainer," Montague explained. "Took him with me to France."

"I have no interest in your servants, Radcliffe."

"Have you not?" Montague poured some coffee and gestured to a seat opposite him. "I've been expecting you. Come, let's discuss this as gentlemen. You won't call me out, you know."

Nathanial remained standing. "You seem very certain on that point."

"Two reasons. First, as you will soon discover, I had no hand in this, and secondly, you know I have more experience in duelling than you. I have no interest in being injured by a man so preoccupied by his wife's health, he forgets to delope."

Nathanial finally drew out a chair. "You can't think you would kill me."

"Not kill. I have no intention of fleeing London again so soon." He paused in the act of buttering his toast. "How's the Duchess?"

"Dead," Nathanial said bluntly, and watched Montague's face pale. There was nothing victorious about his expression, which for a second appeared almost devastated.

"I am saddened to hear it," Montague said with some effort.

"Are you? Perhaps you are." He paused, watching the way Montague turned away as though hoping to conceal his face and the thoughts that lay behind. "You were assiduous in your attentions, after all."

"It is natural for any married woman to have admirers, and singularly dull of them to cling to their husband's coat." Montague recovered some of his colour and took a bite of his toast. "She flirted with me delightfully, you know."

Nathanial did know; he had watched plenty of it. Montague had almost always initiated, but his Theo had entered into it with good spirit. No doubt she enjoyed piquing him as much she did the flirtation itself.

"But let us be clear," Montague said, placing down his knife. "You suspect me of having damaged her in some way."

"She was poisoned. And you were last seen with her."

"Poisoned?" Montague's eyes took on an arrested look, as though he were privy to some secret Nathanial was not. "And you think that it was my hand?"

"Let's not pretend you are an innocent man, or that your interest in her was unconnected to me."

"On the contrary," Montague said, though a thin smile acknowledged the hit. "I found her excessively charming."

"I should know better than most how low you rate the charms of young, innocent females."

"Ah, but she's your wife, Norfolk. How innocent is she really?" He eyed the jam with apparent distaste. "But that is not the point at hand. You suspect me purely because I was there at the point of her collapse, but consider that for a moment. If I had contrived her death, I would have made myself scarce long before the poison took effect. I am not a fool. I know where suspicion must fall."

"If not you, then who?"

"Not my problem," Montague said, although Nathanial suspected he had his suspicions—if indeed he was not the culprit. His expression was bland, but he toyed with his knife, twirling it ceaselessly as though he intended to run Nathanial through with it.

Understanding finally hit Nathanial. Montague was not, as Nathanial had presumed, disinterested. He had developed an attachment.

"I don't blame you for being taken with her," Nathanial said after a moment. "She was remarkably pretty."

"She was."

"You are not alone in finding her charming."

"As her husband, I'm certain you had more chance than I to experience her charms."

Nathanial thought back to that night in Mrs Chichester's gardens, the taste of her that he'd never quite eradicated from his mouth. "She's exquisite."

If Montague noticed his momentary slip into present tense, he showed no sign of it, merely pointing to the door. "I think you've said all you have to say on the matter, and I have no more hospitality to offer."

Nathanial rose and strode to the door, but paused before he passed through. "There's one more thing." He paused, waiting for Montague to glance up. He wanted to see the man's face when he delivered this last piece of news. "I lied before. Theo is alive and recovering. But I warn you—if I suspect you had a hand in this, or any other attempt on her life, you will regret it."

The colour rushed back into Montague's cheeks, and he was silent for a few seconds before giving a languid smile that seemed marginally strained. "You must learn to give better threats, Norfolk. You have no idea of what I might regret."

"I have an idea of what you value," Nathanial said, earning himself a swift, unsettled look. He rewarded it with a cold smile. "It was a mistake to care for her, Radcliffe."

Montague's black brows drew together, but Nathanial left the room before he could say anything further.

It took a further two weeks for Theo to recover enough to contemplate travelling. The Season had not yet ended, but she and Nathanial had agreed that a sojourn from Town was the best policy, and they had settled on Lord Stapleton's invitation as an excuse. That way they could remove from London without raising suspicion.

"Are you perfectly sure you're well enough to travel?" Nathanial said—again—at breakfast. In Theo's two weeks' recovery, he had been nothing but a dedicated husband. He read to her, played piquet and chess and whist, and cancelled an obscene number of social engagements so he could be at her side. The *ton* marvelled at his devotion.

Theo knew it was because he suspected her of being in danger. Although they had not spoken about it since that first night, the very fact he remained in her room, even going so far as to sleep beside her on the bed while she tossed and turned, proved beyond doubt that he feared another attempt on her life.

Still, she liked this new Nathanial. She liked the sensation of waking up in the morning and hearing his soft, regular breathing and feeling his overpowering warmth. *How* he contrived to be so warm, she did not know, but she did not mind.

What she did not like was his endless *fussing*.

"Yes," she said calmly, sipping at her tea. "More than well enough."

He touched a curl that framed her face. "I doubt that."

"Why?"

"Because you are still too pale."

Theo frowned. She had thought, when she'd looked at her reflection that morning, that she had looked better. Almost entirely well, in fact. Perhaps her cheeks were a little more hollowed than usual, her eyes a little too large in her face, but she was already putting on weight again.

"Never fear," he said, leaning past her and flicking her nose as he reached for the jam. "You are still exceedingly pretty."

Her blush sent any accusations of being too pale to the grave. His lip quivered as though he was trying to hold himself back from laughing, and when she fumbled an answer—really, why had her wits left her *then*?—he chuckled.

"We should be ready to leave in an hour. Do you think you can manage that?"

Theo gave him her best withering look. "Of the two of us, *I* am not the one likely to delay our journey."

As it transpired, she was correct: Nathanial got distracted by going over some last-minute documents in his study, and when they at last set off, they were around half an hour late.

The journey took around six hours. Theo did her best to read a book, make idle conversation, or observe the scenery, but somehow, the mere act of travelling sapped her energy; she spent the last two hours asleep against Nathanial's shoulder. He woke her gently, and she wiped her mouth, dismayed to find she had drooled all over his coat.

If she had ever harboured any hope of romance, it was long gone.

He rolled his shoulder before flashing her a smile and handing her out of the carriage to greet their hosts.

Lord Stapleton was a florid man in his forties, with a rounded stomach and expression of perpetual joviality. His wife, in contrast, was a thin husk of a woman draped in shawls and a scowl. They vied over one another to see who could greet their guests first, without seeming to acknowledge each other at all.

Dinner had already been served, so Nathanial and Theo ate alone before joining the other guests in the drawing room. With the Season coming to an end, a shooting party was a welcome reprieve, and the room was full.

To Theo's dismay, Tabitha appeared from nowhere and made a beeline for her. "Duchess!" she said, taking Theo's arm possessively and forcing Nathanial to let go. "I'm so glad you could make it. Was not the journey horrid?"

Theo glanced at Nathanial and bit her lip at his smile. "Terrible," she agreed.

"But now you are here! Things have been so dull in Town now. So many left for the country." She gave Theo a sly look. "Sir Montague remains in London, however. And he has been paying me *particular* attention."

It took Theo a moment to find her voice, dismissing the malice in Tabitha's words. If she was hoping for Sir Montague to offer her marriage, she would be very sorely disappointed. "Oh," she said. Nathanial's jaw ticked, although he was ostensibly in conversation with Lord Stapleton. "Then I suppose I am happy for you."

"Oh, to be sure, I could do better than *him*, although he *is* known to be your husband's heir. Not, of course, that he's likely to inherit." Tabitha cast a meaningful glance at Theo's stomach. Usually, six months into a marriage, a wife had something to show for it.

She imagined rumours were going wild, speculating whether she was barren. No one would ever consider the true nature of the arrangement she shared with Nathanial.

Suddenly, viciously, she wished he had never proposed it.

Before either of them could say any more, Nathanial rose and seated himself beside Theo with his customary careless grace. "Lady Tabitha," he said. "You're looking well."

Tabitha snapped open her fan, which Theo now viewed as a lethal weapon. "Oh, you are too kind, sir. Did you notice I chose my yellow muslin today? I thought perhaps the colour washed me out, but you have quite convinced me to wear it again."

Theo watched in amusement as Lady Tabitha, clearly unwilling to waste this opportunity (even if the Duke *was* married), did her best to charm Nathanial. And Nathanial, with no intention of being charmed, rebuffed her advances with polite civility.

Eventually, Tabitha was called to a game of loo, and Nathanial stretched out comfortably beside her. Theo glanced about the room.

"It was cruel of Lord Stapleton to invite so many unattached young men," Nathanial said with a laugh in his voice, nodding to where Lady Stapleton sat beside a gentleman sat bolt upright and petrified.

"She does appear to be remarkably persistent. Has she forgotten she is married?"

This time, Nathanial really did chuckle, and he leant in so close his breath brushed her ear. "Lord Stapleton does his best to forget, I think."

Theo laughed and rested her head against his shoulder. After the carriage, it felt as though she fit there perfectly.

"Would you like me to carry you to bed?" Nathanial's words were soft, but they sank deep into her. "Or would you prefer to walk?"

"I—"

"I'm afraid the 'bed' part is non-negotiable."

Theo's laugh became a sigh. Leaving the company truly did sound delightful. "I can walk."

"Are you certain? It would cause a delightful scene if I scooped you into my arms right here."

She decided she liked that idea a little too much. Walking was safer. "I still have legs, Nate. I can do it."

"I will make your excuses, then, and see you upstairs." When he leant away, his grey eyes were gentle, and he stroked a finger along the back of her hand. Just once, but her entire body tingled, lighting like a spark set to paper.

"There's no need to—"

"On the contrary. There is *every* need to." His tone was firm, and she knew she would get nowhere by arguing. Reluctantly, she left the cloying warmth of the room, hurrying through the unfamiliar house until she reached the rooms she shared with Nathanial. Barely a minute later, he joined her, and locked the door carefully behind them.

"I know you think I'm being over-zealous," he said, pinching her chin and moving to the bed, stretching across the covers as though he belonged there. Theo's wretched heart gave a pang. "But this is for the best, I promise."

She perched by the pillows. "Are you really so concerned for my safety?"

"Ought I not be? You were poisoned. Is that not enough reason to be concerned?"

Her lips pinched as she thought. "It's quite possible no one intended to poison anyone."

He was so close now, and his hand brushed the sheets by her leg, as though he was tempted to run his fingers across her bent knee the way he did against the soft silk. "Theo," he said, caressing her name with such tenderness, she almost forgot what they were discussing. "I have the utmost respect for your whole-hearted and dim-witted belief in other people's goodness, but on this occasion you must allow me to be right."

"You believe it was deliberate?" He nodded once, curtly. "And," she continued in a whisper, "you believe I was the intended recipient?"

"I think there is no other explanation." The corner of his mouth kicked up. "Unless, of course, someone had intended on poisoning Lady Tabitha."

"Don't be so cruel," Theo said, giggling despite herself. "She is not so bad."

"If you are not an unmarried gentleman, perhaps." His smile faded as she looked down at him, and she was arrested, suddenly, by the shape of his face, all hard lines and edges and unexpected softness. Her fingers tingled with the urge to touch him, and she linked them together firmly in her lap.

"Do you know who did it?" she asked, steering her thoughts back to safer ground.

He hesitated. "No."

"But you suspect Sir Montague?" The words were out before she could stop them, staining the air. Nathanial sat up, on the other side of the bed now, his face a blank mask.

"Does that displease you?" he asked at last.

She reached over to catch his hand before he could retreat any further. "I just want to know why you dislike him so much. I want to *understand*."

He sighed, but his fingers loosened a little under her grasp, turning so they almost—almost—held hands. "It isn't a short story. Perhaps—"

"No! I am not going to wait for another time. Tonight, Nate. Please?"

"Very well, but you should get yourself ready for bed first. I'll visit you shortly."

She clung to him even more tightly. "Do you promise?"

"Yes, you wretch." He brought her hand to his mouth and gave it a swift kiss. "I'll be back soon." And with that, with a lingering glance at her, he left the room.

Chapter Twenty-Two

Theo undressed in record time, sliding under her covers and asking her maid to summon Nathanial. He entered almost immediately, closing the door behind him, and she frowned.

"Did you wait outside?"

"Where else was I supposed to go?" he asked with a small smile. "Now, my love, are you sure you're not too tired?"

"Certain. We are having this conversation, no matter how much you want to put it off."

"It appears I'm distressingly transparent," he murmured, sitting on the bed beside her, one leg dangling.

"Tell me," she urged, looking up at him and the sharpness of his profile. He didn't have a hard face, but there was something cutting about it tonight. "Tell me what happened between you and Sir Montague."

"The truth is, it's hardly my story to tell."

"I know he pursued Penelope," Theo interrupted. "Of course, I don't know the details, but I fancy I know enough."

"The devil is in the details, or so they say." Nathanial took her hand and played with her fingers almost absently. "*Pursued* is not a term that gives justice to the way he persistently attempted to take her virtue."

"Did he succeed?"

"That is not for me to say. And if you bring the subject up with Penelope, I would advise being careful. She is not . . . Let us say she is not Sir Montague's greatest friend."

"I should think not." Theo paused and looked at Nathanial's long fingers wrapped around hers. He hardly seemed to know he was doing it at all, but tingling warmth spread through her body at his touch, and she felt oddly hot. "Is that why you don't like him?"

"In part."

"Is there another reason?"

"There is always another reason," he said, and sighed, glancing down at her and meeting her gaze for one long moment before looking away. "When I was a young man—no more than a child, really—I fancied myself in love. She was a particularly nice, well-bred young lady of unexceptional birth and an excellent education."

Theo found herself hating this nameless young lady already.

"The issue lay that she found her affections to be already engaged—and to Montague, no less."

At least she did not love Nathanial back. Theo wasn't entirely certain why this was important, but it seemed far more pressing than whatever Montague had done to her. "And this was after he attempted to compromise Penelope?"

"After, by a couple of years. My family had all gathered around Pen, you understand, but at that age, I was singularly foolish, as young men tend to be. I loved my sister, yes, but I thought it not unreasonable that a young, hot-blooded man might want more than he could have." Here, he paused, and she placed her other hand across his impulsively. He glanced down at the contact. "I forgave Montague, thinking his transgressions were natural, not considering how easily men could turn elsewhere to satiate their needs."

Theo did not want to think about Nathanial turning elsewhere for his needs, and she scowled. "What of this paragon of all things you thought yourself in love with?"

"Lucy was a dear but at no point did she love me, and in retrospect at no point did I love her. The issue came when Montague, whom she believed *did* love her, took certain liberties. When her father confronted him and demanded satisfaction—"

"No." Theo sat straight up. "*That* was the duel that sent Sir Montague out of the country?"

"It was," Nathanial confirmed gravely. "Lucy was sent into the country to bear his child, and I believe she has since married. Montague chose to flee."

"And now he's back," Theo said wonderingly.

"He heard of my marriage and I presume he wanted to assure himself there would be no heir, as he stands to inherit."

She wrinkled her nose. "He would make a terrible duke."

"I quite agree."

Theo looked down to where their fingers intertwined. "Does that mean you would be prepared to consider children rather sooner than you had originally . . . I know you said you would—that we could—and I . . ." Her voice trailed away as she considered she did not know how, precisely, one enticed one's husband into certain marital acts.

"You wish for children now?" he asked after a slight pause.

"Well, y-yes," she said. "And if we are to ensure Sir Montague does not inherit—"

"If he were the one behind this attack on you, I would agree with your reasoning, however unromantic." The last was delivered with a wry smile. "But I believe the culprit to be someone else."

"Not Sir Montague after all that?"

"I rather suspect a woman of poisoning you," he said, tilting her chin so she looked at him. His gaze followed her features almost dispassionately, as though he was observing her without truly seeing—or perhaps without caring what he saw. "Poison is a woman's weapon, don't you agree?"

"But no woman stands to inherit," she said slowly.

"That does somewhat rather complicate matters."

"Nathanial," she said, half exasperated, half amused. "What are you thinking? What are your suspicions?"

"My suspicions are that you will be safe here—"

"Amongst other women," she protested, "one of whom could be trying to kill me."

"I think not." He dropped a kiss on the end of her nose, and Theo froze at the casual affection of the gesture. "But just in case, be sure not to drink any unattended tea, and that should do it."

"Nathanial," she said as he swung his legs from the bed. More of that unfamiliar fire flooded her, as though by his leaving she was losing something precious; something she couldn't bear to be without. "Don't go."

He paused. "Is there something else you need?"

You.

But, as all men, he was blind to what was right in front of him—and what had, Theo considered, been sitting in front of him for a long time. She steeled herself to make the confession that had burned inside her for weeks, the one that would change everything.

The one she feared, more than anything, to make.

When she said nothing, he turned once again, and she blurted, "It was me."

He froze, and Theo had countless seconds in which to regret saying anything. For too long, he remained in place, and when he turned, his gaze landed on hers with an intensity that shrivelled her up inside. No one had ever looked at her like that before, all smouldering and hot and *angry*.

Heavens above, this was a mistake.

"What do you mean?" he asked in a low voice.

"At the masquerade," she said. "In the gardens. It was me you took there." She inhaled sharply. "And I knew it was you, right from the beginning. That was the only reason I consented to going outside and to— everything that came next."

There. Now she had offered enough pieces of herself to him that she felt bereft; she had opened her chest and bared her heart, and he could see every part of her.

"You knew it was me?" he asked quietly.

"Yes."

"And you allowed me to believe you were consorting with a stranger?"

"You were also . . . I knew what we had agreed about our marriage, what it would be. I thought, if you knew, you would have been angry."

"Allowing your husband to—" Nathanial broke off and swallowed. "That is not a crime, Theo."

"We agreed we would not be as husband and wife."

"We *agreed* that there would be no obligation. Did you feel obliged to go out into that garden with me?" There was real anger in his voice, and he paced across the room with quick, frustrated steps. "I thought you perfectly willing or I would never have—"

"I was! I was willing, Nathanial."

"Then why did you not *say*?" His voice was a trifle unsteady, and that, more than anything else, snapped Theo's resolve. She threw the covers back and went to stand before him, looking up into his face.

So close, as they had been so many times since her illness. Yet this was different, the air charged, awareness skittering down her skin, plunging her deeper into whatever this feeling between them was.

"Because I thought you would not want me if you knew it was me," she whispered.

Nathanial went still. His eyes were wide, tracing across her face, and his breathing shattered. He brushed the back of his knuckle across her cheek, the gentleness of the gesture at odds with the hard press of his mouth. A mouth she knew could be soft. "How could you think I did not recognise you?" he asked, those knuckles now trailing down the column of her neck. "How did you think for even one moment that I did not know you were there, dancing with Montague?"

Theo's mouth was dry. All she could do was stare up at Nathanial. All this time, he had *known*? She felt as though the ground had opened beneath her; that could be the only explanation for the swooping feeling in her stomach as though she was falling.

All along, he had known it was her. Not some nameless lady. *Her.* Theo.

"The only reason I took you into the garden that night was because it was you, love," he said, and her chest cracked. Tears welled in her eyes and she tried desperately to blink them away. He cupped her cheeks, thumbs smoothing under her eyes, swiping away the moisture. "We said we would not be as man and wife, but I do not think there has been a day since we married that I have not wanted you."

She sniffed, an unromantic sound that Nathanial did not seem to mind. The sharp edge of anger vanished from him, and he tipped her chin up as he pressed his lips against hers. Their last kiss had been illicit, forbidden, and he had been furious and wanting. Now, he kissed her like a discovery. Sweetly, so sweetly it made her chest expand with light and warmth so vast she couldn't see the end of it.

This was what she had been craving for so long. Nathanial's lips moving against hers, his fingers knotting in her hair, his breath heavy.

Nathanial, Nathanial, Nathanial.

Yet it wasn't enough. This still wasn't enough.

It was greediness, this desire to have more of him, to take and take until there was nothing left he could give; but she would be guilty of every vice if she could just have him.

The sense of inevitability and falling made her head spin. It made her giddy, and when he turned his attention from her mouth to her neck, she let her head hang back and gave a breathless laugh.

His hand flattened against her back and drew her even closer, until her body pressed flush with his. "Am I amusing?" he enquired, nipping her neck. Her laughter disappeared in a gasp. Heat leeched through the thin material of her nightdress, and she was abruptly aware of how little she was wearing. Her breasts, oddly sensitive, brushed against his chest, and the simple friction set light to the ember of want in her belly.

This was better than last time. Before, it had been new and daring, and the proprietary anger of his touch had been thrilling, but she hadn't been able to give herself to the moment fully. She had been terribly, awfully aware that he had not known it was her. Now, there was nothing in her mind but him and the feel of his hands on her.

All of her.

His fingers combed through her hair and the palm of his hand followed the curve of her hips to squeeze her backside. Heat pooled between her legs and she ached for him. All she wanted, more than anything, was for him to touch her there the way he had before.

Nathanial guided her backwards, until her thighs hit the bed and she toppled over. He followed, his movements a little more controlled, and delicious weight pressed her into the bed.

"Theo," he murmured, his thumb stroking distractingly across her cheek. "Theodosia. Is this all right?"

This was entirely better than all right. Scared to give voice to the rising, swelling emotion in her chest, she caught his face between her hands and kissed him again. Her mouth was inexperienced and clumsy, but he groaned in response, pressing her more firmly into the bed. His body fitted perfectly against hers, hollows and dips equally matching, their lines drawn together.

And Theo allowed herself to be lost in Nathanial, even as emotion swept through her, so raw and great that tears pricked her eyes. Her chest felt full, brimming with joy and aching hurt in equal measure.

She loved him.

The revelation was too big for her to contain, so she clung to him, letting him be her anchor. Tomorrow, she would think about what this meant.

Tonight, there was only Nathanial.

His hand finally reached the juncture of her thighs, and he paused there, tracing small circles over the material of her nightgown. And Theo knew she would not be able to bear it if he stopped now.

"Please," she begged, arching her back and opening her legs.

"Impatient," he murmured, nipping her neck again. One hand cupped her breasts while the other continued its journey down her leg. Finally, he drew up the material of her nightgown and traced up her inner thigh. "Here?" he asked.

"What?"

"Is this where you want me to touch you?" He kissed her again. "Focus, love."

"Yes," she whispered, and he finally moved to where she wanted him—where she needed him. She felt his attention go immediately to that point of contact, to the way his fingers slid through her slick flesh.

"Theo." He caught his breath. "You're ready for me."

Theo wasn't sure exactly what that meant, but she knew she wanted him, and she desperately wanted whatever came next. Impatient again, she turned her attention to his waistcoat, unbuttoning it with fingers that were not strictly steady. Nathanial's chuckle ended in a groan as she tugged his shirt up and placed her hand flat against his stomach.

Ridges. Lines. Hard and soft in juxtaposition. With a growl, Nathanial removed this final layer, baring him to the world and to her. For one long moment, she allowed herself to drink him in. When they had last been together, he had remained fully clothed throughout; and the moonlight, regardless, would have been insufficient lighting.

But here, she was at liberty to observe his male beauty. Here, the candlelight burnished his body, gilded his edges, paid homage to the dips and shadows that characterised his chest. He was broad, she noted, with bronzed skin and muscles that tensed as she slid her hands along them. She had not thought male skin would feel so smooth.

"You're beautiful," she murmured, before fancying it wasn't something she ought to say to a gentleman. But when she glanced up, it was to find him smiling down at her, a tender expression in his eyes.

"As are you." He kissed the corner of her mouth. "So very beautiful."

Though she didn't believe for a minute that he *meant* those words with the same whispered adoration as he had said them, they still made her blush, and an entirely different sort of pleasure unfurled.

He had called her pretty before, but never *beautiful*. When this was over, she would treasure those words.

Her hands dipped in their exploration, across the ridged muscles of his stomach and lower, to the tops of his breeches. He hissed a low breath and caught her hand, bringing it up between them. When he shifted, pressing more firmly against her bared leg, she felt his arousal, hot and thick. She spread her legs wider, allowing him to settle between them. He groaned.

"Nathanial—"

"I'm trying to go slowly," he said, kissing her again.

She wiggled under him, encouraging him to touch her more thoroughly. "Why?"

"Because this is new for you. I want it to be pleasant."

This was more than pleasant. Or at least, it would be, if he were not overly concerned about her delicate sensibilities.

Sensibilities that had either fallen by the wayside or were not as delicate as he imagined.

"Perhaps . . ." Theo was no expert in these matters, but it appeared as though there were several impediments to their goal. "Perhaps we ought to remove our clothes?"

He chuckled. "You are so impatient, my love." With quick, practised motions, he lifted her from the bed and removed her nightgown. Her hair fell across her shoulders and the air felt cool against her breasts, which he gazed at hungrily. "I have been dreaming about these." He tweaked a nipple and she moaned. "For a long time."

She had not considered he might have expectations. A little self-consciousness pierced her fierce want. "Are they to your liking? I am not sure—"

"They are perfect. You are perfect." He flicked his tongue across her breast and she gripped the bedsheets. But the touch was light then gone. He traced slow circles across her body, skimming every inch of her sensitised flesh, or so it felt, except for the part she needed the most.

Theo thought she might explode with frustration. "I'm not sure I like your idea of *slow*, Na—"

He slid two fingers back through her core, and everything inside her went still. He rasped a laugh, planting kisses down her neck as he traced those same circles between her legs, coaxing pleasure and wanton sounds from her she could not even attempt to withhold.

From the way he watched her, dark eyes fixed on hers, drinking in her every reaction, she did not think he minded.

Still—this was altogether too much like the last time, when he had focused all his attention on her, and she had not been given the opportunity to touch him in exchange. Daringly, she stroked a hand along the hard length in his breeches. His fingers stilled on her.

"Careful." His voice was low, more a rumble in his chest than sound. She felt it everywhere. "I do not have the self-control you think I possess." He resumed his caresses, and the heat that pooled inside her grew at his words, at the ceaseless work of his fingers.

"What is the need for self-control?" she asked, stroking him again.

He removed his hand, much to her disappointment. But before she could do much more than make a noise of discontent, he had placed his hips there instead, his arousal pressed against her core. "There is a necessity," he said, and rocked against her.

This was just like it had been in the gardens, yet somehow this felt far more intimate than it had then. *Then* she had been pressed against a statue, aware they were doing something illicit outdoors and that their identities were concealed.

Now, she was in a bed, and he was kissing her with far more tenderness, and somehow far more need, than he had then. And with every slow, gentle thrust against her, the friction of his breeches, the pressure of that length, rubbed against her with such insistence, she lost herself in the overwhelming sensations.

The low noise he made in his throat as he raised his head to look at her face, almost undid her entirely. "Theo," he said, her name a blessing and a curse on his tongue. "You will be the death of me." He kissed her again, warm arms caging her, holding her in a way he had not done the last time. He was everything, everywhere, and she dug her nails into his shoulders, pulling him closer, needing to feel the weight of him, to feel every laboured breath, the tiny sounds of pleasure he made every time she shifted.

She hovered on the edge, so close to falling—or perhaps splitting apart entirely.

"Nathanial," she said urgently. "Nate."

"Look at me," he said roughly. "Look at me, Theo."

She did, marvelling at what she saw. His face was flushed, his pupils so wide his eyes looked black, and he looked at her as though she was the only thing in the world he could see.

And she loved him. Wildly, uncontrollably, every second more than the second before. The thought sent release barrelling through her, and she shattered. Her body shuddered, out of control, arching into him, and he groaned. His rhythm fractured as he pressed against her so hard she saw stars.

In this, they were one. United as they had never been before. And it was so wonderful, it felt so perfect, that she found herself wiping away tears.

"Theo." He caught her wrists and held them to one side so he could see her face. "Are you all right? Did I do something to hurt you?"

"No. *No*. Nate, it was . . ." She hardly knew how to explain it, this sensation that they had been joined in an irrevocable way, even if there was still an odd hollowness inside her, as if they had come close to filling every part of her but not quite. Still, it was . . . "It was *wonderful*."

A sigh of relief brushed across her face, and he gave her a brief kiss before rolling to one side. They lay like that, side by side, his fingers still wrapped around her wrist, until their breaths slowed. Then Theo, curious and uncertain, rolled to face him, propping her chin on her wrist.

"Nathanial?"

"Yes?"

"Was that . . . Did we . . ." She hesitated, not sure how to frame the question. There were many things she wished her mother had told her, and the mechanics of such things numbered among them. "Does that mean . . .?"

"No, not quite." He struggled with his words for a moment before a rueful smile crossed his face. "You wretch, making me try to explain this."

"Well, how should I know?"

"No reason, I suppose." He pressed a kiss to her forehead. "But you may be assured of one thing, Theo—when we come together as husband and wife, you will not have to ask that question."

"Does that mean we wi—"

"Yes," he said hastily. "But not now. And not here."

Theo smiled shyly at him. "When we are home again?"

"When we have discovered who was behind the poisoning, and once we're sure it will never happen again," he said, "*then* I will make you mine, Theo. But not before."

"Why?" she asked, a plaintive note in her voice that made him rumble a laugh. "What is the harm in it now?"

"Because, my dear, I do not want to lose more than just my wife if something more should happen to you."

Theo snuggled against his bare chest, and he wrapped an arm around her. "Then we should find whoever was responsible sooner rather than later, so there is no more danger."

"Yes," he said, a smile in his voice. "We should."

Chapter Twenty-Three

Hunting was not Nathanial's favourite sport. He was a good enough shot and knew how to handle a gun, but there was a lot of tramping over mud and uneven land, and more pressingly, time away from Theo.

He could still smell her on him. Even now, out here in the warming summer air, in the middle of a field that had once been occupied by sheep, he could smell her. If he closed his eyes, he could hear her, too, and that made him want to never leave her side. Hunting be damned.

Except, unfortunately, hunting could not be damned, and neither could Stapleton's generosity. Nathanial had come under the guise of wanting to try the hunting, and the hunting he would try.

"Ready!" the groundsman called. Nathanial cocked his gun and raised it as the beaters chased the partridges out. He followed their path with the barrel, exhaled, and fired. The bird tumbled out of the sky and at a whistle, one of the dogs ran to collect it.

"Excellent shot, Norfolk," Stapleton said.

Nathanial wiped the sweat from his brow and gave a nod. It was going to be a hot day. He wondered what Theo had elected to do that morning. She'd mentioned something about writing her sister and mother a letter—probably to avoid spending time with Lady Stapleton and Lady Tabitha. He couldn't blame her.

Another wave of birds took to the sky and Nathanial readied his gun with the help of the servant to his side. The moment Theo had recovered and his inquiries in London returned, giving him an indication of the type of poison and its source, they could leave Caddington Hall and return. Or even, perhaps, visit Havercroft. The Season was nearly over, after all, and he was more than ready to return to a quieter way of life.

Perhaps there—

Shots rang out from the assembled gentlemen, and impact thudded into Nathanial, earlier than expected. He always braced himself against the knock from his gun, but he hadn't pulled the trigger yet.

In the distance, he heard shouting. The gun fell from his hand. He staggered. He looked down, frowning. There was something on his chest, growing with every second.

The world rolled around him, and as he hit the ground, he stared at the sky, wondering how such a bright day could be so faint, and why it hurt to breathe.

Theo was in the drawing room when they brought Nathanial's body in. She *knew* she was in the drawing room because she distinctly remembered the way her teacup cracked against the carpet as she dropped it.

That sound echoed in her head as she followed the shouting into the main hall. She remembered each moment distinctly, edged like those broken china pieces. There was Nathanial lying on a makeshift stretcher, blood staining his brown coat, his eyes closed. Someone had attempted to bandage the wound on his shoulder, but blood soaked through, and there was so much shouting, so much panic.

Theo didn't know where to look.

All she knew was that this was her husband, and her place was beside him. When they took him upstairs, she followed, the banister smooth against her fingers as she trailed her hand along it. Habit—that's what her life was made up of now. Habit that kept her breathing, kept her moving, kept her upright.

"Duchess," Lord Stapleton said upon seeing her in the bedroom. "Duchess you ought not to be here. My dear!" His call, abrupt as it was, summoned his wife like a haunting wraith. "Please could you escort the Duchess downstairs?"

"Certainly," Lady Stapleton said, reaching for Theo's wrist with long, pale fingers. "Come with me, sweet thing, and we shall give you a hot cup of tea."

"He is my husband," Theo said. Of all the things in this world rocked with colour and too much noise, that was the only one of which she was certain. "He is my husband and I shall remain with him."

By now, the men had placed Nathanial on the bed. Some shouted for water. Others demanded a physician. The panic was tangible, like the tang of an extinguished candle.

He could not be dying. It didn't seem possible. Not after everything they'd been through.

Footmen hurried into the room with a bucket and fresh linen, and Theo approached the bed. Nathanial was barely breathing. The veins in his eyelids were blue, but his pulse throbbed in his neck. She watched it to ensure it wouldn't stop.

"When will the physician arrive?" she asked, her voice cool and clear.

"In minutes, Duchess," a man said. She didn't look to see which one.

"Then until he arrives, clear the room of this noise."

At a gesture from Lord Stapleton, almost all the men filed out. "You do not need to do this," he said, but she flicked her gaze to him, and whatever he saw there caused him to stop.

"He is my husband," Theo repeated. "And I shall tend to him."

Even the strongest stomach could not have felt nothing when Theo removed the makeshift bandage from Nathanial's chest. Blood oozed from a wound so jagged she thought she might be sick from the horror of it all.

But his heart was beating, she told herself. There was hope as long as his heart continued to beat.

"Tell me," she said to Lord Stapleton, who hovered by the door like a particularly troublesome fly. "How did this happen?"

"I don't know," he confessed, mopping his forehead with his handkerchief. "One minute everything's going smoothly, the next he's on the floor with a hole punched in him. Begging your pardon, ma'am."

Theo's hands trembled as she pressed linen against the wound and the blood—so much blood. "From which direction did this shot come?"

"It's hard to say, Duchess. We were so concerned with getting him back to the house as soon as possible, we hardly knew."

Theo stared at the red stain on the white cloth. There was blood on her hands and dress, too, but that hardly seemed to matter. All that mattered was that Nathanial survived.

The iron in her spine threatened to melt, and she pinned her lips together. Here, there was no one to rely on—no parent or older brother or husband who might take the burden away. Nathanial had thought them to be safe here, and he had not thought himself in danger at all, but that had been a mistake, and one he was paying for.

She could trust no one.

Her calm in danger of unravelling, she sat beside his bed and watched the movement of his chest, refusing to acknowledge the grey tinge to his skin or the shallowness of his breaths.

Her fingers were cracked with blood.

Time passed in fits and starts, and she could not have said how long she sat beside her husband, willing him with every fibre of her being to keep breathing, to stay with her, but eventually there was a call of "the physician", and the door opened to admit a portly man with a briefcase.

"So this is my patient," he said. "And his lady wife? My name is Dr Follett."

Theo stepped back to allow him room to examine Nathanial. "I am the Duchess of Norfolk, and this is my husband, the Duke of Norfolk."

"You stopped the bleeding," he said with a trace of approval in his voice. "Well done."

"Will he survive?"

The doctor removed the cloth from Nathanial's wound. The wound was not neat, but at least it was in his shoulder. If it had been further down—

Theo did not let herself think that.

"I believe we will require a surgeon," the doctor said, raising Nathanial's head and listening to his breath. "We must remove the shot as far as we can."

"Yes. Of course." Theo bowed her head, her breath shaky as she released it. "I will fetch Lord Stapleton."

"Thank you, Your Grace."

Outside the room, Lord Stapleton paced, his ruddy face pale. "Well?" he demanded when he saw her. "Is there news?"

"The doctor would like to see you. I believe he wishes to summon a surgeon."

"A surgeon?" Lord Stapleton's jaw dropped before he recovered himself. "That is to say—of course. I will send for one right away." He rubbed a large hand over his head as a maid approached. "Ah, Miss Finch. Show Her Grace to her room." His voice lowered as he looked at her. "I thought you may wish to clean up, Your Grace."

Theo did not have the energy to do so much as smile as she followed the sharp-faced maid down the hall and to a new room. She took in none of the furnishings as she clasped her hands tightly, interlacing her fingers until they ached. "Thank you," she said. "I will ring when I require Betsy."

"Very good, ma'am." The maid curtsied and left the room with a click of finality, and Theo was alone.

Alone.

Merely a few rooms away, the physician was doing all he could to save Nathanial's life, and she wasn't there. She was here, in this room, alone, with no way of knowing if he lived or died, with nothing to aid her but prayers that had never yet been answered.

Her hands shook, and she pressed them to her chest, above her heart. It seemed impossible that anyone could have survived something like this. He had been *shot*.

A moan burst from her lips, and her trembling knees refused to hold her upright any longer. She sank to the floor, covering her face with her hands.

Nathanial couldn't die. He *couldn't*. Not when they had only just reconciled.

Not when she had only just realised she loved him.

Life would lose its sweetness if she was forced to go through it alone. And no matter how many people she surrounded herself with, if she didn't have Nate, she *would* be alone. He was her sun, and she kept orbit around him in breathless circles.

She needed him.

He couldn't die.

The last of her control snapped, and she dug her nails into her skin as she wept. Grief surged through her with unrestrained clamour, and her prayers were disjointed, a mixture of pleading and bargaining. If pledging her eternal soul would guarantee he would survive, she would do it. She would do anything to keep him alive, even if that meant she couldn't be with him.

The world could not stand to lose him. And neither could she.

When at last she rose, she was hollow. Ribbons of pain wrapped around her chest; they were the things that held her together and broke her apart all at once. She still had Nathanial's blood on her hands, so she made that her first task. Wash, scrubbing with soap until every last hint of red had been dug from under her nails.

Splash cold water on her face, soothing her swollen eyes and tight skin.

Ring the bell pull and summon Betsy to her, to release her from a gown that felt as though it was constricting her. Let it pool around her feet as she stepped out. Allow Betsy to pick out a new dress, and stand mute, like a doll as she was dressed.

Betsy touched the cold skin of her arm. "Ma'am?"

Theo blinked, looking once more at the figure in the mirror. She didn't recognise the woman standing there, with such emptiness in her eyes, her skin pale, regal despite the crippling weight on her shoulders.

"He will be okay," Betsy said, though her voice trembled. "The surgeon has been."

"He's been and left?" Theo asked, her voice suddenly sharp. How long had she been sitting on the floor? "And? Do you know anything?"

"Nothing, ma'am—just that the Duke's condition is stable."

Stable. Nathanial was stable.

As soon as Betsy was done buttoning her dress, she turned for the door. "Thank you, Betsy. I'll see His Grace now."

"Of course, Your Grace."

Theo nodded, and after a tiny hesitation, swept from the room. Fragile calm suffused her, but it would be the work of a moment to destroy it.

"Ah, Duchess," Lord Stapleton said, meeting her in the corridor. "I see you've had time to change."

"How is my husband?" She didn't recognise her voice, so low and steady was it.

"He is as well—as well as can be expected. Come, you must see the physician. I was on the way to fetch you, as it happens."

Theo accepted his arm and they went together to Nathanial's room. The door was open and the physician was standing in front of the bed, watching his patient critically. On the bed, Nathanial was covered by the sheets, but the torn remnants on his shirt were on the floor, along with the bloody water she had used. There was a little more colour in his cheeks.

She felt the breath whoosh from her lungs.

"Your Grace," the physician said, finally turning and giving her a perfunctory smile and nod of the head. "Apologies for sending you from the room earlier."

"How is he?"

"You got extremely lucky. The wound is severe, but not, I trust, life-threatening. There was no exit wound and the bullet has been removed. He has lost a lot of blood, naturally, but he is stable."

"Will he make a full recovery?"

"I am hopeful, though nothing is certain at this stage. I have recommended a draught for him to take when he wakes, and I suggest he avoids red meat until he has recovered." The physician took another look at Nathanial. "It's possible he may become feverish. As I say, the wound *is* severe. If that happens, send for me at once."

"Would he survive if he did?" Theo dared ask.

"I could not say," Dr Follett said bluntly. "It is too soon for certainties."

Her prayers so far had been answered. Nathanial was still alive, his chest rising and falling with each breath. Her offers of pledging her soul had worked; she would keep bargaining, keep promising Heaven her eternal servitude if only he would be well.

"He cannot be moved, of course," the physician said. "Not for several weeks."

"His Grace is welcome here as long as he wishes," Lord Stapleton said hurriedly. "As long as he needs. And you, too, of course, Your Grace."

"Thank you," Theo said.

"I will come back tomorrow, unless his condition changes," the physician said. "If you're concerned for his welfare, send for me, no matter the time."

"You're very good," Theo said, inclining her head. The physician bowed and left the room with Lord Stapleton, leaving her at liberty to take the seat beside her husband. Beside Nathanial. She took his hand, pressing her fingers against his fluttering pulse. Not strong, but present. Alive.

When they had come here, he'd presumed the person behind her poisoning had been a woman, but he had been shot, and she was certain it was no accident.

There were no women at the hunt today.

The culprit was a man. And he was here. The only thing she knew was that Sir Montague was not one of the party; he could not have been behind the gun unless he entered the land illicitly. Theo did not know how possible it was for someone to do that. Given the size of Lord Stapleton's estate, she did not think she could discount it.

"They shall not win," Theo whispered to Nathanial's still, waxy face. His hair was damp with sweat, sticking to his forehead, and she brushed it back. "You shall live."

He made no sound but the breaths that whispered from between his lips.

Chapter Twenty-Four

The next day brought no change. In the afternoon, a full day after he was brought to her, she felt she might leave him to spend some time in company.

This desire was motivated by two reasons. The first was that she wished to thank Lord Stapleton, who had been assiduous in his attentions, offering her every comfort, even if she wished he would not.

The second was that she intended to find out precisely what had happened on the hunt with Nate. After his accident, the shooting party was being cut short; only Theo and Nathanial had been invited to stay. If she was going to find out anything, it would be that day.

Most of the party were in the drawing room when she descended. There was a cheerful game of loo at one end of the room, presided over by Lord Stapleton, and at the other end of the room, reclining gracefully before a roaring fire, was Lady Stapleton.

A sweep of the room convinced Theo she would do better avoiding the game, which afforded her no opportunity to speak with anyone in private, and so she advanced towards Lady Stapleton, who held up a bejewelled hand in greeting.

"Duchess," she said with her typical languor. "Pray sit with us. Tell us how the Duke is faring."

Theo took the chair Lady Stapleton had indicated, which just so happened to be beside Lord Brockenhurst, a pale man of indeterminable age. His hair was greying but his thin face was relatively unlined, and bronzed from days out in the sun.

Hunting, no doubt.

"The Duke's condition is unchanged," Theo said, "which I have to hope is good news."

"Indeed it is," Lord Brockenhurst said. "There can be no doubt. The age-old adage of no news is good news is true in this case."

She gave him a grateful smile. "I believe so."

"And allow me, Your Grace, to tell you how very sorry I am this came about in the first place. Shocking business!"

"Shocking *indeed*," Lady Stapleton said, not to be outdone. "And to think it happened here of all places." She could not have said more clearly that she wished Theo and her troublesome, injured husband would leave, and Theo had to bite her tongue before she said something uncharitable.

"It was an unfortunate accident," she said, looking carefully into Lord Brockenhurst's face. He had been present at the shooting yesterday, and it seemed to her as though a flicker of discomfort crossed his face. "But it is a comfort to me—and to Nathanial when he wakes—that he has so many good friends."

Although she aimed this barb at Lady Stapleton, it was Lord Brockenhurst who flushed. "Exceedingly good fellow." Apparently embarrassed by the strength of his feeling, he coughed. "Wouldn't have wanted it to happen to anyone."

"Especially in such a way," Theo said. "The bullet has been removed, but he is not out of danger yet."

"Suspicious dealings," Lord Brockenhurst said, then started. "Beg your pardon, Your Grace—forgot the company."

"Suspicious in what way?" Theo asked innocently.

"Shouldn't have said anything," he said, eyes widening like a trapped rabbit. "Don't heed me, Your Grace."

She tried to calm her pounding heart, though she was dizzyingly aware of the strength of her pulse in her neck and felt certain everyone around could hear it too. "Are you trying to say that hitting N—the Duke was not an accident?"

"Couldn't have been an accident," he said apologetically. "He was off to the right, see. And strikes me no one was aiming that way. Birds were all ahead."

"If no one hit the Duke by accident, it must have been on purpose," Lady Stapleton said with sudden zeal. She sat up, languidness forgotten. "You were present, Lord Brockenhurst. Who do you think it could have been?"

The unfortunate Viscount shifted uncomfortably in his seat. "Can't say, my lady. That is to say, I don't know. It wasn't Lord Stapleton, though, I'm sure of that," he added earnestly. "He was beside the Duke the entire time and I was at an angle to see . . . there was no chance, Lady Stapleton."

"Well." She pinched her lips. "I'm sure I must be grateful."

"If you were at an angle to see it couldn't have been Lord Stapleton," Theo pressed, "could you see where the shot did come from?"

He shook his head emphatically. "If you want to know, speak to the beaters. Might be they saw something, or . . ." He tugged at his cravat uncomfortably. "Hesitate to suggest any gentleman here would wish your husband ill, Duchess."

"Of course not," Theo murmured, forcing her hands to unclench from around her skirts. If no one in the house *had* aimed at Nathanial, that had meant the shot, and the danger, had come from elsewhere. A servant, perhaps, paid off? A local man armed with a gun and instructed to secretly enter the estate?

She was no closer to discovering the culprit.

After a few more moments of idle conversation, she excused herself. Lady Stapleton seemed all too eager to send her away again, and although Lord Brockenhurst pleaded with his eyes, begging her to stay, she was resolute on returning to Nathanial's side.

"I have been away too long," she said as she stood. "Give my apologies to Lady Tabitha when you next speak with her. I'm sure she will be sorry to miss me."

Or at least sorry to miss the excuse of gossiping with her about Nathanial's accident and his chances of survival. That was just the sort of thing Tabitha would enter into with gusto.

"Duchess," Lord Stapleton said as she reached the door. "Are you leaving us already?"

"I'm sorry for being such poor company," Theo said, putting her hand in his as she held it out. He was a kindly man, really, and reminded her of the father she might have had, if her father had taken any real interest in her.

"That's not what I wanted to say," he said, squeezing her hand. "I have a daughter a trifle older than you, you know. Married, of course. Every time I look at you, I see her, and . . . I wouldn't wish this on anyone."

"Nor I."

"But worrying yourself over him will not change his condition. And I would not want you to suffer over it. Allow my men to keep watch, and get some sleep, Duchess."

"You are very kind," she said with a small, genuine smile. "But I would not rest if I were not with him."

"Even a few hours—"

"Even a few hours," she repeated. "I know my limits, my lord, and I would beg you to trust them as I do."

He nodded and released her hand. "Then I can only hope you will sleep tonight, my dear."

She nodded and went upstairs, dismissing Nathanial's valet and taking her place beside him again. A truckle bed had been placed in the corner of the room, but she preferred to sit beside him, listening to the way he breathed. At first, it was slow and steady, but as the hours passed, he became increasingly disturbed. He tossed his head, murmuring incomprehensible things under his breath.

"You must not," he muttered as she placed a hand on his forehead. "Do not touch her."

"I am here, Nathanial," she said, but no matter how often she tried to soothe him, his worries seemed to remain. She tipped some water down his throat, and when that did little to calm him, rang for a maid.

"Send for the doctor and wake Lord Stapleton," she commanded, feigning a calmness she didn't feel. "His Grace is feverish."

"Yes, ma'am." The maid bobbed a curtsy and she was left alone again. With Nathanial, who barely seemed a companion in his delirious state.

Lord Stapleton came almost immediately and clapped a hand on her shoulder. "How is he?"

"Not well, I fear." Theo was not often conscious of a wish to scream or sob, but today she wished she could do both. Nathanial lay prone on the bed beside them, blood leaking through the bandage as his movements disturbed his wound, and nothing she said could touch him.

"Dr Follett will arrive soon," Lord Stapleton said. "He will see us through."

Theo lay cloths soaked with lavender water over Nathanial's forehead, although he often tossed them off, and held his burning hand. Lord Stapleton, kindly yet impatient, paced the room and passed her instructions to the servants.

Thankfully, there was less than an hour of this before Dr Follett arrived, the same briefcase by his side.

"So he has contracted fever, has he?" he asked briskly. "Yes, I can see he has. I was afraid this would happen, but it is no matter. We aren't in too much danger yet."

"What can we do?" Theo asked, her voice a trifle unsteady.

"I've already contacted the apothecary and requested a saline draught and a paregoric solution, which he will send here directly. In the meantime, you may give him some barley water. And an orange, perhaps, if you have one."

"At once," Lord Stapleton said. "That is, I cannot be certain we have an orange, but we can acquire one, and the cook—I shall ask directly."

Theo fixed her gaze on Nathanial's face, which he seemed to be moving with increasing distress. "Don't touch her," he muttered. "I won't allow it."

The doctor seemed unfazed by Nathanial's murmurings; he merely took his wrist and felt for his pulse. "A little elevated," he said, "but not dangerous yet."

"What should I do?" Theo asked. "Tell me, sir. What do I do? If you order me from this room, I won't go."

The doctor gave her a small smile. "No, I fancy you won't. Be still, Your Grace; there is little more you can do than you are doing now. Pray he sleeps, for his sleeping will be calmer than his waking moments."

Nathanial's eyes flew open. "Thirsty," he said, his fingers tightening around Theo's hand. "I must—"

"Shh, my darling," she said, pushing at his shoulders when he looked like he would rise. He met her gaze, but there was no recognition in his eyes. "You will have water soon. Be calm, Nate, please."

"The draught will soothe him," the doctor said. "If not, the paregoric will make him sleep. It's too early to fear."

When would it be *not* too early to fear? At which point could she give into the dread which crawled under her skin, begging release?

Lord Stapleton returned with barley water and an orange, and once he had consumed the barley water, Nathanial settled for a while. At dawn, as the sky paled in the promise of another fine day, the apothecary arrived with the two bottles the doctor had asked for.

"You may give him the saline draught when he is showing signs of distress," the doctor said. "Not more than every four hours, but do keep giving it to him.

He may have tea or barley water as refreshment, but no wine."

"I understand," Theo said.

"I shall give him a dose of the paregoric solution now, which will make him sleep, and you would do well to sleep, too, Your Grace."

Theo attempted to protest, but Lord Stapleton added his entreaties, and she was forced to yield. She *was* tired, but nothing would have convinced her to give up her position beside Nathanial if the doctor hadn't pointed out she would be of little use tomorrow if she didn't sleep now.

She lay on the truckle bed provided as Nathanial's valet took his place once more, convinced she would not sleep. Yet the moment she closed her eyes, she was lost to the world.

Chapter Twenty-Five

Theo woke to full sunshine. Somehow, she'd slept until late morning, and she leapt from the bed, throwing a dressing gown over her nightgown, and hurried to Nathanial's side. By some miracle, he seemed no worse than he had the previous evening.

"How is he?" she asked the valet anxiously.

"As well as can be expected, Your Grace. He has eaten the orange, as you can see, and I believe that did him good."

"Did you give him his medicine?"

"I did," he replied imperturbably, "and he is due another dose soon."

Theo took the chair on Nathanial's other side. Her gaze was not a practised one, and she did not know how a man this injured and ill was supposed to look, but she could not help noticing how pale he was, and how prominent his veins seemed to be under his skin.

"And the doctor?" she asked. "Has he returned?"

"He will return this evening unless we send for him sooner, Your Grace."

Theo took Nathanial's hand, finding his pulse just as the doctor had done, and found it erratic. "Oh

Nate," she murmured. Perhaps this was the moment she should give into hysterics; she had an inkling that hysterics were very much called for in these kinds of situations. Novels had taught her that, and so had the smelling salts left carefully on the nightstand for when she inevitably succumbed to that female temptation.

But the smelling salts alone made her resolve not to become in the least hysterical, no matter *how* tempting it might be. Besides, she did not believe Nathanial had given in to tears when she had been ill, and if he could maintain his composure, so could she.

"Thank you," she said to the valet. "I can take it from here."

He inclined his head. "Yes, ma'am."

The door closed behind him and although Theo had sent him away, she immediately wished she wasn't alone with a man whose breathing seemed increasingly laboured.

"You shall not give in," she told him fiercely, holding his hand against her chest. Someone had changed his bandages, she noticed, and there was no blood on them now. That was something, at least—

and she needed something. She needed all the somethings she could get.

Nathanial, if anything, appeared to fall back asleep. Theo took refuge in being irritated, knowing that if she stopped allowing herself to be annoyed even for a moment, she might lose herself in the grief that beckoned ever closer.

"You stubborn, odious man," she said, and for a moment she believed he might have heard her. "You bring me here for safety and wind up getting shot. Do you know how selfish that is? How inconsiderate?" She looked down into his face and the way his eyes darted under the blueish lids. In a quieter voice, she said, "Do you know how much I love you?"

The room was silent but for his wheezing breaths.

The days crawled by. Something of a routine emerged. Theo sat by his side all day, changing the cloths on his head, and sometimes rolling him over to place wet cloths on his back, although she could not do so alone. At night, she slept on the truckle bed in the corner for a scant few hours while a servant watched over him.

His condition worsened.

At first, she barely noticed. He hadn't seemed to see her when he looked at her the few times he was awake, although he had responded to her soothing. But as time went on, he stopped responding to the sound of her voice, and seemed to believe the world was alive with danger.

"It's to be expected," the doctor had said on one of his visits. "His condition will worsen before it improves."

If it improves, Theo had thought, and the undercurrent of dread that had been alive inside her since Nathanial's accident turned into fear.

Until, one morning five days after Nathanial's fever had begun, Theo woke to silence. Her neck was sore from having slept on the uncomfortable chair by the bed—now she understood why Nathanial had taken such objection to the armchair in her room—and for a moment she merely tried to ease the crick with her fingers, digging right into the muscle.

Then, she noticed the quiet.

For so long, her days had been ruled by the wheezing, rasping breaths of an invalid. In some of her more desperate moments, she had counted them, determined they would not fail when she stood guard. Now, those breaths had quietened. Not gone, but quietened.

She was out of her chair before she knew she'd moved, her cramped muscles complaining, and pressed a hand to Nathanial's head. It was warm, but not hot. A comparable temperature to her own.

The fever had broken.

At the feel of her hand, his eyes opened, finding hers, and for the first time in a long time, they were clear. "Theo," he mumbled.

Theo *should* have stayed calmly by his side and told him clearly and concisely what had happened. Instead, she burst into tears, shocking them both, and threw her arms around him. He made a tiny noise of pain as her body connected against his, but his arms came up around her.

"You fool," she sobbed into his shoulder. "First you got shot, then you got a fever . . . Do you know how worried I've been?"

"I'm here," he murmured, one hand stroking her hair. "Theo, my love, there's no need to cry."

She knew that, she did, but her relief was strong enough to provoke tears and, embarrassingly, shuddering sobs that racked both their bodies.

But through it all, though he was no doubt weak from lack of food and disoriented, Nathanial held her close, reassuring her with murmured endearments, every breath whispering another promise against her ear.

He would be well. He would survive.

With difficulty, she pulled away and stared at him through blurry eyes. He was thinner than she remembered, even though she had watched him slowly waste away. Then, he had been unconscious, in the grip of the fever. Somehow, it felt different now he was awake.

"Water," she said, recalling herself. "You should have some water. And food. I'll call for some broth to be brought up."

"Theo."

Her hand shook as she poured him a glass, just as he had done all those weeks ago when she had

325

awoken from her illness. "Here, Nate. Drink this. You'll feel better."

"Theo—"

She pressed the glass to his lips and after a moment, he drank, allowing her to care for him as she had so many times before. But when he finished, he reached out and took her arm before she could reach the bell pull.

"How long have I been feverish?" he asked, his eyes searching her face.

"About five days."

"And you have been nursing me all that time?"

"Lord Stapleton helped. He has been very helpful." She pulled her wrist away and hurried to the bell pull, yanking at it with more force than strictly necessary. When she returned to the bed, he was watching her with concern.

"You look pale," he said.

"I can guarantee that is nothing to how you look," she said tartly, but she took his hand and carried it to her cheek. "How do you feel?"

"No worse than I look, I imagine," he said dryly, and patted the bed beside him. "Come, join me. You look as though you have had less rest than I."

She shook her head. "How can you worry about me now? You were shot."

"I have not forgotten."

"You might have *died*."

He attempted a smile. "Has anyone ever told you your beside manner is abhorrent." He tugged at her wrist until she obeyed his summons and sat on the bed beside him. "I'm sorry I worried you," he said gently. "But I won't have you sacrificing your health for mine."

Theo lay on her side facing him. Though he had been awake for only a few minutes, he already looked exhausted. Perhaps this was how she had looked when she had awoken. "Sleep," she told him.

"Only if you join me."

Sensing he was stubborn enough to refuse if she did not agree, she nodded. "Very well."

"You will stay with me?"

"Yes, Nate. I will stay."

His eyes closed with relief, but his grip on her hand didn't slacken. "Good," he murmured, and she worried he was delirious again. "I like waking beside you."

"There's something else," she said, hating that she had to mention this now.

His eyes fluttered open. "Another death threat?"

"No, I—"

"Has someone else poisoned you, my love? I warn you, I cannot exact vengeance in this state."

She sighed in exasperation. "Be *serious*, Nate."

"Very well." His fingers toyed with her hair even as his eyes fluttered closed once more. "What else have you to tell me?"

"I sent word to your mother that you were ill," she said apologetically. He winced.

"No doubt she is on her way."

"With your sisters. I'm sorry."

"All three?" He groaned. "Would that I had waited another day to wake."

"What will you tell them?"

"Enough of the truth as will satisfy them," he said without opening his eyes. "It was a hunting accident and I contracted a fever from my wound."

"Do you believe it was an accident?"

There was a grim cast to his mouth, and a muscle clenched in his jaw. "No," he said after a moment. "I don't believe it was an accident at all."

Chapter Twenty-Six

Juliet Stanton rifled through her letters, flicking past the invitations, the bills, and the occasional note from an ardent lover. To cool their passions, she made a point of never replying within two days.

However, along with the more regular missives was the letter she had been looking for. Written on coarse paper, the direction scribbled in a clumsy hand, it looked entirely out of place. When Juliet saw it, she dropped her other correspondence and flicked it open, reading the two brief lines inside.

Eyes unseeing, she dropped the letter into her jam and stared straight ahead, the fingers of one hand curling around her knife. Seconds later, the peace was shattered by a scream.

"That *devil*," she raged, driving the point of her blade through the letter, and cracking the plate. "How *dare* he?"

Her servant, a stoic man she had hired for his discretion, did not so much as flinch as she hurled her plate and everything on it at the wall.

"Peters," she said, chest heaving. "Bring the carriage round."

"Yes, ma'am," he said, inclining his head and leaving the room. Finally alone, Juliet vented her fury in another earth-shattering scream, and retrieved the letter. The two lines had been written by a hand clearly ill-used to holding a pen.

The Duke met with an accident, the note ran. *His family left for the country. Looks serious.*

Met with an accident. Juliet had been around long enough to know what lay behind those simple words; and if the Duke's family had left Town to see him, including the sister with a new baby, it must be serious.

Montague had not visited since the day of the picnic.

She hadn't expected him to, considering she had handed him the drink that had so *almost* killed the new Duchess, but his continued absence with this news only meant one thing.

He had been responsible for this. For acquainting Nathanial with his *accident*.

Really, it had only been a matter of time before he tried something drastic, but she had thought their agreement to prevent his marriage from producing an heir, would have been of more use to her.

Before she left for the carriage, she tucked a small pistol in her purse and changed into a drab dress, a veil over her face. Now Montague had reached the end of his usefulness, she would have to ensure he wouldn't do anything else drastic.

Montague's apartment on James Street was dim and still when she arrived. If she hadn't known he had nowhere else to go, she might have suspected he, too, had left Town for the summer. As it was, however, she presumed he was merely recovering from a late night of excess.

"Tell Sir Montague that a lady is here to see him," she said as she swept past the butler and took stock. It was a regular bachelor's house, and after a little deliberation, she walked through to the study. All she would have to do was beg him to take a walk with her, and as soon as they were somewhere undisturbed, she would shoot him and run for a constable.

Or perhaps she would shoot him here and now and have done with it. No servants knew who she was, and she would be able to slip from the house easily enough. Once outside, she could hire a cab.

The door opened and Montague entered the small space. She had forgotten how tall he was, and for a moment she wondered if one shot would be enough. The pistol was small and she couldn't risk his survival.

"Well," he said, a sardonic smile on his lips. "To what do I owe this pleasure?"

"I thought you must have heard," she said, sliding a hand inside her reticule. "Nathanial's family have rushed to the country after a certain accident."

His brows rose. "An accident?"

"Well no, Montague. I don't believe it was."

He had the audacity to look almost amused as he strolled forwards, and she fumbled for the trigger. "So you presume I'm responsible for my dear cousin's hunting accident?"

"Hunting?" This time, it was her turn to raise an eyebrow, though her heart pounded in her mouth. "I had not known it was while hunting."

"Where else might he be shot?"

"Do not pretend you were ignorant of this."

"I hardly see what business it is of mine," he said languidly.

"Of course you would deny everything, even to me." Anger replaced her fear, and she strode in short, frustrated circles, her skirts swirling around her legs. "Even to me, you will not be honest."

Montague raised a brow. "Even to you? What do you suppose you have done to gain my trust?"

"We had a common goal."

His hand flashed out and caught hold of her wrist, pulling her into him. "You made a mistake coming here," he murmured.

"Do not think to lecture *me*," she snapped. "I will do as I please."

"I'm afraid I can't allow that. Not after the last time you took matters into your own hands."

Her heart stuttered. "I don't know what you're talking about."

"Liar," he said, in a low, seductive voice one might use on a lover. "I was most impressed, you know, with your gall in handing *me* the poisoned lemonade."

"Is that what you think?" This conversation wasn't going the way she had planned, and although her free hand was wrapped around her pistol, her skin was so slick with sweat, she half thought it would slide from her grasp.

"I don't just think," he said, tilting his head as he looked down at her. His fingers tightened almost

333

painfully, and he took hold of her other arm, moving it away from his body as though he knew what she had in her bag. "Tell me, did you hope he would fall into your arms when his precious wife died?"

"I—"

"Let us not play games. I know you love him."

She had never given name to the emotion she felt for Nathanial. Perhaps it was love, or perhaps it was possession, but it didn't stop her from saying, with all the coldness she could muster, "And you? I've seen the way you look at her."

A look crossed his face that made ice form in her veins. For a second, his eyes blazed with fury, before the emotion passed, leaving a cruel amusement in its wake. "And how do I look at her?"

"As though you want her."

He seemed to consider for a moment. "Perhaps I do. Why, Juliet, are you jealous?"

"Of course not! She's nothing—a chit in her first Season who knows nothing of the world."

"True," he agreed, transferring both her wrists to one hand so he could take her chin. The pistol slipped from her grip, and his fingers were tight enough to be painful. He forced her to meet his gaze. "Yet she has charms you would barely be able to comprehend."

"I never thought you were in the petticoat line."

"As I said," he said, a humourless smile twisting his lips, "you cannot comprehend it."

"If I had known she would twist you around her finger, I'd—"

"You'd have what?" He forced her hands together away from him when she tried to fight, and for the first time she truly appreciated his strength and power. She tried to control her breathing. "You wouldn't have tried to murder her?"

"I—"

"Even to me, you will not be honest," he mocked. "My, how the tables have turned."

"Montague, please," she said when his grip on her chin didn't ease. "Let's talk about this as adults."

Both brows rose this time. "Oh, but we are. And you, Juliet, are going to listen to me."

All she had to do was reach for her pistol, but he was looking at her with more of that amusement, as though he could read every thought that crossed her head.

She hated him.

If she had the pistol pointing in his direction, she would have shot him there and then without a single regret.

But to achieve that, she would have to make him believe he had intimidated her into obeying him. "Very well," she said, dropping her gaze demurely.

"At the outset, I knew our goals did not align," he said, the hand from her chin sliding to her throat. She struggled, briefly, but he squeezed, long fingers wrapping almost entirely around her neck, and she froze again. "I concluded I would bear with you until you outlived your use. At the picnic, you did just that."

His grip on her hand was too tight; without alerting him to what she was doing, she couldn't point the pistol in his direction. "If that were true, you would have visited me and told me yourself."

"With Theo out of the city and beyond your reach, there was no pressing obligation."

"Far more worth your while to attack Nathanial," she spat.

"Yes," he agreed pleasantly, even though the look in his eyes was anything but pleasant. There was such yawning darkness there, as though she was looking into the mouth of a chasm that held no end. His fingers tightened around her throat, and she doubled her efforts to twist the pistol to face him. All she had to do was pull the trigger.

"She will never love you," she said, her last act of defiance. The pistol's barrel inched around. Just a little further—

Montague leant down as though he was going to kiss her, and his nose almost brushed hers. "No one will ever love you again."

Chapter Twenty-Seven

Mere hours after Theo had forewarned Nathanial that his family were likely descending on them, they arrived, his mother in full sail and his sisters following behind. For Nathanial, at least, it was a familiar image, but poor Theo shrank back. Especially when his mother bypassed him and plied her with questions.

If he were less of a gentleman, he might have continued to pretend he was asleep, but Theo was pale and exhausted, and he could not allow her to shoulder the burden of his family as well as her—entirely justified—fears for his health and safety.

So he opened his eyes. "Peace, Mama," he said as she demanded from Theo a list of his symptoms and ailments. "I'm recovering."

His mother let out a little scream and fell to his side. "Oh Nathanial!"

Elinor, a little further back, had clapped her hand over her mouth, and Penelope was weeping into a little handkerchief.

"What a maudlin sight," he said dryly, offering his other hand to whichever sister came to claim it first.

"Anyone would have thought you had come to mourn my passing. Weep over my deathbed, if you please, and not here."

"When Theodosia sent us word that—" His mother broke off, sharp eyes assessing the bandage around his chest. In truth, his wound ached like the devil and itched something terrible, too. The doctor had assured him that they were healing pains, but it was taking all his self-control not to rip the blasted bandages away so he could address the itch.

"She told us you'd been hurt in a hunting accident," Elinor supplied, sufficiently in control to find a chair for Penelope, who clung to his hand and pressed it to her forehead. Only Cassandra hadn't moved, staring at him as though she couldn't believe what she was seeing.

"She gave us leave to think," Cassandra whispered, "that you *were* on your deathbed."

"Poor Theo," Nathanial said, looking for his wife, but she'd slipped from the room. He couldn't blame her. "I think she began to fear the worst and wanted to ensure you were all here in case. No doubt her note was unnecessarily urgent."

"There's not a doubt it was suitably urgent," his mother said in arctic tones, "but the question is why it was not sent before."

Nathanial almost wished he'd kept his eyes closed and maintained the façade of sleep. "You must excuse her, Mama. She was tired, recovering from her own illness, and no doubt didn't want to alarm you."

Elinor was staring hard at him, eyes slightly narrowed. "Odd that you took ill so soon after she did," she said after a moment.

"Odd? Not at all," Nathanial said cheerfully. If there was one thing Theo and he agreed on, it was that his family—or hers—would not be privy to the information that someone was trying to kill them. Nothing could be more assured to cause unnecessary panic. "Although certainly unfortunate."

"She ought not to have nursed you alone," Penelope said, dropping her sodden handkerchief on the bedside table and turning red eyes to him. "What a burden to have borne . . ." She shuddered.

"Lord Stapleton did a great deal as well," Nathanial said. "We are greatly indebted to him. But did you think you would nurse me back to health yourself, Pen?" He pinched her cheek when she didn't reply.

"You know as well as I do that you would have been quite undone when I was at the height of my fever, and we can't have hysterics."

"*I* would not have succumbed to hysterics," Elinor said stiffly. "I would thank you to bear that in mind."

"No, you would have rearranged the household according to your inflexible vision of how things ought to be done, and you would have scolded me until I regained consciousness."

Two pink spots appeared on her cheeks. "Well really, Nathanial—"

"And Cassandra shouldn't have left young William," he said, giving her a kind smile at her doleful expression. "At least, not for the period of time it would have taken to nurse me back to health. So you see, Theo made the right choice in not summoning you here sooner. She afforded you the least amount of worry and inconvenience possible."

His mother speared him with a glance. "You appear to think she acted correctly in all things."

"Mama," he said, conscious of an odd feeling of pride in his chest, "I would not have handed my care into the hands of another person. She did everything

341

that was right and my biggest regret is that her health suffered in tending to mine."

His mother harumphed, but the fire was gone from her voice. "In which case, I'm glad she was here, even if another woman might have given us earlier news of your condition."

"If you mean to disparage Theo as my wife, you may as well leave now," he said, anger in every word, and for the first time, his mother smiled.

"No, I don't mean to do that. She's a good girl, and devoted to you, which I concede has its benefits. A wife should be devoted to a husband where possible, and when the husband in question deserves her devotion." What a lady should do when her husband did not deserve her devotion, she didn't mention. Nathanial didn't dare ask.

"Now," Elinor said, providing another chair for Cassandra and seating herself on the end of the bed. "You must tell us everything."

To Nathanial's disgust, he and Theo were forced to remain at the Stapletons' for another three weeks.

Nathanial graduated from the bed to the chair, and eventually ventured downstairs, but the doctor refused all mention of travel until his wound had sufficiently closed.

But, just as Nathanial thought he might go mad, or might stride out into the estate in the hopes whoever had taken a shot at him might have another go, the doctor proclaimed he was recovered enough to travel.

They left the next day.

"Thank goodness," Theo said, resting her head against the seat. Her face was pale, and her eyes underlined with deep shadows. "If I'd been obliged to spend another evening with Lady Stapleton, I think I would have screamed."

Nathanial gave a slight smile at the idea of Theo, so determined to step into the role of duchess, losing all sense of propriety. "I only wish we could have left several weeks ago."

"We might have been able to if you hadn't been shot," she said tartly, but the glimmer of a smile in her tired eyes belied her words. "It was most inconvenient of you, Nate."

"Believe me, I'm more than fully aware of it."

She drew her finger down the windowpane, tracing patterns he couldn't read. "Are you sure going back to London is the best idea?" she asked after a moment. "You're not yet fully recovered, and—"

"I am not an invalid."

"No, you merely have a hole in your shoulder."

"A healing hole."

"A hole," she repeated, glaring at him. "Several of them, in fact. And I hardly see what you think you are going to achieve in *London* of all places. The Season is over."

If he could have persuaded Theo to visit Havercroft without him, he would have done so, and made enquiries in Town. But she would not have gone, and he did not feel equal to the argument that would have no doubt followed. His Theo was many things, but compliant was not one of them.

Had he known the true state of her stubbornness when he had offered for her, he would have thought twice, which only left him to be grateful he had not known. Just a few months of marriage had served to assure him that there was one woman he could love, and she was sitting at the other side of the carriage.

"We would be better off going to Havercroft," she said. "I haven't seen the estate since our marriage, after all, and I know it's beautiful in the summer. Town is odiously hot and dusty."

"Perhaps after a week or two we could retire there," he suggested.

Her gaze snapped to his, and despite her exhaustion, her eyes were alive with suspicion. "After a week or two of what?"

"What do you think, Theo?" He sighed, but there was nothing for it. And he supposed, if he was being honest with himself—something he had been forced to do alarmingly frequently over these past few months—she deserved to know the precise situation. "I'm intending to investigate who I believe to be behind this." Or rather, how he could *prove* who was behind this.

There was only one person who, to his knowledge, had the motive to want him dead. All he needed to do was find evidence of it.

Theo narrowed her eyes and crossed the carriage to him, her knee brushing distractingly against his. His recovery had made it impossible to further their intimate relationship, but there was no denying he wanted to. And the longer he denied himself, the more desperately aware of her he became.

"You are not adequately recovered," she told him.

"You have been my nurse, and I'm grateful, but I must ask you to trust me to know my limits."

Her eyebrows rose and she took his hand. "I am to trust the man who once broke his leg climbing a tree that he was warned off by both the groom *and* the steward?"

"And my father," Nathanial said, grinning slightly at the memory. "But I believe, my sweet, you were standing at the base of the tree encouraging me and telling me which branches I should climb next."

She glared at him, though a smile quivered at the corner of her mouth. "How ungallant of you to remind me."

"You have always been my partner in crime," he said, and unable to resist the temptation any longer, slid his fingers around the back of her neck, brought her face to his, and kissed her.

At first, she froze, and he wondered if he'd made a mistake. Over the course of his recovery, she had been careful to keep her distance, and he had never approached her, knowing that giving into something like this was the first step along a slippery slope he did not know he could resist for long. Self-control had never been a problem except with Theo. He had never found it difficult to resist a lady before, because he wanted none the way he wanted her. Desire was in him a hunger, an ache, and the only thing that could ever sate him was her.

He trailed his fingers along the hinge of her jaw, and she softened under him, pliant and yielding. When he swiped his thumb across her cheek, she opened her mouth to him, and the sound she made as he met her tongue with his almost undid him.

Lord, how he wanted her. That need had him tugging her closer, skimming his hands down the line of her body, along her waist and the curve of her hips. There was too much material in the way, and by the time his rational body had caught up with his instinct, he was already running a hand down her leg.

And she was cupping his face in her hands and kissing him with such desperation he might have believed she was starving. Which suited him, because he'd been starving their entire marriage, and she was the feast, the antidote to his hunger.

"Nate," she whispered against his lips, but he didn't want to hear what she had to say; some instinctive part of his brain knew it was going to be a suggestion they stop, and he didn't want to stop. Not now—not when they were so close.

His fingers had found her calf now, and he ran his palm along the soft curve, inching up until he found her knee. He took hold of it and eased her around until she was straddling him. The skirts of her dress were in the way, and he bundled them up and off. He needed to feel her, and she needed to feel him, how hard he was for her. He wanted her to feel *everything*.

For a moment, her hips shifted against him, and the sensation was enough to make him groan. But as she did, she leant against his shoulder, and his groan turned into a grunt of pain.

She threw herself off him, eyes wide, hair wild—had he done that?—and panting. Her tongue moistened her lips as she watched him.

Damn. He leant his head back against the seat and tried not to notice how, now the wound had been disturbed, every jostle of the carriage sent spikes of pain through him.

"Nate," Theo whispered. There was something so achingly vulnerable in the sound of his name that he looked at her again and held out a hand.

"I'm sorry."

She took it and pressed it against her lips. "There's nothing to apologise for. I just feel *here* isn't perhaps the best place, and while you're still recovering—"

"You don't need to explain yourself," he said with a wry smile. "I should not have been so . . . carried away."

She edged closer, and placed his hand against her cheek. Her skin was warm and flushed, and it took every modicum of willpower not to lose himself in her again. "When you're better," she said, dropping her gaze so she didn't meet his, "I would like it if you got carried away again."

He could have told her that there was every chance he would get carried away every day for the rest of their life together. He could have told her that he submitted to her in every way; that over their seven months of marriage, she had stolen his heart in a way no other woman had or could.

There were so many things he could have told her, but just as he didn't intend on taking her in a carriage, rumbling along the main road to London, he didn't plan on confessing his feelings in such an inauspicious location.

So he smiled and kissed her fingertips. "When I'm better," he promised, "I will show you just how difficult waiting has been."

Pink suffused her cheeks and she glanced away in pleasure and embarrassment. Nathanial watched the way her lips curved into an involuntary smile, and wondered what he could do to make her smile like that again.

As soon as they knew who was behind these attacks, he would find out, in painstaking detail.

Until then, he would have to learn patience, no matter how little he wanted to.

Chapter Twenty-Eight

It was enough to drive any woman mad, to know her ill and still-recovering husband was intending on investigating an attempted murder when he wasn't even well enough to—

Well, never mind what he wasn't well enough to do. He wasn't doing it and that was that. And if she had any say in the matter, he wasn't going to have a chance to strain himself in an entirely *different* way.

"Your Graces," Jarvis said as they finally arrived at Norfolk House that evening. "It's good to have you back."

"Thank you, Jarvis," Nathanial said, his voice surprisingly easy, though she knew he was in pain from the tight press of his mouth.

The idiotic man, thinking he was well enough for any sort of intimacy in a moving carriage. If she hadn't enjoyed it so much, and if the warmth of being so desperately wanted wasn't still in the pit of her stomach, she would have told him what for.

"Dinner will be served in half an hour," the butler said. "If that suits Your Graces."

For the first time, irritation escaped into Nathanial's expression. "Of course," he said. "We can dress in that time."

Theo could dress in that time. Nathanial, on the other hand, looked as though he needed to lie down awhile before he would be ready to eat.

"I can order your dinner to be brought up to your room on a tray," she said anxiously as they parted to their separate dressing rooms.

"*Our* room," he said. "I'll keep my room made up for appearances' sake, but I have no intention of sleeping alone."

Warmth spread across her cheeks, but she just tipped her head back so she was looking full into his face. "Do you think you can contain yourself?"

"Wretch," he said, but his eyes darkened as they dropped to her mouth, and the now-familiar curl of anticipation unfurled in her stomach. "I suppose I can count on you to stop me."

"I wouldn't be so sure," she murmured. In a bed, which already felt alarmingly intimate, there was rather less incentive to stop than in a rocking carriage. And last time, the only reason she *had* stopped was because she'd hurt him.

He leant down until his lips were a hair's breadth from hers, and when he spoke, his breath danced across her mouth in an agony of temptation. "Perhaps we should skip dinner after all."

And he had the audacity to call *her* a wretch. She was but human, and he was too close—or perhaps not close enough.

But he was injured and tired and they'd been travelling all day.

She wanted to groan at the unfairness of it.

As though he sensed her indecision, and nothing less than full commitment would have prevailed upon him to kiss her, he eased back. "We should dress for dinner or we'll be late."

The desire to groan increased. Before she could overthink, she reached up and kissed him lightly, cupping his face in her hands and holding him still as she drew her teeth across his bottom lip. His breath caught.

"A promise," she said, breaking away. "For later." Then, before the blush on her face could reveal how awkward she felt, she fled into her dressing room and shut the door, leaning against it and closing her eyes as she remembered precisely how his mouth had felt against hers. The ghost of his hands as they had come to cup her elbows and draw her into him.

The night before his accident, he had looked at her as though she was the only thing in his world; as though the sun could have burnt and died and stopped shining, and he might never have noticed.

She wanted him to look at her like that again.

She changed quickly and reached the dining room before Nathanial. When he appeared, his movements were stiff, and she wished they had just taken a tray in her room. The journey had suppressed her appetite, and despite the feast before them—honey-roasted duck, vegetables smothered in butter, fish and parsley, sweet and savoury pies—nothing tempted her.

"Excuse me, Your Grace." Jarvis approached her with a note on a silver tray. "This arrived just now. The boy insisted I deliver it immediately."

Theo frowned as she plucked the single sheet from the tray. No one even knew she was back, but the implication was of urgency.

Was her family sick?

"Thank you, Jarvis," she said, dismissing him with a smile she didn't feel. Her fingers only marginally shaky, she ripped open the wafer and read the few lines written in elegant, faintly familiar script.

My dear Duchess, it read.

No doubt you must be understandably worried about your husband's health in the light of recent events. Believe me when I say they are unconnected to your recent illness.

If you should like to know more, meet me at Victoria Gate tomorrow morning at eight, and I shall tell you everything I know. Come alone.

I remain your loyal servant,

A Friend.

Theo stared at it blankly, reading it again but more slowly. A friend? What friend did she have who would refuse to put their name?

And their claim to know something about Nathanial's attempted murder . . . Could it be true? Did this person have the key to unlocking this entire mystery? Or was this merely a hoax, to either waste her time or put her in some danger? After all, she *had* been poisoned.

But the streets would not be empty at eight o'clock, even in the morning. There would be witnesses, and

Victoria Gate led into Hyde Park, which was hardly an inconspicuous location.

She would be foolish to even consider it. The note was almost certainly a trap.

"Theo?" Nathanial asked, a sharp note to his voice. She glanced up, noting as she did the paleness of his face and the strain in his eyes. This was probably not the first time he had said her name.

The choice whether to tell him or not was made before she'd even considered it. Nathanial could never know about this note. Not when telling him would result in him forbidding her to leave the house, most probably, and hurting himself to discover the letter-writer.

She hadn't yet decided if *she* was going to obey the letter's summons, but if she did, she would at least make that decision herself.

"Oh, it's nothing," she said airily, folding the letter again. Her voice didn't quite obey her, and her fingers shook like autumn leaves in a wind, so she gave him a bland smile she hated. "Annabelle writes asking if I can visit her tomorrow."

"How did she know you would be back?" The suspicion hadn't lightened on his face.

"Oh, I wrote to her a few days ago suggesting we might set off soon. Perhaps she saw the carriage, or delivered the note here in hope."

"Is there something wrong with your family? Your mother's health, perhaps?"

Theo's heart lurched uncomfortably against her chest. How many lies would she have to tell? She wasn't even particularly *good* at lying. "My mother has a trifling cold and wishes to see me. This is the longest I've ever been away from home, you see." She kept her voice light, and eventually Nathanial turned back to his plate, a frown pulling at his mouth.

As soon as this was over, she would tell him everything, and while he would probably be angry— well, there was no 'probably' about it; he *would* be angry—she would have relieved her soul of its burdens and they would be free to live their lives without the threat of danger lurking overhead.

"You seem distracted," Nathanial said as the meal finally ended. "Is your mother's health worse than you're letting on?"

"Unlikely." Theo's smile was lamentably fake. Why had she never learnt that young lady's trick of lying through her teeth? "But Annabelle does love to worry."

"And you?" he asked, his gaze piercing. "Do you love to worry?"

"Me? No, of course not." She forced another smile and glanced away. His suspicion and concern cut away at her until she almost lost her resolve.

Would he ever forgive her for this?

Perhaps she could show him the note, after all. What was the worst he could do? Strain himself going after the letter-writer? Do the exact same thing she was considering, but in poorer health?

There was a possibility he would recognise the handwriting, of course, and so he might be able to inform her decision. But if he didn't, and he prevented her from making this meeting, she might never learn whatever it was this person knew about the accident.

And they had to know something. No one outside of her and Nathanial, and perhaps the doctor who had attended her, knew that she had been deliberately poisoned. For the person to mention that the two events weren't connected suggested they had intimate knowledge of the situation.

Her head was spinning and the food turned to ashes in her mouth.

"Theo?" Nathanial asked, his voice gentle. "Are you quite well?"

"The journey tired me," she said after a moment. She might as well find a reason for her sudden preoccupation, and if she retired now, she would have a few more minutes to herself before Nathanial came up to bed, as he would.

"Of course." His brow didn't clear, but concern now replaced the uncertainty in his expression. "I should have thought—it's been a challenging few weeks for you, too."

She rose, the letter clenched in her fist, and approached him. A gentle smile touched her lips at her nearness. The letter burned her hand.

"Goodnight, Nate," she said, looking down into the face of the husband she had grown to love so dearly. The grey eyes, the dark hair, the softness that she knew she could bring from him like nectar from a flower.

He reached out and stroked the back of a knuckle along her cheek. "You'll see me soon," he said, a teasing note in his voice, although there was still that wariness around the tight corners of his eyes. She smoothed them with the pads of her fingers, feeling the strangest urge to cry.

Her resolve faltered, and she clung to its frayed edges. If she gave Nathanial the letter and absolved herself of all responsibility, she would be opening *him* to danger. That, she could never do.

Before she said something to incriminate herself, she picked up her skirts and walked from the room, feeling Nathanial's gaze on her back with every step.

Chapter Twenty-Nine

True to his word, Nathanial joined her before much time had passed at all, and she was forced to hide the letter inside one of her gloves. Betsy had been apprised of her plans to rise early, and as she and Nathanial lay together, his arm wrapped around her, their breaths mingling, she told him she was slipping away early to see her family.

He didn't object. The guilt settled in.

But even if she hadn't been feeling guilty, clinging to Nathanial's warmth and the soft regularity of his breathing as though she could live in each passing moment forever, she wouldn't have slept. She was, as she well knew, about to do something stupid, and every heartbeat brought her closer to its execution.

Or perhaps hers.

Every thought was a morbid one, and if Nathanial had awoken to see her restless, sleepless worry, she would have told him everything.

But he slumbered on, and when dawn finally broke across the sky, Theo slipped from the bed, sliding a dressing gown over her shoulders, and moved into her dressing room. There, she rang for Betsy, who came bleary-eyed to dress her in a plain, dark dress.

"Are you sure about this, ma'am?" she whispered as Theo descended the stairs in near-darkness.

"Perfectly sure," Theo said, though it wasn't strictly true. She'd read the small note several times that morning alone, and there was little in her life she was *less* sure of.

Yet if she didn't take this step, would they ever find out who was responsible for Nathanial's accident? The grooms at Stapleton didn't know, and neither did the beaters. They hadn't seen anything, hadn't spoken to anyone, and there were no reports of poachers or anyone else on their land the morning of the hunt.

No one knew anything except, apparently, this mysterious letter-writer, and Theo was determined to unravel this mystery.

Just in case, however, she had secreted one of Nathanial's knives in her reticule, and she'd left a letter for him with Betsy, to be delivered if she didn't return within a few hours. All the eventualities she could think of were covered.

Time to find the truth.

The carriage pulled up outside the house as sunlight spilled across the streets for the first time. This was not the grey, foggy day she had feared; the sun burned away the mist, and the sky was a delicate, eggshell blue.

She relaxed into the seat.

Victoria Gate came into sight, far less conspicuous than the Canada Gates beside Buckingham Palace, and the carriage came to a stop. Hawkins, the groom, helped her from the carriage.

"Keep the horses walking," she said, hoping she sounded more confident than she felt. "I won't be long."

"Excuse my forwardness, Your Grace," Hawkins said, his sharp blue eyes fixed on her face. She'd only known him a few short months, but he had already shown himself to view her with fatherly affection. "But might I suggest you don't walk alone at this time of day. I could accompany you."

She gave him a smile she didn't feel. "But then who would care for the horses? They're His Grace's greys, you know."

"I suspect His Grace would rather harm came to his horses than Your Grace."

"I won't be long," Theo repeated, with a little more force. Reluctantly, Hawkins fell back, and Theo walked briskly to the gates. A few businessmen passed her, tradespeople and lawyers, perhaps, dressed smartly in black. Some gave her questioning looks—it was not usual for a lady of Quality to be walking alone at this hour—but none so much as stopped to see her.

She glanced back at the carriage, reassured to find it precisely where she left it, Hawkins standing at the bridle and watching her with uncompromising focus. Relieved, she gave him a little wave and walked through the gates into Hyde Park.

Dew clung to each blade of grass and vibrant leaf; if she had been on any other errand, she might have been tempted to linger and appreciate their beauty. But before she could do more than cast a quick glance around, a voice caught her attention.

"Duchess," he said, a note of surprise in his tone. "You came."

Dismay and fear flooded through her in equal measure as she turned and looked at the man she had barely allowed herself to suspect. "So it was you," she said flatly. "You sent me that letter."

With a sardonic twist of his lips, Sir Montague took her hand before she could twist it away. "How quickly you perceive the situation, little mouse."

"You know something about Nathanial?" She looked up into his face and the twisted smile that was still on his lips. Her fear overpowered her dismay, and she took a steadying breath. "What do you know?"

"Do you trust me?" he asked, dark eyes hooded.

If she could have done, she would have pulled away. Instead, caught like a fish on a hook, she stared up at him. "Trust you?" she whispered. "Why would you ask me that?"

"Because," he murmured, bending down until his face was altogether too close to hers, "it changes how I approach this. Do you trust me, Duchess? Theo." He said her name softly, but there was a curl of menace behind his words that made her heart pound.

No, she didn't trust him. Nathanial did not, which would have been enough by itself now, but Sir Montague had lured her here.

He had still not let go of her hand.

"Release me," she said, her voice breathless and too quiet. Panic swarmed up her tight throat. "Release me or I shall scream."

He sighed. "It would have been easier if you had trusted me." His fingers wrapped around her other elbow. "I'm sorry, Theo."

She didn't even have time to speak before he clamped his hand over her mouth and dragged her roughly off her feet. Her screaming was muffled, lost beneath his rough palm, and for a second, as panic took hold, she couldn't breathe.

Every part of her was cold. He was going to take her somewhere quiet and end her life once and for all. Nathanial had been wrong, after all—Sir Montague had been the man behind her poisoning. He, for an inexplicable reason she did not yet understand, wanted her dead.

And he was going to succeed.

Belatedly, she remembered the knife in her reticule. With her free hand, she stuck her hand into the small bag, Sir Montague's palm muffling her cry as the blade cut her fingers. Trembling, terrified, determination hot amidst the coldness in her chest, she fumbled for the hilt, drew it out, and plunged it into   his   leg.

Chapter Thirty

Theo was gone when Nathanial woke.

He lay alone for a few moments, accustoming himself to being in her bedroom. It was a nicely proportioned room, and he had spent enough time in it while Theo had been recovering that it felt familiar, but there was something different about it in the silence. There was no gentle warmth from her body, no tongue-in-cheek comments about his sleeping habits—he had several, it seemed, that amused her—and no concern for his wellbeing.

He missed the sound of her breathing, which was such a ludicrous thing to miss that he sat up, ignoring the twinge from his chest, and swung his feet out of bed, shuffling through to his dressing room and calling for his valet. Theo had said something about anticipating being back for lunch, which really wasn't too far away. It was ten o'clock now, and he wouldn't even think about worrying until it was twelve, at least.

Of course, the letter hadn't been from her family. Her sister didn't have the power to send such a flush into her cheeks, and he doubted she'd have been so eager to visit her family so early for a mere cold.

No, it was almost certainly someone else she was meeting. A friend or worse. Sir Montague, perhaps—

No. After everything he had told her about his cousin, he doubted she would hurry to meet him. Likely, it was another gentleman she had formed a fancy for.

But he was her husband, not her keeper, and if the thought of her meeting another man made him want to smash something, well, he would merely curb it before she returned.

But no sooner than he had dressed and was applying himself to his cravat, there was a knock on the door. "Enter," he said.

Jarvis, his face carefully blank, entered the room. "Hawkins would like to see you, Your Grace."

"The groom?" Nathanial frowned, decided his neckcloth would pass muster, and turned. "What could Hawkins have to say to me this early?"

"That is for him to say, Your Grace, but I determined it was Urgent Business."

Immediately, Nathanial's thoughts went to Theo— and specifically, the fact that she had called for the

369

carriage that morning. That in itself was unsurprising, as was the fact the carriage and Hawkins had returned without her, but he couldn't prevent the feeling of dread that crept through him.

"I'll come downstairs," Nathanial said, taking the stick that lay propped against the dresser. He preferred not to use it, but it was convenient, he'd found, to have it on hand.

Hawkins was waiting for him in the library, and Nathanial wasted no time in asking, "Is it the Duchess?"

"I'm afraid it is, Your Grace," Hawkins said, rubbing his nose with the back of his hand. He was a burly man of indeterminate age whose crooked nose suggested he had once tried to make a career of boxing. As long as Nathanial could remember, however, he had been part of the household, and he had no reason to question his loyalty.

"Well?"

"She requested me to take her to Hyde Park this morning," he said. The dread Nathanial had been feeling settled into mingled anger and panic. "Around eight o'clock, sir. I suggested she might want an escort, and offered to walk her to her destination, but

370

she appeared to think my services unnecessary and bid me to watch the horses."

Of course she had, the little fool. An attempt on her life wasn't considered danger enough for her to be careful. The Lord help him, he was going to have words with her when he got her back.

If he got her back.

The thought was so terrible, so horrific, he reared back. No, he would find her. There was no other option. He would not allow it.

"And?" he asked, though he barely recognised his voice. "What happened next?"

"Well, you see, that's the thing, sir. She passed through the gates and was lost to sight. I held the horses for her as she bid for an hour, but she didn't return. I handed the horses to a passing boy—they're quite all right, sir—and searched the vicinity myself, but I didn't see her. Thought I should come back and inform Your Grace of the events."

It would be impossible to keep this matter from the servants, no matter how hard he tried. Jarvis would, no doubt, attempt to keep talk to a minimum, but this was severe enough he could not hide it. No one could. Theo was gone.

But now was not the time to panic.

"Very well," he said. "Dispatch as many servants as you can spare to search the area, although I doubt she'll be there now."

"Yes, sir," Jarvis said. "Should I inform the servants whom we are looking for?"

"Tell them Her Grace may have fallen ill again."

"Yes, sir."

Nathanial pinched the bridge of his nose. He had to *think*. Who could have wanted to harm her? The letter she had received last night would give him a clue, but he didn't know where she had put it. Where she had *hidden* it. Last night, he'd felt unequal to confronting her, and she had been just as gently affectionate as always, looking at him in a way that . . . He had felt sure she wanted no other.

He should have found that damn letter.

Using his cane, he pushed himself to his feet as Jarvis cleared his throat. "Betsy wishes to speak to you, Your Grace," the butler said, waving her in.

"Betsy?" Nathanial looked across at Theo's lady's maid, the one who had so often glared at him and made her disapproval plain. "Well? I presume this is about Her Grace."

Unusually, the woman had tears in her eyes, and she held a folded piece of paper in shaking hands. "She told me to give you this if she didn't return in two hours, Your Grace," she said, passing it to him and pressing her hands against her face. "I never thought—she never said—I didn't think she'd be in danger."

Without bothering to respond, Nathanial ripped open the note.

My dearest Nathanial, it began in an achingly familiar hand.

If you are reading this, I conclude I have not returned home, and you must no doubt know I went to Hyde Park this morning, not my mother's house. You see, last night, I received a letter claiming to know something about your accident, and I went to discover what I could. I know you are planning on making enquiries, but you're too hurt, still, and I wanted to spare you that.

If the worst has come to pass, I beg you would not hurt yourself looking for me. Only know that these months married to you have been the happiest of my life. I was looking for a hero, and I had not known I had found one in you.

Your ever-loving,

Theo.

Nathanial stared sightlessly at the paper, unable to focus on the words, unable to look away. His dear, sweet, *stupid* Theo had thought to spare him the pain of investigating by endangering herself, and she could not see how very much trouble she was in.

Only know that these months married to you have been the happiest of my life.

He needed to find her before—

He crumpled the letter in his fist and turned his attention to the butler, groom and lady's maid, who still watched him, waiting for his next instruction.

"Prepare the carriage," he said curtly. The stupid, foolish girl. As though he would rather she put herself in danger for him.

He would have preferred her to be meeting another gentleman. At least then she would have been safe. At least then, she would have come home, and he could have found a way through this.

But knowing she had gone to 'discover what she could' about his would-be murderer meant something far more dangerous was at play. He could be guaranteed of nothing.

"Fetch my pistol," he told Jarvis. "I have a feeling I will need it."

Theo awoke in a carriage. She couldn't recall having been unconscious, but she had certainly awoken, and pain splintered from a point in her temple.

The carriage was not one of her own.

Nathanial had several carriages, but they were all outfitted in a similar way, with burgundy leather seats, his coat of arms mounted on the back, and wide, clean windows. This carriage, however, was dirty. The stitching on the seats had split, revealing the stuffing within, and there was no coat of arms.

The curtains were drawn. Opposite her sat Sir Montague.

He might have looked composed and easy, one leg stretched out in front of him and the other tucked away, if it were not for the blood and makeshift bandage across his thigh. His gaze, when it alighted on her, was not forgiving.

The memory hit her like a bolt of lightning and she looked at her hand—specifically, at the cut that ran across her fingers from where she had gripped the knife. The same knife she had sunk into Sir Montague's leg.

"I took it," he said in answer to her sudden panic. Her reticule was nowhere to be seen. "I confess, I hadn't thought you would think to take a weapon with you. Nor," he added with a grimace, "the capacity to use it in such a way."

"You tried to capture me!" She paused and wrinkled her nose again at her surroundings. "You *did* capture me."

"I did."

Horror pressed against her throat, and she closed her mouth before she could say anything foolish. He'd already hit her once, if the pounding in her head was any indication, and she didn't want to give him any reason to do it again.

If only she still had her knife. Next time she would aim it higher than his leg.

"I won't hurt you again if I can help it," he said.

"If you can help it?"

His voice was grim. "Don't stab me again, and you won't have to find out."

"How could I stab you again if you've taken my knife?" she asked, and the fear in her throat made its wavering way into her words. She clenched her fists until her nails bit into her palms.

"I'm hoping you can't," he said dryly. "But you might as well stop looking at me as though I'm some terrible villain. I've captured you, yes, but note you're unbound and I'm not attempting to force myself on you. That should give you some comfort."

"Little enough," she flashed before she could help herself, and an appreciative smile leapt into his eyes, just for a second.

"I see kidnap has not dimmed your spirit."

"Where are we going? Is this your carriage? *Why* am I here?"

"So many questions."

"I will have fewer if you answer them."

His laugh was pained, but he laughed all the same, and despite herself, she relaxed slightly. "Very well. We are going to Nathanial's Leicestershire hunting box to begin with, and this is a hired carriage. I apologise for the smell."

She drew her feet up. "You may apologise for capturing me."

"Oh, but I feel no need to do that," he said gently. "This, without the unfortunate pain in my leg, is precisely what I had intended."

"But *why*?"

"Because you are Nathanial's wife," he said. "And he is the Duke—a title that without his marriage might have fallen to me."

"All this for a title?"

"All this because my cousin, born with that proverbial silver spoon, was granted leniencies I was not. Because my cousin is the Duke and I am not." His smile was a dark, bitter thing as he looked at her. "And he married you, my little mouse."

There was a look in his eyes that alarmed her. Not because it was violent, precisely, but because it held a heat she was all too familiar with. Nathanial had taught her what expressions like that could mean, and while she might have been amenable to kissing Nathanial in a carriage, Sir Montague was a very different matter.

"What do you intend to do with me?" she whispered.

"An intriguing question," he murmured. "What *do* I intend to do with you?"

Without her knife, which she could see nowhere easily accessible on his person, Theo was helpless. He might be injured, but he was larger than her, and stronger. He had killed a man in a duel, and there was something dark about him that spoke to the primal part of her, telling her to run.

There could be no running from inside a carriage.

Sir Montague gave a low, humourless laugh. "I told you, Duchess, I have no intention of hurting you."

"I suppose I ought to thank you for your forbearance."

"A mouse with the claws of a cat," he said, one side of his mouth curling. "I understand why my dear cousin is so attached."

The thought of Nathanial made Theo want to scream. Had Betsy given him the letter yet? What would he *do*? He wasn't well enough to go gallivanting around the country after her.

If only she had aimed the knife a little higher.

"Why Nathanial's hunting box?" she asked after a moment. "Surely he'll find us there eventually?"

"Sooner rather than later, I hope."

"And once he arrives, what then? What are your intentions?"

"My intentions are to become Duke," he said. He made no attempt to reach forward and touch her, but she felt his gaze skim across her body, and she fought the urge to curl into a ball. "And I intend to achieve that with Nathanial's consent or without it."

She snorted. "You're expecting Nathanial to give up his title for my sake?"

"I have every expectation of it."

"And if he does not?"

"I recommend you do not trouble your head over it." A coldness entered his voice, one that sent goosebumps rising over her skin. This was not the charming, smiling man who had courted her and offered her compliments. This was the creature of darkness that lingered under his skin and did not shy away from causing pain. "But if that *were* to happen, then fear not, little mouse. I would be more than happy to restore you to your current position as Duchess, once the appropriate period for mourning had passed."

Disgust tasted like ash in her mouth. "You would marry me? After killing my husband?" Laughing or crying—both seemed reasonable options, but neither would give her satisfaction. "You cannot be serious."

"Can I not?" Now he reached across the space between them and plucked her hand from her lap, smoothing out her fingers to reveal the life lines on her palm. "I must marry someone, once my position as Duke is assured, and of all the ladies I have encountered thus far, you are the only one to occupy my attention for more than a month or so."

"I?" Theo tried to snatch her hand back, but he didn't let her. "Let go of me."

"I would make you happy, Theo."

"Don't call me that, don't—" She finally succeeded in wrenching her hand from his grip, and she cradled it against her chest, watching him all the while. Her rejection didn't seem to have discomposed him; he leant back against the seat, the tiniest of smiles playing around his mouth.

"You can hardly say you were never drawn to me," he said. "The moment I arrived in London, you made your preference known."

"A mistake," she said, wrapping her arms around herself. *Then* she hadn't realised the man she could fall in love with was lurking—unromantically—in her house the whole time. "And a flirtation, Sir Montague. Nothing more."

"No?" He moved to her side and sat beside her, his knee brushing against hers. She wondered if she could open the door and throw him out. "When you accompanied me to the masquerade despite your husband's disapproval?"

"A mistake," she repeated.

"The mistake was mine for letting you out of my sight."

"If you think I would have done anything with you, you are very much mistaken," she snapped. "And you are mistaken now."

"I haven't asked you for anything, little mouse."

"Then sit back where you were before and let us talk of something else."

With a laugh, he did as she requested, although she noticed his movements were stiff. Perhaps the pain in his leg meant he was feeling less amorous.

"You said in your letter that you had some information for me," she said. "Were you behind my poisoning?"

"I?" There was a tightness around his eyes that hinted at pain, but their expression gentled as he looked at her. "No, Theo. That was not me. But rest assured I handled the situation—the person who harmed you cannot any longer."

"And the shooting? Nathanial? Was that also—"

"No. That, I can lay claim to."

"You admit it so easily."

"I have no desire to deny it. I rather suspect you will not attribute a conscience to me now, and we are past the point of lying. I was the one who arranged for Nathanial to be shot that day, and I was very nearly successful."

"Then how can you expect me to believe you won't hurt me?"

"Are you really so blind, Theo? Can you not guess?"

Perhaps, on second thoughts, it would be better not to know. "If you had succeeded in your aim of killing Nathanial," she said simply, "you would have killed me,   too."

Chapter Thirty-One

It was a little after one when Nathanial arrived at Montague's lodgings, and it was to find the house shut up. The butler made a half-hearted attempt to prevent him from entering, but soon stepped aside. Nathanial stalked through the house, noting the threadbare carpet, the smudged wallpaper, and the worn furniture. Montague wasn't plump in the pocket, and no doubt he intended to bolster his income with Nathanial's wealth. Or perhaps his title direct.

What would he do to Theo to achieve his goal? He'd suspected his cousin of harbouring feelings for her, but this behaviour didn't suggest fondness. Unless his fondness had taken an entirely different direction.

White-hot anger flared, and he clenched his fists, forcing it back. *If* Montague had forced Theo into— anything—he would see to it Montague paid dearly.

There were few rooms in this house, and he even flung open the door to Montague's bedchamber, uncertain of what he was likely to find there; to his relief, he found nothing. No abandoned earrings, no shoe lying carelessly across the floor, no signs of a struggle having taken place.

Wherever Theo was, she had not been taken here.

A brief search of the desk in Montague's dressing room yielded results: a half-written letter. The ink was smudged, but Nathanial made out enough to see that Montague anticipated being in Leicestershire over the course of the next week.

Leicestershire. There could be nothing for him there.

Unless . . .

When they were children, or as close to children as they could be while still maintaining an independence, Nathanial and Montague had thrown countless parties at his hunting lodge under the guise of hunting. Back then, Nathanial had been trying to establish his reputation without clearly knowing what his reputation should be. He was the only son of a duke and he knew that made his consequence large.

Montague, as with all things, was content to encourage all forms of licentiousness.

If Montague *had* gone there, it would be bold of him, but it would probably work. The retainers there knew him, and if he said he had come with

Nathanial's favour, they would most likely believe him. *Especially* if he had Theo in tow.

Using his cane, Nathanial hobbled out of the house and back into the carriage. "Leicestershire," he ordered. "As fast as you can. Spare no expense."

"Very good, Your Grace."

Nathanial settled back against the leather seats and closed his eyes.

As Theo had predicted, the hunting box was not nearly as small as its name suggested. In fact, as they approached, it looked rather more like a small country house, with six large windows at the front and two Grecian pillars crawling with ivy.

It was, however, unhelpfully in the middle of nowhere. Good for hunting, no doubt, but rather less felicitous for escaping. Trees surrounded the house on all sides, and although they had passed signs for Melton Mowbray, which she surmised to be a town of some size, it was not close enough for them to reach easily.

"Remember," Sir Montague said, his fingers gripping her shoulder tightly. His face had grown steadily paler as the journey had continued, but aside from changing horses and a quick meal, he had stopped for nothing. "We are here with Nathanial's approval and he will join us later."

She shrugged his hand away. "And if I should not play along?"

His mouth was a thin, white line. "Don't try me, Theo. The servants are frail, and my patience is running low."

Gone was the almost effortless charm from earlier. This was not a man for whom forbearance was his primary feeling.

The carriage stopped and he opened the door. With considerable effort, judging by the way his nostrils flared, he descended the steps and held out a hand for her. She glanced at the front of the house, but the housekeeper was already toddling towards them, and there was nothing she could do but accept his assistance.

His fingers tightened around hers in clear warning.

"Master Montague," the housekeeper puffed, holding out her hands to him. Sir Montague had briefly explained that he and Nathanial used to visit often, but Theo hadn't expected the housekeeper to be quite so pleased that he was here.

She scowled.

"Mrs Clayton," Sir Montague said, taking her hands with a smile that almost banished the darkness in his eyes. "Mr Clayton."

Mr Clayton, presumably, also emerged from the front door and shuffled towards them. According to Sir Montague, they had been tending to the hunting box as long as he could recall. Or perhaps, Theo thought uncharitably, since the dawn of time itself.

"We weren't expecting you," Mrs Clayton said, her rheumatism-twisted hands giving Sir Montague's one last shake before turning to Theo. "And you must be the Duke's bride."

With Sir Montague's gaze on her, Theo dropped a slight curtsy and held out her hand. "Pleased to meet you."

"Aye, and pretty behaved she is too," Mrs Clayton said approvingly. "Come in, come in. Is the Duke with you?"

"He'll be coming shortly," Sir Montague said. "Tomorrow, I believe."

"Oh, well, we'll have to hire a serving girl from the village, or maybe two. Take the trap now, Tom."

Mr Clayton nodded. "Yes, dear."

"And a manservant, if you would. I think Peter in Scalford would do nicely."

Theo stored Scalford away for later perusal. Perhaps it was closer than Melton Mowbray. Could she find a way of driving the trap there herself?

"Now, you stay seated in here with the fire going, and I'll put fresh linen down," Mrs Clayton said, ushering them into a small drawing room. The fire was puffing with smoke, and as soon as the housekeeper left, Sir Montague prodded it. More smoke billowed into the room.

Theo folded her arms. "What now?" she demanded. "Am I to be your prisoner?"

"You are my guest."

"In my husband's house."

"You will be gratified to know how soon I anticipate his arrival." Sir Montague lowered himself into a chair, his leg stiff. Through the rip in his calfskins, she noticed the bandage he'd wrapped around himself was stained with blood again. "Sit down," he said, the sharp edge of impatience in his voice. "You will gain nothing by standing around."

Theo held her ground. "Why, will you hurt me if I don't do as you say?"

"I certainly won't make things pleasant for you."

After a moment, she sat on the dusty chair and stared at him. With an injured leg, he was less of a threat, but she couldn't be certain he wouldn't overcome the pain to keep her there. That seemed entirely something he would do.

"You should have given these poor people warning we were arriving," she said.

"How could I, when I barely knew myself until we were on the road?" He leant his head back and closed his eyes. "I had no guarantee you would come, and I only knew of your arrival in London because the boy I employed to watch the house told me of the carriage."

"All this was achieved on a *whim?*"

"Not a whim, but I could hardly know when my plan could come to fruition. And I wanted to give Nathanial no indication of what I was planning." His smile was wolfish. "I couldn't have him disrupting me, could I?"

She cast another glance at his leg. In her opinion, stabbing him had been a disruption in its own right. "I wonder," she said, giving his person a quick once-over, "what your intentions are when Nathanial arrives?"

"A worthy question, little mouse."

"He will not come unarmed," she continued, hoping this would be true. Surely he wouldn't be so foolish as to come here without at least one gun. She knew there were two pistols—beautiful things—in Norfolk House. Two guns. Could she take one?

Or could she somehow avail herself of Sir Montague's?

She looked at him again, wondering where he might be keeping a pistol if he did have one.

"Fear not," Sir Montague said, a sardonic note in his voice now. "I won't let your husband shoot me, though that's what you wish, isn't it?"

Theo didn't reply. What could she say, except to agree?

"I am also armed," he said. "Both with a pistol and the knife you were so good as to give me."

Despite herself, she flushed. "Well, you should not have tried to capture me."

To her surprise, he laughed. "Touché. You may reassure yourself on one point, however. You defended yourself admirably."

She looked at Sir Montague's coat again, negligently open, and thought she saw the gleam of a pistol butt protruding from his waist. If Nathanial truly was coming, and Sir Montague seemed certain he was, he probably thought he needed to rescue her.

But perhaps, she didn't *need* to be rescued. Perhaps she could rescue herself.

Chapter Thirty-Two

Theo had hoped to have a chance to escape that night, but when Sir Montague accompanied her to her room and, unchivalrously, locked the door, she swiftly saw there was little chance for escape. Her room was devoid of weapons and the only thing outside her window was the ground, two storeys down. Even the fireplace was small and narrow, and there was no way of climbing up.

And, she thought ruefully, being trapped on the roof overnight was hardly an improvement on her situation.

Mrs Clayton had been surprised to find Theo had no luggage, but Sir Montague had explained that away with tales of ill maids and unfortunate accidents, which explained the injury on his leg. Blinded by trust, Mrs Clayton had accepted his word, provided Sir Montague with bandages and hot water, and offered Theo a nightgown that swallowed her whole. The next morning, she would be obliged to wear the same dress she had arrived in, creased and crumpled.

Still, after a night of tossing and turning and planning, she had a plan.

If she was lucky, which given her track record seemed unlikely, Sir Montague would be in so much pain he would remain in his room. If he was not, however, she would have to rob him of the ability to hold her captive.

And to do that, she would need his gun.

When she descended, finding her door unlocked once more, it was early enough that breakfast had not yet been made. However, it was not so early that she did not encounter Sir Montague, something she should have predicted from the moment she found her door unlocked. He limped to greet her as she entered the library where he sat, a little too far from collapse for her liking. A pity.

"Duchess," he said with his usual sardonic smile. "You rose early."

Theo looked up into his face and tried to remember the days when she had believed him her every romantic ideal. If she was going to be convincing, she needed him to believe she had a fondness for him.

As she held his gaze, a frown touched his brows and the rather hard expression in his eyes melted into cautious confusion. He had offered her marriage, and she believed him. All she would have to do was use that affection for her against him.

At the thought, her stomach twisted.

"I wanted to know what would happen next," she whispered, still looking up at him. "With you and Nathanial."

"He must be gratified to know he has inspired such dedication in his wife."

She licked her lips and his gaze darted down to the movement. Suddenly, the room felt too tight and they felt too large in it. Sucking in a large breath, she stepped back, only to find a shelf preventing her from moving away.

Sir Montague didn't move, watching her with mingled suspicion and hope.

"I like a title," she said, and swallowed. "And he has been kind to me."

Her heart was thudding so loudly she felt sure he should be able to hear it. And when his eyes narrowed, she knew she had gone too far; she had been too suggestive when she should have been subtle. Would he use her dagger on her? Or perhaps the pistol she was attempting to steal?

Her fingers trembled.

He took a step forward. "What game are you playing, little mouse?" he murmured, leaning closer. His gaze dropped to her mouth again, but this time, the glance was deliberate; a warning about his intentions. She stiffened. "I warn you, you might not like the rules."

Her heart stuttered before picking up at twice the rate, tapping staccato against her teeth. He was so close now, and from the way his pupils bloomed in his eyes, he was just as aware of their proximity. She reached up and placed both hands on his chest, feeling the way his heart pounded under the material.

She had thought, given his presumably extensive experience in this area, he would be suave. But he seemed as taken aback by her gesture as she was nervous, and he hesitated as she flattened her palms against him.

In order to get his pistol, she would have to reach down into his pocket, but there was no chance she could do so without him noticing.

Which meant she would have to distract him in other ways.

Seducing one's husband was one thing; seducing one's kidnapper was entirely another.

"What do you want, Theo?" Sir Montague asked, his voice low and rough.

She stepped even closer, until a mere inch separated their bodies. It felt natural now for her hands to slide down his sides to his waist, and his gaze didn't flicker.

Almost there.

His lips parted slightly, and she knew he would try to kiss her momentarily—and no doubt would presume her amenable, given their current position.

Her hand slid down even lower, almost brushing his pocket.

"If you become Duke," she whispered, "will you make me your Duchess?"

His gaze didn't stray from hers. "Yes."

Something about the unhesitating way he said that made her chest hurt, but she slid her hand into his pocket. The pistol was cool against the palm of her hand, and she gripped it as his breath shuddered and her mouth came within brushing distance of his.

"Theo," he said again, then seemed to realise what she was doing. He cursed and jerked back, but he was too late. She held the gun. Rage and betrayal flickered in his dark eyes as she levelled it at him.

"I do not need a man to save me," she said, her voice quiet but clear. Her finger curled around the trigger and she prayed it was loaded, because she had no way of knowing otherwise. The way his gaze flickered to the pistol then to her face, and the way he came no closer, suggested it was.

Good.

"So it seems," he said dryly, but there was an undercurrent of anger to his voice that scared her. He swept into a mocking bow. "My congratulations, little mouse. I have been outplayed."

If only it were that easy. Despite his words, bitterness suffused his words, and any hint of ardour was gone. Cruelty and anger fought for dominance in his expression, and she tightened her hold on her gun.

"Come any closer and I'll shoot," she said, hoping it was true. "I won't have you harming Nathanial any more than you already have."

"I was not the one who pulled the trigger."

"You ordered the shot to be taken."

"Did you know he came to see me after you were taken ill? He accused me of having harmed you and told me you were dead. For sport, one presumes." His lip curled. "If I did not already want his title, I would have wanted him dead for that alone."

"For a few minutes of fear?"

"I have always had a damnable temper." He did not phrase it as though he thought a temper was any bad thing. "And when I think he took you from me without even availing himself of a husband's right? You must have been deceived indeed."

When I'm better, I will show you just how difficult waiting has been.

Sir Montague gave a short, sharp laugh. "What excuse has he given you? Do you believe he loves you? Poor, sweet child."

Theo jerked back, colliding with the bookshelf behind her. She didn't think Nathanial *loved* her, precisely, because the word 'love' encompassed so much—more than she could ever deserve. But she did believe he was fond of her.

No, he *was* fond of her.

"If you don't believe he loves me," she said, sucking in a deep breath, "why did you kidnap me?"

"Because a man always seeks to protect what's his, little mouse." He advanced closer, closer, until he was close enough to touch her, reaching out and brushing back a curl. "Even when she isn't any longer."

She jabbed the pistol against his stomach, her shaking hands unable to raise the pistol any higher. "I'll shoot."

His hand fastened over hers, squeezing her fingers until they hurt. The anger in his eyes swamped any fondness that had once been there. Her little trick must have hurt him more than she had supposed.

"No you won't," he said, and his voice was mocking. "Do you know how I know, my sweet thing?" He leant in even closer, until his breath skimmed her cheek. "Because you have excellent moral fibre, just like your husband, and that will be your undoing."

Moral fibre? Theo wanted to snort, but instead, she did the only thing left to her.

She   pulled   the   trigger.

Chapter Thirty-Three

When Nathanial reached his hunting lodge, everything was silent. The morning sun glowed softly against the walls, illuminating the ivy he had commanded be cut down. Another time, he might have reflected angrily on Mr Clayton's inability to run the place with only the help of his wife—or perhaps it was the other way around—but today he had no thought except for what he would find inside.

If he would find anything inside.

His limbs were stiff as he climbed out of the carriage and surveyed the silent house before him. Nothing stirred. For a moment, he thought he might have been mistaken. Perhaps Montague hadn't brought Theo here after all; perhaps that had been a false clue left to send him in the wrong direction. Panic tasted sour in his mouth as he hurried to the front door.

It was unlocked.

"Mrs Clayton?" he called as he strode inside, one hand on his cane and the other on his pistol. "Mr Clayton?"

"Your Grace!" Mrs Clayton said in delight, bustling out from the servants' door. Keys jangled from around her neck. "Sir Montague said you would be here today, but I didn't expect you so early. Will you have breakfast?"

Nathanial blinked at her. "Sir Montague . . . said I would be here?"

"Why, did you not expect him to tell me?" She clucked at him. "Though I must say you could have sent us a letter or—"

"Never mind that," he said, waving away her chatter. For the first time, her gaze latched onto the gun in his hand and her eyes widened.

"Is everything quite well, sir?"

"No," he said grimly. "Where is Sir Montague and where is the Duchess?"

"They're both in the—"

A shot cracked through the air like a thunderbolt, and Nathanial didn't wait for the rest of her sentence. He turned, wound forgotten, and sprinted in the direction of the library. His breaths came short and fast, and even though the hallway was not long and the library not too far distant, his mind had ample opportunity to throw images of what he might find.

Theo lying on the floor, blood pooling about her prone body.

Theo stumbling back, eyes wide, her hands clutching her chest.

Theo, Theo, Theo; in every vision it was Theo, her wound too great for any doctor to heal—too great for her body to recover from.

And in every iteration, it was Montague standing over her, emotionless, a gun in his hand.

Nathanial flung open the library door, and stopped.

Theo was there, just as he'd imagined, her face white and her eyes wide and dark—darker than he'd ever seen them. Her head turned at the sound of the door, but she didn't seem to recognise him.

And before her, staggering against the bookshelf, an expression of almost comical shock on his face, was Montague, a red stain erupting on his waistcoat.

Chapter Thirty-Four

Theo couldn't quite process what she had done.

The gun was in her hands, which suggested she had been the one to shoot Sir Montague, but nothing quite felt real. The air was too thick, and she was struggling to drag it into her lungs, because she was falling, falling, falling.

A voice. Her name. She snapped her head up, but the figure in the doorway was blurred. Something hot ran down her face as she blinked, and the figure lurched forwards. Towards her. Hands outstretched, saying her name again in a pleading way that tugged at her heart.

The gun toppled from her fingers, landing on the carpet with a dull thud that radiated through her.

Sir Montague fell to his knees. Blood stained his brocade waistcoat, and he pressed his hands to his stomach, pulling them away with an expression of confusion, as though the redness there didn't make sense.

Theo wasn't certain she was breathing.

"Theo," the voice said again, and now there were hands on her face, turning her to look at him. Familiar grey eyes greeted her, filled with concern and anguish and an expression she couldn't name, that put air back into her lungs and spurred her mouth into speaking.

"Nate," she whispered.

"Are you all right? Are you hurt?"

At the mention of hurt, she looked back at Sir Montague, still on the floor. The detachment faded, replaced by alarm. She had done this. *She* had done it.

As though Nathanial sensed her shifting mood, he released her and knelt by Sir Montague's side. "There's a lot of blood," he said grimly.

Sir Montague raised his head. Every breath was ragged, and Theo thought she could hear something liquid bubbling at the back of his throat.

He couldn't die. Not now. Not because of *her*.

"Theo, fetch Mrs Clayton," Nathanial said sharply. "Tell her to send for a doctor."

"Trying to save my life, cousin?" Sir Montague's snort was weak. "I beg you wouldn't bother."

"Theo," Nathanial said again. "*Go*."

Her feet moved before her mind did, consumed as it was by the sight of Sir Montague lying on the floor, bleeding out against the rich, green carpet.

She had done that.

And Nathanial was here. How he had come to be here now, she didn't know, but she could cry at the sight of him, coolly peeling back Sir Montague's shirt to reveal the wound, unhesitating in everything he did.

But she couldn't cry. Not when Sir Montague's life hung in the balance.

She had *shot him*.

Mrs Clayton hovered outside the library door, her hands fluttering beside her mouth, and Theo drew herself up. She was a duchess.

"There's been an accident," she said, her voice cool and clear. "Send for a doctor immediately."

Mrs Clayton's eyes darted from the doorway, through which little was visible, to Theo's face. "I'll get the stable boy to take the trap into the village," she said. "Dr Brayburn resides there, and—"

"Thank you," Theo said, cutting her off. "Do it now, please."

"Of course, Your Grace." She bobbed a harassed curtsy and waddled down the corridor, calling for her husband in a loud, brash voice.

Theo slipped back into the library and closed the door behind her. "She's sending for a doctor," she said, her voice not quite sounding like her own.

Nathanial glanced up and nodded. "Help me remove his coat." He paused as he withdrew a knife from Montague's pocket and held it up to the light. A frown caught the corner of his mouth. "This is familiar."

"That's because I took it," she said, coming to kneel beside him.

"I see." In a quick, easy motion, he sliced through Sir Montague's coat, followed by his shirt. "Help me hold him up so I can remove these."

The last thing she wanted to do was lift up a man twice her size, who thanks to her might soon be a corpse, but there was no one else to help, and Nathanial had given her the instruction in the steady understanding she could obey.

She took a deep, shuddering breath, and raised Montague's shoulders, allowing Nathanial to peel his clothes away. "I'm sorry," she said, her voice breaking. "I never intended . . . I'm so sorry."

Sir Montague's lips twitched into a ghastly facsimile of his languid smile. "An excellent shot, Duchess."

A muscle in Nathanial's jaw ticked, but all he said was, "Hold these strips, Theo."

They worked in silence, wrapping Montague's ripped shirt around his stomach, the binding tight and quickly stained with blood. There was so much of it, coating Theo's hands, hanging pungent and coppery in the air until she wanted to vomit.

Montague didn't wake. She wasn't sure if he ever would again.

Finally, Nathanial rocked back on his heels, and Theo slumped against the ground. Her hands were shaking. If Montague died, she would be responsible. She would be a murderer.

She rose, stumbling from the library, away from the body and the proof of what she had done.

"Stay with him," Nathanial commanded behind her, but tears were blurring her eyes, and she couldn't see who he was addressing.

It didn't matter.

Her shoulder knocked against a wall and her knees gave out. Sobs, ugly and raw, burst from her throat, and she pressed the heels of her hands against her eyes.

"Theo," Nathanial murmured, wrapping his fingers around her wrists and pulling them from her face. "My sweet, foolish darling." He eased her against him, his arms settling around her back, and with a gasp, she submitted to his embrace. He smelt like home.

"I'm so sorry," she sobbed. "I'm so sorry."

"Shh. Shh." With one hand, he stroked her hair; the other locked around her waist, holding her more securely against him. They were on the floor, the marble cold against her legs and Nathanial's legs on either side of her. His arms cradled her. And for the first time since Sir Montague had caught her, she released the fear that had been building in her chest. She cried, not caring Nathanial's shirt was wet under her face, or that the rough material made her skin itch. She cried until there were no tears left and all she was left with was an aching hollowness that devoured her heart.

This was her fault.

Nathanial shifted under her, and she tried to draw back in alarm. "Am I hurting you?"

His arms tightened, holding her in place. "Don't think of it."

"Nate—"

"Let me hold you. It's all I thought of doing since I discovered you were missing." His lips brushed her hair, and his voice broke. "You stupid, stupid girl."

She pressed her face more deeply into his uninjured shoulder and choked back another sob. "I know."

"I thought I would never see you again. I thought—" His breath caught and he drew back so he could tip her face up to his. His thumb swiped tears from her face as he kissed her, seeking and giving assurance with every movement of his mouth. When he pulled away, hers was not the only face that was wet. "I thought I'd lost you."

Theo closed her eyes.

"I can't be without you," he said, his voice raw and ragged, each word ripped from him. "I thought about it, Theo. I thought about what my life would be without you in it, and I couldn't. You had my heart before I knew I'd given it, and you have it still. You might—" He broke off, swallowing hard. "You might not love me in return, but—"

"I do," she said, taking his face in her hands. His eyes widened and met hers, wonder and adoration in them like the rising sun. "You married me to rescue me, Nate, and everything since . . . How could I not love you? How could I ever love someone else?"

There was blood on his face from her hands. Sir Montague's blood. And she was certain there was blood on her dress. But when Nathanial reached up to brush her cheek with his fingertips, so lightly and gently she might have imagined it, she forgot to care.

"And your heart?" he whispered.

"In your keeping," she whispered back, their breaths mingling. She rested her forehead against his and closed her eyes. "As it has been for longer than I care to remember."

"Montague—"

"I don't want him to die, but that doesn't mean I love him." She hesitated. "I never did."

His sigh was heavy, one of relief, and his nose nudged hers. "I'm not ashamed to admit I'm glad."

She wanted to remain in his embrace forever; she wanted to forget the rest of the world existed and lose herself in him. And, by the way his arm tightened around her, he wanted that, too.

But all too soon, Mrs Clayton's frantic voice rang out, "The doctor is here!" and Theo could no longer forget.

"I won't go upstairs," she warned as Nathanial eased back. "I did this."

He studied her face for a moment before nodding. "Then let us go." His thumb rubbed her cheek one last time before he climbed stiffly to his feet. She followed, sliding her fingers through his. Together, they walked to the library.

Theo had expected a country doctor, more accustomed to dealing with farmers' wives than gunshot wounds, but she encountered a thin, greying man with sharp eyes and a manner of calm command. He betrayed no surprise or alarm and wasted no time asking questions. Instead, he removed the bindings around Sir Montague's stomach to reveal the wound.

It was just as Nathanial's had been those weeks before. The flesh around the entry point was singed, and although it was no longer actively bleeding, it looked red and raw and pulverised.

"You may have been lucky," the doctor said. "The bullet missed his stomach."

"Will he survive?" Theo whispered. Nathanial squeezed her hand.

"If he wakes," the doctor said dispassionately.

The hours seemed to pass slowly and yet too fast. With help, Nathanial and the doctor removed Sir Montague to a bed, and the doctor assured them he would remain until the morning. With nothing further to do, and exhausted, Theo and Nathanial retired to bed. They lay together, wrapped in each other's arms, the reality of what she had done colouring their every thought.

"If he dies, will I need to flee?" she whispered against Nathanial's chest.

"No."

"How can you be so sure?"

"Because I will not allow it."

Theo pressed her nose against his neck and his arm tightened around her waist. "You cannot force the law to bend to your will."

"If it comes to court, and it will not, I will ensure that the world knows what Sir Montague attempted to do to you. They will be lenient."

"What about Sir Montague?" she asked. "If he survives."

"He will leave the country and never return."

She nodded. That seemed fair. Closing her eyes, safe in Nathanial's arms, she attempted to get some sleep.

As dawn glowed its promise on the horizon, a knock sounded at their door. "Forgive me for waking you," Mrs Clayton said, "but Sir Montague is awake."

Theo's heart jumped into her mouth, but she and Nathanial said nothing as they threw robes over their nightwear and hurried into Sir Montague's room.

Just as Mrs Clayton had promised, Sir Montague was awake. At their entry, his eyelids fluttered. "The devil's in my gut," he rasped.

Nathanial turned to the doctor. "How is he?"

"Recovering, sir. It will be a slow process."

"Thank you. You may go now and rest. We will send for you if his condition changes."

The doctor bowed and left the room. Nathanial turned to Sir Montague, and even in the dim light, Theo could see the anger across his face. "You are fortunate," he said, crossing the room to stand by Sir Montague's side, "that my wife shot you so I do not have to."

The whisper of a smile, though it was more of a grimace, crossed Sir Montague's pale face. "Fortunate indeed."

"Juliet?" Nathanial asked curtly, and Theo startled. To her knowledge, he had not so much as seen her since Theo was poisoned. "Was she behind it?"

"Handed me the poisoned cup herself."

"And?"

"Dead."

Nathanial stiffened, then nodded, as though this did not come wholly as a shock. Theo gaped at them both.

"For Theo's sake, you may remain here until you are well enough to travel," Nathanial said. "Then you will leave. I don't care where you go as long as I never have to see your face again. If I do, they will hang you for your crimes. Do you understand?"

Sir Montague closed his eyes. "I understand."

Without so much as another glance at Sir Montague, Nathanial strode to the doorway. "Come, Theo."

Theo lingered, looking at Sir Montague's white face and pale lips. He did not look like a villain now; he looked like a man who had lost everything.

His eyelids fluttered open. "Duchess," he said, looking at her. The fire was gone from his dark eyes, and unexpected pity stirred in her chest. "Forgive me."

Nathanial made an impatient noise. "You have done too much to be so easily forgiven, Radcliffe."

"A mortal wound in exchange for kidnap," she said. "Consider us even."

She took Nathanial's hand as she left the room.

Chapter Thirty-Five

Montague survived.

Nathanial was fairly certain this was a good thing. His wife wasn't a murderer, and while she expressed no desire to be a part of Montague's life, she also didn't want him dead.

He, however, would have been more than happy to orchestrate Montague's death himself. That seemed a fair exchange.

As it was, he satisfied himself that he, and Theo, would never have to see his cousin again.

After three days ensuring Montague wasn't going to die on his property, Nathanial removed Theo and himself to Havercroft. Partly to escape Montague's lingering and unwelcome presence.

Partly because Nathanial wanted to be far from the events of the year when they finally consummated their marriage.And the sooner they did *that*, the better.

Theo peered out of the carriage window as they approached the house. "I've seen it so many times before, but this feels different, somehow."

"Probably because you're now its mistress."

She flicked her gaze to him, a teasing smile curving her lips. "As good a reason to marry as any."

"A better reason than most, given the size of my estate."

Her laugh was rich and beautiful. For the first time, he realised how little he'd heard it over the course of their marriage.

That was another thing that would change.

They pulled up outside the front doors, where the servants were lined up to greet their new mistress. Nathanial offered her his hand, and with his bride by his side, turned to face his childhood home.

How many times had he and Theo run wild through this house and across the land? She had been here almost as often as he had as a boy, and it felt only right she was here to stay.

"Roland," she said, greeting the austere butler with a gracious smile and a nod of her head. A twinkle in the back of her eyes, saved for Nathanial, was the only thing that marred her presentation of a great lady, and he knew no one else would notice.

If only his mother could see her now.

"You've seen the house plenty of times before," he said as he led her into the hallway. "I won't bore you with a tour." At least, not of the downstairs.

There was plenty upstairs he wished to show her.

She looked around, at the arching ceiling and the paintings on the walls. "I'd forgotten how grand it is."

"Do you like it?" The words were almost involuntary, falling from his lips before he'd realised they had formed.

"How could I not?"

He had fully intended on being a gentleman and allowing her to accustom herself to the house and her responsibilities before making any advances, but the artless way she said it, as though it was inconceivable that she would *not* like his ancestral home, snapped something in him. He scooped her into his arms, ignoring the slight ache in his shoulder.

"Nathanial?" Theo wrapped an arm around his neck, a breathy laugh escaping her. "What are you doing?"

"Taking you to the only part of the house you have yet to visit."

Her eyes, molten in the light, widened. "Oh."

"I made you a promise," he told her as he mounted the stairs, "that one day I would show you how difficult it has been to wait."

"*Oh.*"

"I am a man of my word, Theo."

The arm around his neck tightened, and she exhaled a long, shuddering breath against his throat. "I would not have you any other way," she said, and the huskiness in her voice spurred him on.

But when she started pressing tiny kisses to the side of his neck, pulling his cravat out of the way so she could have better access, he came to a stop. "I do not have infinite patience," he said, though his words sounded more like a grunt.

"You have tried mine for entirely too long," she murmured, kissing up to his ear and the sensitive skin there. This was tenderness in its purest form, combined with a sensuality that tempted him to give up on reaching his bed. He let her down for a moment before picking her up again, this time so she could hitch her skirts up and wrap her legs around him.

The bed was categorically not necessary.

She made a pleased sound in her throat at the way he caught her mouth with his, kissing her until the gallery around them swam and he couldn't breathe. Or perhaps he'd forgotten—breathing hardly seemed a priority when her lips were so soft and her hands clung to him.

"Nathanial," she panted, breaking away. "Here?"

"We may as well give my ancestors something to frown over."

"*Nathanial.*"

"This house is ours and we may do what we like in it." He paused and looked down into her flushed face. She'd never looked lovelier than she did now, in his arms with flared pupils and a voice that quivered with desire.

He wanted to take her here. He wanted to push her skirts up around her thighs and bury himself inside her. He wanted his name to be on her lips.

But she deserved better; for him to take his time as he claimed her.

Mine.

It was primal, this need to have her as his own, just as urgent as his need to offer her the last part of his heart.

"I love you," he said roughly, and carried her the rest of the way to his bedroom.

Nathanial's bedroom was large and spacious, with a gilded mirror hanging above the fireplace and chintz chairs around a walnut table in the corner. However, Theo did not spare them more than a passing glance. The only thing that occupied her attention was the bed. The mattress was as wide as it was long, and the decorated roof was so high she couldn't see the detail close enough to appreciate it fully.

Not that she had much opportunity as Nathanial laid her down, wincing slightly as his shoulder pained him, and pressed kisses across her jaw. Her legs were still wrapped around his waist, and she wondered if there was a way to remove her clothes without painstakingly undoing all the tiny buttons down the back.

Really, someone ought to have thought this through.

As though he knew what she was thinking, he drew her skirts further up her thighs, revealing her legs to the cool air. Or perhaps the air was warm, and it was her that was burning up.

He toyed with the top of her stockings. "While these are delightful," he murmured, "I really think we could dispense with their services."

"I'm wearing a dress, stays and a chemise, and your priority is my stockings?" Unable to help herself, she grinned up at him, her chest bursting with such fierce adoration she half thought her heart would explode with the force of feeling. "Of everything I'm wearing, I mind those the least."

There was a wicked twinkle in his eyes that made her stomach twist with anticipation. "Oh, I intend on removing it all."

"Soon?"

"Impatient, my muse?" He used the name as an endearment, as though the memory of their first joining brought him only pleasure. "Half the joy comes in the anticipation."

"We have had five months of it." To prove her point, she tightened her legs around his waist, holding him to her as he had been before. In a different bed, certainly—far less grand—but the feeling was the same.

Consumed.

There was a slight growl to his voice as he said, "Today, I want to worship you as you deserve to be worshipped."

Well, Theo couldn't complain at *that*.

He moved torturously slowly, as though his entire being was focused on the feeling of his lips against hers, the slow sweep of his tongue; an endless provocation, calling to mind all the other things he could do if he had but the inclination.

And the fire that had remained banked within Theo grew stronger with every movement of his mouth, with the soft travel of his hands down her body, starting from her shoulders and trailing down her arms to her waist, her legs, exploring the skin just above her stockings. His fingers toyed with the lace and silk almost idly, as though he barely noticed what he was doing.

It transpired Theo *could* argue at the idea of being worshipped if it involved so little touching.

"Nathanial," she groaned as he kissed her again, leisurely, as though they had all the time in the world. "Please."

His lips curved against her mouth. "Say it again."

"Please."

His smile was all delight and desire that made her catch her breath. "Your wish is my command, Your Grace."

Never had those words taken on a more sensual meaning.

This time, when he kissed her, it was with the edge of intention, and she responded in kind, running her hands along his chest, avoiding his wound, to his stomach, and further down, to his breeches and the bulge that she knew now was an expression of desire just for her. It twitched under her curious fingers, and he groaned.

"Lord, Theo," he said, and there was no sensual promise in his voice now. It was raw and full of need, and he ripped off his cravat, then his waistcoat, followed shortly after by his shirt, tugged over his head with such impatience it stoked the fire in Theo's stomach. It was the first time she had seen his wound in weeks, and she sat up now, her gaze fixed on his shoulder.

He caught his breath, holding it as she reached out and touched the puckered skin. His eyes were dark and heavy on her face. "Does it hurt?" she asked.

"Very little."

She had almost lost him; the wound would never heal, and she was, in a way, relieved. They would never forget what they had been through, and what they had gained by his recovery and everything that had happened since.

She didn't want to forget. Not the pain or the joy that had followed after.

Would her happiness now be as potent if she hadn't suffered the pain of loss and despair? They had fought for this moment, and it was all the sweeter for it.

"Theo," he said quietly.

"I love you," she said. He stiffened. "Every inch, Nate."

His hand came up to cup hers, holding it against the wound. "I would do it all again," he murmured.

Before she could cry during their joining—three for three really would be unacceptable—she kissed him. Tenderly, cupping his face in her hands as he pulled her closer. His arms wrapped around her, holding her against him, and this time she felt no impatience.

A lifetime was more than enough time for them to explore each other's bodies with aching precision. For now, she was content to be in his arms, his mouth against hers, his hands flat against her back.

Eventually, however, those hands began to move, applying themselves to the buttons down the back of her dress, moving steadily downwards. Once it was loose, he pulled it over her head and tossed it to one side. Her stays went the same way, as did her stockings, until she only wore her chemise.

Nathanial pulled her pins from her hair until it tumbled down her shoulders. "If I could have my way, you would never leave this room."

"Ask nicely," she said, running her hands through his hair. "You never know what boons I might grant."

He laughed at that, but then he slid the chemise up her body, and his laughter died as he looked at her. "Theo," he said unsteadily. "Theo, my love. You are the most beautiful lady I've ever had the privilege of seeing."

"Nathanial—"

He kissed her, swallowing her protest. "And I shall spend the rest of my life reminding you of it."

She slid her hands down her chest, savouring the feel of his soft skin under her palms, to the material of his breeches. "I cannot be the only one exposed."

"This time," he murmured, "I would not have it any other way." He kept his eyes on hers as he shifted back until he was standing. In a few quick motions, he removed his breeches, and then he stood before her, all bare skin and muscles and arousal.

She ached for him.

"Nate." Her throat was dry and she held out her hands for him. "Please. I want to know everything."

He took her hands, kissed them, and joined her on the bed, lying beside her. The tips of his fingers were whisper-soft as they brushed her loose hair back from her face. "Do you trust me?"

He had asked her that before, and she had pledged her trust without knowing all she knew now. This time, she was in possession of all the facts, yet her trust was just as immediate, just as implicit. "You know I do. Completely."

A tiny smile crossed his face, and the hand on her face moved down her body between her breasts to her hips. He traced small circles across her skin until she moved, parting her thighs and inviting him to the place that had been throbbing for him since they began.

As he slid his fingers into her slickness, he kissed her, capturing her moans and swallowing them. The world stopped, all thoughts suspended as he stroked her, his breath harsh and fast against her neck. She felt his arousal against her leg, moving against her as though he couldn't help himself.

This time, the pleasure gathered faster, building and tightening inside her in what felt like seconds. His nose brushed against her neck, as he slipped a finger inside her. Then another.

"Nathanial," she gasped.

He made a noise of approval. "That's right."

It was indeed right; she could think of nothing more right than this moment, and she fumbled for his hand, linking their fingers, needing to hold onto something as he coaxed her over the edge.

Her back arched and her body shuddered entirely out of her control. If she'd had her faculties, she might have felt a quiver of embarrassment, but there was nothing in her head but Nathanial and his hands on her, wringing pleasure from her she had never known existed.

This time, when it was over, she didn't cry. There were no tears; the feeling in her chest didn't allow for anything but smiles. He skimmed the back of his knuckles across her cheek.

"There's more," she said, though it was more of a question.

"There's more," he confirmed.

"Show me."

In answer, he ran a hand down her leg, finding the crook of her knee and guiding it over his hips. She shifted to allow for the movement, and found herself straddling him. Both his hands settled on her thighs as he looked up at her, eyes burning, so beautiful she could hardly breathe.

"This may hurt," he said as he eased her up and placed himself at her entrance. "But in this position, you're in control." As though to prove his point, he removed his hand from her hip, the message clear.

This time, Theo felt no hesitation. *Do you trust me?* he had asked.

The answer would always be yes.

Obeying the prompting of her body, she lowered herself onto him, the stretch almost painful. He filled her, and it filled a space she hadn't even known ached for him. This was everything she hadn't even known she'd been missing; the truest act of love, and the joy of it filled her almost as entirely as he did.

Underneath her, he was utterly still, muscles tense, as she eased further down, the stretch almost painful—the brink of pleasure and pain. He sucked in a breath as she paused, bracing herself with a hand against his chest, and seated herself fully on him.

He ran a reassuring hand up her side. "Does it hurt?"

She experimented shifting her hips, and discovered that the delightful friction chased away any lingering thoughts of pain or tightness. She did it again and his eyes fluttered shut as he released a long, controlled breath. His hand tensed on her side.

"Look at me," she said, just as he had said the last time they had come together. He opened his eyes as his other hand stroked along her legs, and the expression in them made her skin feel hot all over.

It took a moment for her to find her rhythm. He kept patiently still, smoothing her hair away from her face and running his hands all over her, until finally, he moved to meet her.

This time, his groan sounded utterly involuntary, and the tension low in her belly tightened.

She understood, now, why this was called lovemaking. In this, there was equal measure giving and taking, yielding and submitting, owning and possessing. In this, they were one in the most primal of ways; she would always carry a piece of Nathanial with her, and her with him. For the first time in her life, she had been made complete, offering herself to a man who offered himself in return.

His breath was ragged against her face, and he slid his hands down to her waist, his fingers digging into her skin. "Theo," he groaned, and the sound of her name said in such a way set her alight. "Theo."

"I love you."

He cursed, low and harsh, and the sound was enough to undo her. Release barrelled through her body, and he rode out the way she shuddered on him, telling her how beautiful she was, how much he loved her, how much she wanted this.

When the final wave of pleasure drained from her, he rolled them over, until his body pressed against hers just as it had before. This time, however, he was inside her.

And oh—if she thought the last time had been wonderful, this was incendiary.

Nathanial linked their fingers and kissed her as he found his rhythm. Theo held him, loved him, and he soon followed her over the edge with her name on his lips.

After a moment that seemed to stretch forever, Nathanial slid away and she curled against his side. His chest rose and fell rapidly, matching hers, and she felt her heartbeat in her chest, her ears, thrumming through her entire body alongside a lethargy that dictated she remain here for a long time. Perhaps forever.

She wasn't certain she minded.

It transpired, somewhat to her surprise, that heroes did not come in the form of handsome strangers to sweep her off her feet. *That*, as Annabelle had once predicted, was less like romance and more like abduction.

Lazily, she traced a heart across Nathanial's chest. He turned to face her. "You're not crying this time," he said, a teasing note to his voice, but there was a look of anxiety in his eyes as he searched her face.

No, heroes came in the form of old friends, in deep and abiding love.

They came in the form of husbands.

"We are truly married now," she said, smiling up at him. "You can't take it back."

"Even if I could, I would not.

"Very gallant."

"When we married, you asked for romance." He kissed her fingers, one by one. "I shall do my best."

Another thought occurred to her, and she propped herself up on her elbow so she could look at him. "You said something else, too."

"Heavens, Theo. I said a great deal of things and meant very few."

Despite everything they had just done, a blush suffused her cheeks. "You said that you didn't want children at present, and that you didn't expect me— well, that is to say . . ."

"Yes," he said dryly. "I understand you perfectly."

"But now I *am* performing my wifely duties, does that mean—"

"Theodosia, if you refer to this as your wifely duties again, I shall renounce you as my wife."

"You can't do that," she said, and smiled at his scowl. She pressed a kiss to his arm. "Besides, you didn't answer the question."

His groan was more than a little theatrical, but when he looked at her again, he was biting back a smile. "I suppose we can hardly prevent them now, my love."

"Natha—"

"And yes, I want to expand our family." He kissed her again, long and deep. "Though heaven help me if they're anything like you were as a child."

She slapped his shoulder. "You were worse."

"You're right," he said, his lips a hair's breadth from hers. "I was reprehensible. And do you know, Theo, I think I might be reprehensible again."

Theo could not find it within herself to mind.

Thanks so much for reading! If you enjoyed it, please considering leaving a review!

If you're interested in a spicy epilogue, sign up to my newsletter. You'll get your hands on other bonus content, be the first to hear about future releases, and have the chance to sign up for ARC opportunities!

Want to read Annabelle's story? Click here. (It's spicier!)

To Marry the Devil

14th May, 1802

"Enter."

Jacob Barrington pushed open his father's study door with more than a little trepidation. The room was a forbidden one, although he sometimes stole inside for fun, snapping his father's quills and emptying his ink. A rebellion against the inevitable.

Even at fourteen, he knew there was only one possible reason he had been called to this study. He had been punished for no shortage of sins over the years. Most he had deserved—he *had* stolen his brother's precious poetry book and dropped it in the pond, he frequently stole food from the kitchens, and he took considerable delight in causing mayhem.

The thing he did not deserve was his father's unrelenting, blazing hatred. He received that, anyway.

As always, his father was sitting behind his desk. It was an old desk, made of rather fine mahogany, with papers piled high. Jacob had once rifled through them when he had broken into the study through the window, but he had found nothing interesting.

Nothing that warranted his father being locked up in this room for so many hours every day, avoiding everyone in the house except Cecil. Jacob's perfect older brother.

He took his time advancing into the room. A carriage clock ticked ominously on the mantel and a fire burned in the hearth despite the heat of the day. The room was swelteringly hot, although there wasn't so much as a bead of sweat on his father's pale, iron face.

Demons were used to the heat. When Jacob was little, he'd fantasised about his father being an instrument of evil, sent from Hell to terrorise everyone except Cecil. As a child, that had been his favourite explanation for his father's bouts of cruelty and violence.

Now he was older, he knew better. His father was just a man who fed on pain, and Jacob's was his favourite flavour.

He stopped just before the desk. His father's grey eyes narrowed.

"You called for me, sir," Jacob said stiffly.

"That was five minutes ago."

"I came as soon as I received your summons." Jacob paused long enough for the insult to sink in. "Sir."

His father's lip curled. "Your insolence has no bounds, I see. I presume it was you who entered this office while I was in London?"

Jacob didn't break his stare. Not yet, but soon, he would be old enough to fend his father off, and he counted the days. "That was me, sir."

"As I supposed." His father took one of the broken quills and twirled it in his fingers. "Cecil informs me you have not attended your lessons this week."

Jacob clenched his fists. He had never understood why Cecil, superior only in his bookishness and age, was so revered while he was so reviled. In his father's eyes, Cecil could do no wrong. Cecil was the heir, the golden boy, the apple of his father's eye. Jacob, as soon as he had come into the world with his mop of dark, unruly hair and deep brown eyes, had been deemed a disappointment.

It had not taken him long to learn that, if he wanted anything for himself, he would have to take it. His mother had never shown him any interest and the servants, scared of his father, had ignored him. Cecil only paid him attention to tease or lecture him.

Or, apparently, to tattle to their father.

"He told me I was not required to attend," Jacob said stiffly. He, unlike Cecil, had never been bookish, but that did not mean he didn't enjoy his lessons. At least his tutor treated him with a modicum of respect—a rarity in this house.

"So," his father said in a deceptively quiet voice, "when faced with your shortcomings, you would choose to blame your brother."

Jacob's back stiffened. "It's the truth."

"What would you know of the truth, boy? You were born a lie." Eyes glinting with an anger Jacob had never fully understood, his father planted both fists on his desk and pushed himself to his feet. "It would have been better if you had never been born at all."

Jacob could smell sherry on his father's breath, but the words still ricocheted deep inside him, lodging in his chest like broken glass. He had long known that his father would have preferred him not to exist, but he had never understood *why*.

His father's thin, cruel mouth puckered in distaste. "Turn around," he ordered coldly. "Take off your shirt."

Briefly, Jacob considered rebelling. He was almost as tall as his father, though nowhere near as wide. It was likely he could have put up a small fight, but in the end his father would win. And then he would be that much angrier.

His father's eyes narrowed into grey, endless slits. They reminded Jacob of the time he had shorn slivers off the lead drainpipes with his pocket knife. Just as sharp. Just as poisonous.

He turned, shrugging out of his waistcoat and tugging his shirt over his head. His breath came too fast and his chest was tight. Afraid, even though he would never have confessed to fear, his muscles bunched in anticipation of the pain.

"You are a disgrace," his father said without inflection as he brought the cane down hard. Pain lashed, a visceral, unsteady thing that filled his veins with fire. His free hand curled into a fist as he fought not to cry out.

"Father," he began. "I—"

"Do *not* call me father." For the first time, rage coloured his voice. The cane swished again and lightning flared across Jacob's back. Despite the lip caught between his teeth, he made a mewling sound of agony. "You're a coward," his father continued, tone biting, the words falling almost as hard as the cane's metal tip. "And you are unworthy of the name of Barrington."

A different kind of hurt settled in Jacob's chest— not the sting of pain, or the aching sensation of being beaten, but something colder that wrapped around his heart with frosty fingers and ate away the last of his desire to belong. He had known for a long time that they would never accept him, but this beating was the final straw, and his desire for acceptance was the camel's back.

If they would refuse to love him, he would not love them. If they thought he was bad, he would be worse; if he was to be hated, he would give them something to hate.

And he would make them all regret every day he carried the name Barrington.

Also by

Finders Keepers

In Search of a Hero
To Marry the Devil
The Picture of Desire

Companion novellas

His Ample Desire
To Have and to Hold

Made in the USA
Las Vegas, NV
08 October 2024

96508686R00260